Potions Are for Pushovers

Also by Tamara Berry

Séances Are for Suckers

Potions Are for Pushovers

Tamara
Berry

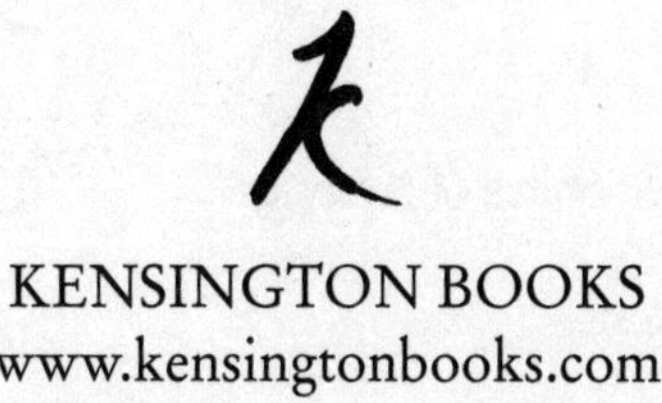

KENSINGTON BOOKS
www.kensingtonbooks.com

KENSINGTON BOOKS are published by

Kensington Publishing Corp.
119 West 40th Street
New York, NY 10018

All Kensington titles, imprints, and distributed lines are available at special quantity discounts for bulk purchases for sales promotion, premiums, fund-raising, educational, or institutional use.

Special book excerpts or customized printings can also be created to fit specific needs. For details, write or phone the office of the Kensington Special Sales Manager: Attn. Special Sales Department. Kensington Publishing Corp, 119 West 40th Street, New York, NY 10018. Phone: 1-800-221-2647.

Kensington and the K logo Reg. U.S. Pat. & TM Off.

Library of Congress Card Catalogue Number: 2019944527

ISBN-13: 978-1-4967-1963-8
ISBN-10: 1-4967-1963-8
First Kensington Hardcover Edition: December 2019

ISBN-13: 978-1-4967-1966-9 (ebook)
ISBN-10: 1-4967-1966-2 (ebook)

10 9 8 7 6 5 4 3 2 1

Printed in the United States of America

Potions Are for Pushovers

Chapter 1

"Is the cat part of the ritual?" The tall, gaunt man taps his fingertips on the mantelpiece, uneasily eyeing the sleek black feline at his feet. "It keeps looking at me. Why does it keep looking at me?"

"She won't cause you any harm, Mr. Worthington," I reply, though I, too, have a habit of treading warily where that animal is concerned. For reasons known only to herself, my cat refuses to leave the room whenever I receive a visit from a client. Like a brothel madam overseeing her domain, Beast—as I've aptly named the creature—won't leave until payment is secure and services are rendered. "Her presence merely seals what is already strengthened between us. Did you bring the money?"

Mr. Worthington pats his breast pocket. "Small, unmarked bills, as you asked."

I nod once. Small, unmarked bills are my favorite kind. A little bulky to carry around, yes, and a pain when trying to buy anything bigger than a breadbox, but I find them essential for daily living. Not even Inspector Peter Piper, the village watchdog and my ever-attentive nemesis, can raise a hue and cry if I stop by the grocer's with a purse full of five-pound notes.

With a careful glance at Beast, who has moved to position herself in the doorway to the kitchen, I reach under my couch and extract a small wooden box scratched all over with cryptic markings. Even *I* don't know what they mean, so you can imagine the effect they have on my visitor.

"What's that?" he asks, his voice wavering.

I place the box on the coffee table and push it toward him. "You asked for the most powerful elixir I can make. This is it."

Intrigued despite himself, Mr. Worthington leans forward and examines the box. He's careful not to touch it, though. Glancing up at me, he breathes, "And this will do it? If I drink it, she'll come back to me? Forever?"

I nod. "Forever."

"When should I do it?"

Considering I'd already cornered his beloved and locked her up while he went on a fruitless errand to plant a handful of flax seeds at the evergreen crossroads, I'd prefer it if he drank the tonic sooner rather than later.

I gesture at the box and begin a low, humming chant that amounts to the Latin version of *Annie*'s "Tomorrow." "*Cras cras cras te amo*," I say.

Mr. Worthington's dark, watery eyes fly open. He makes as if to flee from the room, but Beast is sitting perfectly still, blocking the kitchen as she watches the proceedings. Since I'm closer to the front door than he is, my nervous guest is trapped. I nudge the box one last time.

Reluctantly, he lifts the box as if he expects it to burst into flames at the least provocation, then slides it open to reveal a vial of purple-red liquid nestled in a bed of straw. The liquid is composed of vanilla, sage, cinnamon, and a hint of boiled beets for color. It doesn't taste great—the sage overpowers what might otherwise be quite tasty—but it won't hurt him any.

"*Tu tantum diem*," I continue, accidentally slipping into the song's catchy beat. At this, Mr. Worthington shoots me a slightly suspicious look, but he lifts the bottle to his lips and, after a tentative recoil, kicks it back.

He pauses, as if waiting for something miraculous to happen. I mentally will Beast to indulge us with a well-timed meow or even a haughty twitch of her whiskers, but she doesn't move. *Stupid cat.* The next time I unwittingly adopt a witch's familiar, I'm getting a dog. A sweet, cuddly, highly trainable dog.

"That's it?" he asks, disappointment drooping the corners of his mouth. "I thought it would feel different."

I place a hand to my temple, which anyone who's used one of my potions before would recognize as a signature move. "Don't be surprised if you and your Regina are restless for a few days. That's the natural side effect of the binding spell taking hold."

"Restless, yes." He looks down at his hands, which are showing a psychosomatic tendency to twitch already. "Is there anything else I should know?"

"Only this, Mr. Worthington. You'd better take good care of her from now on. Provide her with extra love, lavish her with extra attention." My voice picks up a hard note, and I stare at him until he's forced to blink in return. "A spell like this can only work if your intentions and your actions remain pure. If you mistreat Regina in any way, she could fight the spell. It won't break—it's much too powerful for that—but it may turn darker and more sinister than even I can control."

"Yes. Yes, of course. I understand." He can't drop the box or the empty vial fast enough after that. After a few muttered promises to provide all the love and care Regina requires, he places the envelope of money on the table and beats a hasty retreat. He tries to leave the way he came in, through the back kitchen door, but Beast still blocks the way. The front door is the only way to go.

Since my cottage is located on a remote road between a bona fide English castle and the small village I've only recently begun to call home, there's little chance of him running into anyone he knows. Still, he casts a suspicious look in either direction before dashing out the door and down the lane, determined to put as much distance between us as possible.

"All this trouble for a runaway pig," I mutter, standing in the doorway as I watch him go. "He could have saved himself a lot of time and effort if he'd just fixed the fence himself."

Not that I blame him too much. That fence had been broken in three places. It took me almost as many hours to repair it.

Mr. Worthington's feet leave a trail through the mud-soaked earth, but I'm sure it'll be washed away by the rain before the hour is up. I'd been warned that springtime in Sussex was a wet affair, but nothing could have prepared me for just how damp everything would get—or how poorly an ancient thatch roof would stand up to it.

"Well, that's one more satisfied customer." I shut the front door and sag against it. When I'd envisioned my life in a quaint English village, I'd pictured long, drowsy days under handmade quilts and cups of tea by the bucketful. Although it's true that I've consumed more caffeine than is wise under current health guidelines, sleep hasn't been as forthcoming as I'd hoped.

And not just because of the stream of foot traffic at my back door, those hesitant knocks and wringing hands, the whispered requests for health, money, affection, *love*. No, it's the other thing that keeps me lying awake at night.

Nighttime is usually when my sister, Winnie, visits me.

My *dead* sister, I should say.

A not-so-hesitant knock at that same back door almost causes me to jump out of my skin, a tiny scream emitting from my lips. Beast casts a disdainful look at my cowardice, but I ignore her. If I took to heart the judgment of every creature—living or dead—around here, I'd be crying into that bucket of tea right now.

Lifting a hand to my head, I make a quick adjustment to my ornate coil of braids. I also check my reflection in the paned glass to make sure my blood-red lipstick is still intact. One of the most difficult parts of being the resident psychic-cum-village-witch is that I always have to be "on."

"Enter," I call in a voice I hope is deep and mysterious. It needs to be both for me to effectively sell my trade around here. The quaint cottage I call home doesn't exactly exude mysticism, since it's all cheerful calico and farmhouse chic, complete with an AGA stove taking up most of the kitchen.

Still, I like it. It's cozy. And since the previous owner had to sell in a hurry, I got a great deal on the purchase price.

"Oh, good. You're home." The door flies open to reveal a beautiful young woman so layered up under her raincoat that she barely fits through the door. As soon as she crosses the threshold, she starts shedding those layers, unwinding scarves and shrugging out of sweaters. "Your house is always so hot, Ellie. How can you stand it?"

"Hello, Rachel." I lean forward and accept the girl's hug. Her tawny hair tickles my nose, the light scent of my signature lavender water not far behind. "I see you're wearing the attraction elixir. How's it working?"

"Like rubbish," she says and laughs so merrily I can't take offense. "Not a single boy asked me on a date all week. But I sold three bottles to the other girls at the art gallery. Are you sure you did the spell right this time?"

I heave a sigh. "I danced naked under the full moon for two hours. If that didn't do the trick, I don't know what will."

"Perhaps four hours are required. I'd be happy to help next time." The other voice that appears at my back door is just as familiar as Rachel's. It also causes another tiny scream to leave my lips.

"Nicholas!" I cry and launch myself into his arms. "You're home early!"

My reward for such an unbridled show of enthusiasm is to be lifted up off my feet and soundly kissed. I'm never sure how appropriate it is to use tongue while in the presence of a man's niece, so I pull away before our embrace becomes unseemly.

I might be the village witch, but I'm also a *lady*.

"Why is it that the naked moonlight dancing always seems to take place while I'm away?" Nicholas murmurs as he sets me back on my feet. "Just once, I'd like to witness this particular ceremony for myself."

"Alas, you can't," I say in the same mock serious tone as his. "It's a sacred ritual conducted between me and the lunar goddess."

"Pity. The lunar goddess has all the luck."

I don't allow myself to be cast into *too* much alt at this comment. Although the great Nicholas Hartford III's work means he's rarely around when one wants him, I've been seeing him long enough to know that it's never a good idea to take him at his word. He sounds solemn, yes. He looks solemn, too, what with his dark suit and tie, his well-lined face drawn into an expression of inscrutability. Even his eyes are a steely, impenetrable gray. But woe to the woman who assumes there's anything trustworthy about that deadpan exterior. No one commits to irony quite like him.

"If you're not here to sing my elixir's praises, to what do I owe this honor?" I ask.

Aware by now that anyone living at Castle Hartford is sadly undernourished, I unwrap a plate of sandwiches and place them in front of Rachel. My neighbors might be wealthier than the rest of the entire village combined, but they're not known for serving haute cuisine. Or any cuisine, really. Rachel barely waits until Nicholas and I join her at the table before digging in.

Around a mouthful of chicken salad, she says, "Grandmother sent me. She's supposed to help plan this year's spring fête, but the first meeting is tonight. She can't make it."

I blink first at Rachel, and then at Nicholas. "Um, okay. Are you taking her place?"

Rachel laughs. "Are you joking? Sitting around with all the village biddies, discussing how many tea cozies we need to knit this year? I'd rather be dead."

Catching Nicholas's gaze and all the meaning contained within it, she sobers. There's already been enough death around this place—and in their lives—to make the topic a sensitive one.

"What I mean is, it's not my style." She swallows a bite of her sandwich and turns a pair of pleading, violet eyes my way. A striking girl even without the purple-tinted irises, that extra bit of color makes her downright gorgeous. "Besides, I'm busy with my new internship at the gallery in London—I'm up to three mornings a week now. And Uncle Nicholas is always flitting around for work, so Grandmother thought perhaps you'd like to go instead."

"A family emissary of sorts?" Nicholas suggests dryly.

A smile brightens Rachel's face. "That's it! Seeing as how Ellie is one of us now."

"The last time I checked, my name was still Eleanor Wilde," I say, repressing a strong urge to laugh. This family can't even volunteer for a local tradition without turning it into a battle of strong wills. "Not Hartford."

"Well, obviously, but everyone knows Uncle Nicholas is nutty on you. Well, you *are*, Uncle Nicholas, so it's no use looking at me like that. Besides, they don't actually care which one of us is there, just as long as someone goes. They'll be glad to have you."

Her words are kind, but not a single one of us believes them to be true. I've only lived in the village for a few months, but one would hardly call my welcome a *warm* one. Invitations to parties haven't exactly been forthcoming, and the stream of clients to my back door is really more of a trickle.

But, "If it's important to Vivian, of course I'll do it," I say. I made the decision to move here and embrace the full pastoral lifestyle—adopted cats and leaking thatch roofs and all—and I intend to stick to it. "But I can't knit, and I doubt they'll want me to be in charge of making the punch."

The relief that moves over Rachel's face wipes a good half a decade off her already young eighteen years. "Oh, you don't have to do anything but raise your hand when they call for a vote and praise Mrs. Cherrycove's biscuits when they're passed around. But no matter how hungry you are, don't eat them. Grandmother chipped two teeth last year."

Her errand thus discharged and most of my sandwiches in her stomach, Rachel rises from the table with a bright smile. "You'll have to leave in ten minutes if you want to make it on time. Uncle Nicholas can walk you." She waggles her fingers in farewell and heads toward the back door. She pauses long enough to call over her shoulder, "I'll just leave this open, shall I? We wouldn't want you to be late to your meeting."

"You Hartfords," I mutter, rising to shut—and lock—the door behind her. "All alike, commanding every situation to suit your own needs and then making it look like you're doing *me* a favor. She gets that from you."

Nicholas watches me from his seat at the table, a smile playing on the edge of his lips. "You don't have to go. It would serve my mother right for sending Rachel to do her dirty work."

"Oh, I don't mind. Not really. It'll be a good opportunity—I need to drum up some more business if I want to pay the gas bill next month."

Nicholas opens his mouth to speak, but I forestall him with a glare and a shake of my head. "Don't say anything. That was an exaggeration. I'm *fine*."

"It does seem a pity for all that space in the castle to go to waste."

I cross my arms and glare harder. "I like it here, thanks."

"And my mother is always saying how much she misses having you around."

"I had tea with her last week, and she literally told me how much better she likes me when she doesn't have to see me every day."

He chuckles obligingly, but his expression is one of painful—and rare—earnestness. "You'll tell me if that changes? I mean it, Eleanor. After everything you've done for the family, offering you sanctuary is the least I can do."

The sanctuary he's speaking of is both literal and metaphorical. Literal, because he would gladly coerce his poor mother into having me as a permanent houseguest up at Castle Hartford despite her protestations. Metaphorical, because all it would take is a few firmly worded hints, and every home in the county would fling its doors open to me.

In a way, I suppose it could be considered a bonus—an extra payment for the job I did last year removing a ghost from his home. Nicholas Hartford III had little idea what he was getting into when he hired me to travel from New York to England and rid his castle of its restless undead, but there's no denying I accomplished what I set out to do . . . even if his ghost *did* end up being nothing more than your usual, garden-variety murderer.

I had little idea what I was getting into, either, especially since I've given up my wandering lifestyle for a taste of something more sedate. Not *too* much more sedate, obviously, but there's no denying that my life has undergone a drastic change. I'm no longer Madame Eleanor Wilde, spiritual medium dedicated to eliminating the world of its phantasmagoric plagues. Now I'm just a potion-pushing village eccentric everyone is a little wary of during the full moon.

It's not a *bad* change. Just new. I'm not used to permanence.

I am, however, used to taking care of myself—a thing I intend to continue even without the inordinate ghost-exorcising fees to support me in the manner to which I'm accustomed.

"I'll have you know that business has been booming lately." I give a haughty toss of my head. "In fact, I helped Mr. Worthington tame his runaway pig today. They're bound body and soul now."

Nicholas laughs, the harsh lines of his face relaxing into their usual calm. "Regina? Impossible. That animal has been escaping her pen for years. Nothing short of chains will keep her in one place."

"Nonsense. She needed a sedentary spell, that's all."

"You fixed the fence, didn't you?"

When I don't reply, Nicholas laughs again. He also glances at his watch and rises to his feet. I can read his elegant body language well enough to accept that however glad he is to see me, we'll need to get going if I'm going to make it to the fête planning committee on time. Punctuality is bred into his uptight British soul.

"I hate to be the bearer of bad tidings, but you've just committed yourself to a lifetime of fence repair," he says. "Everyone around here knows she eats through the posts."

I halt in the middle of wrapping myself up in a warm woolen shawl. "She *what*?"

"Bites through them like they're butter. My poor Eleanor."

He leans forward and presses a kiss on my forehead, but I push him away. I'm not fooled by that romantic gesture. He's mocking me. "You laugh now, but how will you feel when the whole village knows I'm a fraud?"

"My dear girl, I've been telling them that for months." He adjusts the shawl, his hands lingering reverentially on my shoulders. "Maybe now they'll finally start to believe me."

Chapter 2

I've lived here long enough to know that any community event, from AA meetings to CPR classes, will be held at the large, imposing stone church in the village square.

My first few visits to those hallowed walls brought a quake to my knees, since I wasn't sure how the church would react to a woman who makes a living as a traveling medium and then decides that practicing witchcraft offers better long-term stability. However, I've since come to look at that ancient Anglican structure as home.

Strange, I know. But my entire life is nothing if not a testament to the weird and wonderful.

"Ellie! How good to see you!" Annis, the vicar and one of my dearest friends, is standing in the church antechamber when we arrive. She wraps her arms around me in a hug and holds me in place much longer than a fête committee meeting necessitates.

I like it, though. There's something about that short, round, sunny woman that makes me feel as if everything is going to be okay.

"And Nicholas." Annis pulls away and makes to embrace the great Nicholas Hartford III with the same loving ebullience. "Don't tell me you're coming to help plan the festivities. The last time anyone saw *you* inside this place . . ."

Nicholas accepts Annis's hug with complaisance but shakes his head at the rest of her greeting. "I'm here merely as convoy. My mother regrets that she'll be unable to participate this year, so she's sending Eleanor in her stead."

Since Annis has known the Hartfords from her cradle, she's not fooled by this formal speech. "Oh, dear. What did they do to force this on you, Ellie?"

I laugh. "I don't know. That's the problem. I've always believed myself to be a woman of fierce independence, but ever since I met this sorry lot, I find myself doing the exact opposite of what I intend."

"Alas, it's part of their charm. Come in, come in. Everyone is gathered in the basement. I'll keep the doors open for five more minutes, and then we'll get started."

Although I've become inured to the fact that I'm now friends with a vicar, I haven't yet grown accustomed to performing public displays of affection in front of one. I restrict myself to smiling up at Nicholas and saying good-bye.

He suffers no such qualms and leans down to press a kiss on my cheek, his telltale scent of bergamot wafting over me. "I'll be back at nine to walk you home."

It's a sweet gesture—if slightly archaic—but I decline. "Thank you, but there's no need. I have one or two things to do around the village afterward."

One of Nicholas's heavy brows comes up. "Fence repair, perhaps?"

"Very funny," I mutter. And, because checking on Mr. Worthington's pig is precisely what I intend to do, I point a warning finger at him. "For your insolence, I bring a pox down upon your household."

"Excellent. Should I expect something along the lines of chickenpox, or are you going full smallpox?"

"Chicken, of course. I'm not a monster."

This kind of exchange is one we often share. Nicholas believes in magic, mediums, and mysticism even less than I do—in fact, it's what drew him to me in the first place. Although my worldview has shifted since our initial meeting, and while I've come to learn that there are many things about our universe that defy rational explanation, he remains steadfastly disbelieving.

Considering what he went through this past winter, I can understand the chip-sized burden he carries on his shoulders. It took me a long time to come to terms with the loss of my sister and believe in the miraculous again. I'm not going to rush him.

Unfortunately, our playful exchange is witnessed by one of the more respectable families in the village. Standing a few feet away are Mr. and Dr. MacDougal, the local schoolmaster and family physician, respectively, along with their preteen daughter. They take one look at me cursing Nicholas's entire household and give us a wide berth as they enter the church doors. Annis flashes me an amused look and goes to greet them with her calm, friendly air, but the damage has already been done.

"Now look what you made me do," I say irritably. "All my credibility is gone, and the meeting hasn't even started yet."

"Don't be absurd. You never had any credibility to begin with."

Though true, it's not very gentlemanly of him to say so, so I send him off with a glare. He makes no mention of when he'll see me again, but it doesn't bother me—at least, not much. Our arrangement is that we have no arrangement. I'm living in his home village because I like the setting and the people. He comes and goes as his work and family demands dictate. We're nothing more than ships passing in the night. Ships that occasionally share waters, yes, but all attempts at defining our romantic entanglement stop there.

It has to. Women in my profession can't afford stability. An air of mystique is our most valuable asset.

Familiar with the church's layout, I make my way past the rows of heavy wooden pews toward the basement. Like many of the structures around here, the lower level is the most modern one, updated from the dark, dank hold of centuries past to display fluorescent lighting and high-traffic beige carpet. The scent of percolating coffee assails my nose as I walk in to find about a dozen local residents settling into a ring of folding chairs. Some of the women have brought knitting with them; others sit chatting as they wait for the meeting to start.

After grabbing a paper cup of coffee and stirring enough sugar and cream in to dilute the burned taste, I decide to sit between the gently snoring General von Cleve, who can be trusted not to recognize me even though we've met several times before, and Mrs. Brennigan, a fifty-something woman with brindled hair who's one of my regulars.

"Oh, Madame Eleanor!" she cries, shifting her chair over to make room for me. She bears the lightly floral scent of my lavender water. She's also glowing with the kind of vitality that can only come from regular visits to the marriage bed. I hate to boast of my own success, but there's no denying she looks, well, *happy*. "I had no idea you were interested in village affairs. Isn't this a little . . . tame for someone like you?"

I plaster on an appropriately mystical smile. "I'm interested in all things ritualistic. Local traditions and customs are fascinating to a woman like me, especially since so many of them can be traced back to the early pagan rituals."

She blinks.

"Springtime is an especially potent time of year. Renewal and rebirth—they're everywhere around us. Can't you feel it?"

"Not really, no," she says baldly. "We've been doing this fête every year for two decades, so the only thing I feel about it anymore is bored."

"Hear, hear!" mutters the general under his breath. He still bears the hallmarks of a man sound asleep, but one of his rheumy eyes opens long enough to wink at me. *Huh.* Maybe he does know who I am, after all.

"Then it's a good thing we have Eleanor to help us spice things up a bit this year, isn't it?" Annis asks from directly behind us.

I turn, flustered. "Oh, I'm not here to—"

"There's nothing wrong with our customs," Dr. MacDougal says from the other side of the room. She's an austere woman in her early forties, sharp eyed and sharp tongued, but somehow attractive in spite of it. Maybe even because of it. It's difficult to imagine her handing out lollipops and soothing children over their scraped knees, but I bet she's a killer at vaccinations. "In fact, I'd like to know under whose authority she was invited. I understood the fête planning committee was for local residents only."

Being excluded from public events isn't a new thing for someone like me. I might not bear a scarlet letter in the middle of my chest or ride a horse through town wearing nothing but my long, dark hair, but I do have a tendency to flaunt convention. It's understandable that a few backs get put up along the way.

Before I'm able to defend myself, however, the youngest MacDougal turns on her parent.

"Oh, don't be so fusty," the girl says. Like her mother, she's thin and sharp and, to be honest, a little intimidating for a twelve-year-old. However, that's where the similarities end. She's covered from head to toe in freckles, her hair an orangey red that resembles a flame whipped into a froth. She turns to me with a crooked, toothy smile and says, "I think what she's doing in this village is *smashing*. She actually cares about making people happy."

To be fair, I mostly care about making a living using the only real skill set I have in this world, but I appreciate the gesture.

"Lenora Marie . . ." her mother begins.

Her father clears his throat and adds, "Don't speak to your mother like that."

Mrs. Brennigan, bless her, rises to my defense with a staunch, "But it's true. She *does* care. She's done more for me in the past few months than the rest of you have done in years."

Unfortunately, she's no match for a stout, beetle-browed woman two seats down waving her knitting needle at me like it's a lance. "I think she's giving me the evil eye. Does it look like she's giving me the evil eye?"

Behind me, Annis clears her throat in a gentle, unobtrusive way. It's a testament to her role as theological guide to this community that the room falls silent and stays that way for a full ten seconds until she's ready to say her piece.

"I understand that Madame Eleanor's spiritual leanings are somewhat contradictory to the tenets that you and I hold dear." She places a hand on my shoulder. I can't decide whether it's to comfort me or hold me in check, but it serves to do both. "But I believe—as I'm sure you do—that people of all faiths and backgrounds are welcome in our village. What better way to make her feel welcome than to allow her to contribute her share to our continued success?"

It's a lovely speech, and I'm appropriately misty eyed at a woman of such moral superiority leaping to my defense. It might have even worked on the crowd, too, except the woman who accused me of giving her the evil eye slumps in her chair at that moment, a hand clutched against her chest.

"Sarah?" The woman seated on her right is Penny Dautry, a local villager and baking wizard. She dives for Sarah's purse, her hands shaking as she searches for something inside it. "Sarah, where are your pills? Did you remember to bring them?"

"It's her heart," the general mutters. "The doctor. Let the doctor see to her."

Dr. MacDougal rises nobly to the call, getting up from her

chair and going to the woman's side with a competence I can't help but admire. As she lays the woman's body out on the ground and begins talking to her in a low, capable voice, I can even forgive her for saying I'm not a resident here. She's that good.

I've never seen a heart attack in person before, but I never believed them to be as violent as the one that takes hold of Sarah. In fact, after one glance at the wrenching spasm that upends the contents of her stomach, I take it upon myself to clear the room.

"Let's go upstairs and give them some space," I say, not wholly for the doctor's benefit.

"Yes, let's," Annis agrees. More to the point, she begins corralling her parish in a herd and pushing them toward the door. "You can wait in the pews while I call an ambulance. I'm sure Dr. MacDougal has things in hand down here."

I don't know how true that is, but the doctor pays us no heed as we file out of the room. Of everyone, Lenora seems the most upset, which is understandable given her age and the fact that her parents are the ones who have gone to the rescue. As she files through with the rest of the group, her face ashen, I sling an arm over her shoulder.

"It's a good thing your mother was here," I say in a tone that carries nothing but friendly cheerfulness. "If I were to have a medical emergency, she's exactly who I'd want to be sitting next to."

"You'd better not," Lenora says in all seriousness. "I doubt she'd bother to save *you*."

I'm not sure whether to be insulted or not, but there's nothing malicious about the frank way she looks up at me.

"She's going to be okay, isn't she?"

I glance over Lenora's head to where Dr. MacDougal has started chest compressions. The girl shifts as if to turn with me, but I keep my grip firm on her shoulder. There are some things a child should never have to see for herself.

"She's going to be fine," I lie. "I'm sure it's just something she ate."

"It was something she ate."

I pause in the middle of bringing the cup of tea to my lips.

"Not here, of course." Vivian Hartford waits until I take a sip of the tepid liquid before speaking again. I'm well onto the tricks Nicholas's mother likes to play by now, so I know that the cold tea and stale cake are meant to dissuade guests from visiting during mealtimes. "It's just what they're saying in the village. That Sarah Blackthorne was poisoned."

"Poisoned?" Even though the tea tastes perfectly normal, I set the dainty pink cup back on its saucer. "What kind of poison?"

"Rat killer? Arsenic? I don't know. What sort of poison do people use to commit murder in this day and age?" Vivian blinks at me, an expectant air in every line of her bearing. Although the older woman delights in being an oddity, and is wearing some kind of bizarre tennis dress and bolero jacket combination to prove it, I like her. And not just because she believes I know all the tricks to modern-day homicide.

"I think prescription narcotics are probably the best way to go," I say after some consideration. "I mean, it would be easier to frame as an overdose that way, don't you think?"

She purses her lips. "Well, yes, but it's not always easy to get your hands on that type of thing."

"I'm pretty sure it's easier to get Vicodin than it is arsenic. But then, I'm just spitballing here."

Our conversation is interrupted by a low, cool voice from the hall. "I'm not going to ask," Nicholas says as he moves smoothly into the parlor. It's the room most often used at Castle Hartford, a truth borne out by the shabby blankets cast over chairs and half-read books left open on their creases. It's easy to be fooled by such bourgeois comforts, but there's a real Aubusson carpet underfoot and I'm pretty sure the vases flanking the fireplace are from the Ming dynasty.

Perfectly at ease in these elegant surroundings, Nicholas leans down and kisses first my cheek, then his mother's. "Actually, I *am* going to ask. Mrs. Blackthorne?"

Vivian makes a tsking sound before pouring a healthy dollop of brandy into her tea. "Yes, the poor thing. Not that I cared much for her—not since that time I caught her drowning a litter of kittens down by the bridge—but they say it was a rather gruesome way to go. Was it, dear?"

This question is put to me, but I find myself unable to answer. For one, I was well out of the way by the time she passed, sitting upstairs with the rest of the parishioners. For another, I'm still caught up on the kittens.

"Didn't you stop her?" I ask, thinking of my own surly Beast. I like to think she'd fight hard before she'd let anyone—human or otherwise—thrust her into the great beyond before she's good and ready. "Surely there's an animal shelter that would have taken all those kittens in."

"Well, of course I did. Why do you think I asked you to go to the fête committee in my place? She and I haven't been able to share a room ever since." Vivian's eyes narrow, revealing a side to herself I've never seen before. "She had the gall to call me a busybody and lodge a complaint with the city council. I'd have poisoned her myself if I'd thought about it. And none of that Vicodin nonsense, either. Something slow, I think. And painful."

"If I might make a suggestion, I'd keep the death threats to a minimum until the coroner comes back with his results." Nicholas's tone is both mild and mocking—a combination he has perfected.

"Nonsense." Vivian brushes him off with a wave of her

hand. "I can name you at least half a dozen other people who would have been glad to bump her off. Do you think I ought to write them down? It might help the police with their investigation. You're friends with Inspector Piper, Eleanor. What do you think?"

I sit back in my chair, taking everything in with a slightly bewildered air. I should know by now that nothing that takes place in this village is as straightforward as it seems. The problem with people who have lived in the same small town for years, sharing births and deaths and mundane daily activities, is that they have a tangled history it would take a professional taxonomer to organize.

"Um, I wouldn't call Inspector Piper my *friend*," I say.

Nicholas laughs outright. "I don't think Inspector Piper cares for any of us. Let's not interfere until we're asked, shall we?"

It's solid advice, and it behooves us all to heed it. However, a knock at the front door and Rachel's chummy "Hullo, Inspector" in the distance cause events to transpire sooner rather than later.

"Oh, no," I mutter, slinking low in my seat. I scan around for some means of escape, but this is one of the few rooms where the secret passageway that runs through the castle walls *doesn't* exit. "Quick—where can I hide?"

Nicholas pours himself a cup of the lukewarm tea and settles in his chair with nothing but expectation of enjoyment at the events to come. "Now, now, Eleanor. I thought you were the one woman in the world who didn't fear the bogeyman."

"I don't fear the bogeyman," I say, rising hotly to my own defense. "The hand of the law, however . . ."

The hand of the law, such as it is, enters a few seconds later. At first glance, the yellow-vested police inspector standing in the doorway looks like nothing to be wary of. He's thin and wiry, more weasel than man, his eyes shiftily taking in the room. There's nothing intimidating in his stature or his neutral expression, or even in the way his hands reach for his coat pocket in an unconscious tic. He quit smoking a few months ago when I pointed out how small his chances were of winning back his ex-wife otherwise, but the habit of reaching for his cigarettes remains.

Inspector Piper's commitment to his habits is what alarms me. It's how he works. He'll follow a lead and repeat every possibility over and over until he's worn a path in his case. And for some reason, those paths have a tendency to lead straight to me.

His next words confirm it.

"Ah, Ms. Wilde. I'd hoped to find you here."

"Hello, Inspector." Resigned to my fate—and to the fact that no one else in this room is going to play the role of host—I get up and pour him a cup of tea. "Won't you have a seat?"

"Thank you." He sits and accepts the cup but doesn't drink. He's been a visitor enough times to know better, too. "I assume you know why I'm here?"

"Poor Sarah," Vivian says in a convincing show of sympathy. "What a terrible tragedy for the community. She'll be greatly missed."

Even Nicholas looks surprised at his mother's willingness to play by the rules, his eyes meeting mine in a flash of humor. That humor turns to downright mischief when Vivian adds, "Settle a question for us, if you please. Was it arsenic or prescription drugs that did her in? Eleanor seems to think she'd have more luck with the latter."

Inspector Piper pauses in the middle of setting his cup aside to stare at me. "Is that so? What kind of prescription drugs do you normally use to poison people?"

I pass a hand over my eyes with a groan. "We were talking in hypotheticals, I swear."

"*Hypothetically*, what would you use? From one professional to another?"

I see nothing for it but to play along. "If my goal was to escape detection, which I assume is the goal of most poisoners, I'd go for the obvious. Vicodin, OxyContin, Percocet. Anything that could be ruled an overdose."

Inspector Piper nods along, not the least shocked at my ready knowledge of prescription painkillers. The amount of time I spent in hospitals and nursing homes with my sister turned me into something of a savant.

"If my goal was to out and out murder a person, however, I'm not sure what I'd use. Hemlock, maybe? I don't know. I've never been tempted to kill anyone before."

Nicholas coughs and casts an obvious look at his mother, who's absorbing my confession with unwarranted glee. "Not even once?" he asks.

I smother a laugh. Vivian isn't the least bit traditional or motherly, but I adore her, as he well knows. I have a thing for people who are unapologetically honest about themselves.

"What would *you* use, Inspector Piper?" I ask, turning the question back on him. "From one professional to another?"

"Oh, I'd never use poison," he says, almost cheerful. "It's too cowardly, a woman's weapon of choice."

At that, Vivian's backbone begins to emerge. "Well, honestly. I don't think you're qualified—"

I'm about to rally behind the old girl, but Nicholas interrupts before either of us can *really* start to show our hackles. "Is that what we're looking at? Was Mrs. Blackthorne poisoned? Eleanor seemed to think it might have been a heart attack based on what she saw last night."

The inspector turns his head and carefully studies me. He also whips out his ubiquitous notebook and pen, though I swear most of the time he draws pictures of animals instead of taking statements. "Is that so? What makes you say that?"

I find I'm not wholly comfortable with conjuring up the images from last night. In the broad light of day, chatting with Vivian and Nicholas over cups of tea, it's easy to turn the woman's death into an oddity. But I had a difficult time falling asleep last night, unable to forget the way her whole body went stiff or the wrenching way her stomach had convulsed all over the floor.

"She clutched her chest," I say. "And the general said she had a weak heart. That's all. I wasn't there long enough to see much else. *Was* it poison? There was coffee there, but we all drank some. It can't have been that."

He doesn't answer me. Instead, he reaches into his coat pocket. For a moment, I think he's indulging in his nervous tic again, but he extracts a vial and sets it on the tray next to him.

I recognize the vial in an instant. It's identical to the one I gave Mr. Worthington yesterday, a craft bottle I buy in bulk. I like it because it has a square shape that I can easily affix labels to, and it can be stopped with a simple piece of cork. Very rustic and authentic—perfect for potion making of all kinds.

I immediately rear back. "She was never one of my clients. In fact, I got the strong impression she disapproved of me. She'd go out of her way to cross the street whenever we happened to pass."

"So you admit to dispensing illegal substances throughout the village?"

Well, I can hardly unadmit it now, can I? "It's not like I'm peddling *cocaine*. It's artisanal water."

Nicholas's low chuckle is swiftly hidden under a cough.

The inspector's cough is much more authentic. "Artisanal water?"

"Yep. Just plain, ordinary tap water infused with botanicals." I then add, "*Local* botanicals," lest he think I'm importing strange concoctions from overseas.

"Local botanicals?"

I'm not loving the way he's parroting my words back at me, or the fact that they're all phrased as questions. On a cognitive level, I know it's how Inspector Piper gets responses out of people, in much the same way I use dramatic pauses and warbling messages from beyond. On a visceral level, I can't help feeling he's about to drag me to the jailhouse and swallow the key.

To show him that I'm above such petty interrogation tactics, I reach for the bottle. He doesn't stop me, so I pull out the cork and give it a tentative sniff. There's no liquid left, but I use such strong concentrations of, uh, local botanicals that it can be difficult to get the smell out. The overpowering burst of lavender that hits my nose is a confirmation of it.

"Just as I suspected." I hold it out to him. "This is my attraction elixir."

He doesn't sniff the bottle, although both Vivian and Nicholas oblige me.

"And before you say, '*Attraction elixir?*' in that odious way, I should note that it's meant to be worn as perfume, not consumed as a tonic," I say. "It's used to attract potential mates. Male ones."

I don't have to glance over at Nicholas to know that he's struggling to keep himself in check. His laughing silence conveys enough.

"I've had a very high success rate with it," I add with a blatant disregard for truth. Rachel's lack of dates at her art gallery has been weighing heavily on me, but not so much that I'm willing to admit as much out loud. I still have to make a living, after all.

The inspector raises his pen over his notepad. "And what, if you don't mind my asking, goes into an attraction elixir?"

"Actually, I do mind you asking. It's a trade secret."

"Lavender is my guess," Nicholas supplies as he hands the bottle back to the inspector. "And far too much of it. Though how that could be considered a local botanical at this time of year is beyond me."

"Nick, you wretch!" I cry. And, because there's no way around it now, "It *is* mostly lavender. Which, by the way, I buy in dried bundles from the sweet old lady who makes that soap from sheep's milk and sells it at the Saturday market. *Locally*."

"What else goes in it?" the inspector asks.

I shift uncomfortably. "Well . . ."

"A woman is dead, Ms. Wilde."

"Um, vodka?"

Nicholas releases another one of those laugh-coughs.

"And?"

"That's all, I swear! It's just lavender, water, and vodka. I mean, I also perform a sacred lunar goddess ritual over the batch, but that goes without saying."

Inspector Piper eyes me doubtfully. "And what is a sacred lunar goddess ritual?"

Nicholas supplies the answer for me. "She dances naked under the light of a full moon. Or so I've been led to believe. Unfortunately, I've been out of town every time a full moon hits. I've rescheduled all my meetings so I'm sure to be at home for the next one."

I turn to glare at him, determined, as usual, to give him a piece of my mind. However, the look in his eyes stops me before I get the first word out. It's such a warm look, a *hungry* look, that I can hardly be blamed for my lack of follow-through.

I have never, in all my life, danced naked under a moon of any kind—waning, waxing, or bursting with sensual brilliance. If he promises to watch with that gleam in his eyes, however, I might have to take up the habit. This whole ships-passing-in-the-night thing is really starting to take its toll on me, sensual brilliance–wise.

Inspector Piper clears his throat, drawing my attention back to the present—and the fact that I'm being questioned for a murder in front of Nicholas's mother.

I nod at the bottle. "Even if she *did* drink it, which I expressly tell my clients not to do, all that would happen is she'd get a slight buzz and feel like her mouth was recently washed out with soap. I'm sure if you take it in for one of those forensic tests, they'll tell you the same thing."

"The last time I investigated a crime you were tied to, you wanted me to bring in a sketch artist and DNA-sniffing dogs," the inspector says.

I know I did, and it was good advice, too. Especially since the sketch I ended up commissioning on my own *solved* the entire murder. "So?"

He gets to his feet and slips the bottle back into his breast pocket. "You seem to have a skewed idea of the kind of budget I operate under." He nods first at me and then at the pair seated on either side. "Thank you for your time, Ms. Wilde. You've been most . . . informative."

"So that's it?" Vivian says, disappointed. "You aren't going to tell us how she died?"

Inspector Piper's eyes open in mild surprise. "She was poisoned, naturally."

"And?" Vivian urges.

Inspector Piper's next words are for me. "And cursed. According to Mr. MacDougal, Ms. Wilde gave her the evil eye right before her attack."

All eyes in the room—evil and otherwise—turn to me at once. I groan.

"If I could curse people with just a look, believe me, you'd all be the first to go." I stare at them as if to prove it. As expected, no one is moved, not even to blink. "See? I'm harmless."

Harmless I might be, but I'm also wary of being investigated for a crime I had nothing to do with. Hoping to catch a private word with the inspector, I walk him to the door.

"What was the actual reason for your visit?" I ask as we move through the huge foyer. It's always been my favorite part of the castle, all cavernous and gloomy and echoing. "You know very well that my elixir isn't poison. Not even the worst criminal in the world would kill someone with a substance she's known to sell to anyone with twenty pounds and a broken heart."

"Twenty pounds, huh?" he asks with a pat of his breast pocket. "That seems awfully steep."

"I use the good vodka." I pause. "Seriously, though—what did you *really* come here to ask me?"

Inspector Piper studies me with the intensity I've come to expect from our interactions with one another. He hates that I'm just as good at this investigative stuff as he is, even without years of academy training and a badge hanging around my neck. I'd feel bad for him, but he must know by now that a person doesn't become a successful fake psychic without *some* natural talent. I'm better able than most to take a step back from situations, to detach myself emotionally and watch for the inevitable clues that people let fall.

It's not a skill that comes from a happy place. I've always felt like an outsider looking in, more attached to my dead sister than any living human being.

Aw, thanks, Sis. I'm attached to you, too.

There's also that. Winnie's ability to communicate with me from beyond the grave is what some people might consider a real boon in my line of work.

"I can't confirm the type of poison that was used until the toxicology results come back, but I believe we're looking at something organic. Something *local.*"

My breath catches in my throat. "Oh, dear. Not the sweet old soap lady?"

A ghost of a smile crosses his face. "I'm not ruling anyone out just yet, but I doubt Aunt Margaret was involved."

"Wait—what? She's your aunt?"

My tone is sharp, mostly because I'm annoyed with myself for not realizing it earlier. Now that he mentions it, there is a slight resemblance—the thin lines of the nose and cheeks, the calm way they appraise the world around them. All similarities end there, however. Margaret knows all kinds of useful things about where to find flowers and roots, and is more than happy to share her knowledge with me. Getting information out of Inspector Piper is like squeezing granite and hoping for honey. He shares that trait with Nicholas.

"If you're interested in the local flora, why don't you just ask her for her input?" I demand.

"I already did." His tone contains nothing but mildness, but there's a worried pucker to his brow that doesn't normally reside there. "And while we're on the subject, I'd also strongly suggest you stop selling your potions for a while."

"But that's how I make a living! Do you want me to starve?"

He casts an obvious look around—at the splendor of Castle Hartford and all the bounty contained within it. There's no denying that the contents of this room alone could provide enough income to feed both me and Beast until our dying days.

My hackles rise anew. Although I might be a charlatan and a cheat, I'm not a gold digger. I'd no more live off Nicholas's generosity than I would ask Inspector Piper to let me come live with him.

"I can't stop working every time there's a suspicious death within a hundred-kilometer radius," I say. "And I'm pretty sure you can't make me without some kind of legal order."

"You mean a legal order like a request to see your business license?" he returns calmly. "Or perhaps your VAT certificate?"

I don't allow my shoulders to slump. Of course I don't have a business license or any kind of tax-paying system set up, but that doesn't mean I'm going down without a fight. "I'm a *witch*, Inspector. Our relationship with government entities has long been fraught with dissent. Need I remind you what they used to do to my kind? Crackle, crackle, burn, burn."

My attempt at turning the tides of history in my favor fail.

"Until the investigation is over, Ms. Wilde. That's all I'm asking. Then we can, uh, re-visit the idea of you establishing a business in the city. A *legal* business."

He tips his hat to me like a Victorian bobby of old and takes his leave. I'm tempted to go home and start brewing the biggest batch of herbal elixirs this county has ever seen, but common sense soon warns me that I'm not likely to find many buyers for my wares. Not with a woman dead from poison and nary a suspect in sight. Even if I include a list of ingredients on the label, I don't see a whole lot of people lining up to ingest anything that doesn't come from their own hands.

Whether I like it or not, I'm going to have to wait for a conclusive end to this investigation before I can get back to work.

"Oh, dear." Nicholas appears in the foyer, watching me watch Inspector Piper depart. "You don't look as though you enjoyed that interview. Shall I start pulling together the bail money? We have one or two family heirlooms I'd love to have an excuse to unload. There's a picture of my great-uncle Harold that used to give me terrible nightmares as a child."

"Very funny," I mutter. Even if I *did* need bail money, Nicholas wouldn't have to sell anything to get his hands on it. He's a legitimate millionaire, though a less flashy one I have yet to meet. His clothes are expensive and well tailored, and he has a private jet he takes on his many world travels, but all ostentation ends there. "He told me I have to stop selling my potions until the mystery is solved."

One ironic brow lifts. "Because you're a suspect?"

"Yes? No? I can't tell, but it's not as if it matters anyway. No one is going to buy my stuff if they believe I poisoned Mrs. Blackthorne." I perk at a sudden thought. "Unless I came up with an antidote. Do you think—?"

"No, I decidedly do not."

I sigh. "You're probably right. I'm just going to have to ride this one out, I guess."

The mocking laughter on his face drops only to be replaced by a more earnest regard. I find myself recoiling from it, since I know what's coming next. In an effort to stave him off, I fling up a hand. "No. Don't."

"Eleanor . . ."

"I don't need your help," I lie. "I still have plenty of money in my savings account from my ghost-hunting days, and I've been making a killing on those elixirs lately."

"A killing?" he asks. "Are you certain that's the word you want to use?"

As it's been effective at stopping him from making an offer I have no choice but to refuse, yes, it's absolutely the word I mean. Since I know he meant nothing but kindness, however, I tiptoe and reach to brush a kiss on his cheek.

I mean to end the kiss quickly—and to escape the castle before our conversation reaches a heavier, more intimate tone—but his arms wrap around my waist to hold me pressed against him, my toes only lightly touching the floor. As if that weren't enough, a slight turn of his head brings our lips into direct contact. As always, his kiss is firm but gentle, a polite request that could, with the right persuasion, turn into something more.

Although I'd be happy to do some persuading in the ordinary way of things, I only allow myself a slight nibble and a sigh before pulling away again.

"Thank you, Nicholas," I say. "You're sweet to be concerned about me, but I don't need your generosity."

"Oh, it's not generosity. I don't want the people of the village thinking I can't keep a woman properly, that's all."

I laugh, more grateful than he realizes that he made this easy on me.

"Don't worry," I say and indulge in one more embrace—this

time with enough persuasion to leave us both wishing his mother wasn't sitting and drinking tea upstairs. "I promise to parade through the streets dripping with jewels and furs at least twice a week. Three, if you promise to kiss me like that again."

"You drive a hard bargain, Madame Eleanor, but I think I can oblige," he says.

And he does.

Chapter 3

"So now, not only am I *not* allowed to sell any of my potions, but my reputation is in tatters." I throw myself onto my bed and stare up at the ceiling, where a watermark in the shape of a giant cross looks down on me. I'm going to need to get that thatch looked at soon, or one of these days, I'm going to wake up to a deluge overhead. "Half the townspeople are afraid I'm going to poison them while they sleep, and the half who aren't—mostly Hartfords, by the way—don't believe in witchcraft in the first place. I'm ruined, Liam. *Ruined*."

My brother, never what one would call a sympathetic man, sighs into the phone. "I told you it wasn't a good idea to move there permanently, remember? It's all that bad energy hanging about the place."

"Please. You don't believe in bad energy. You just don't like that I'm living my bucolic British dream without you."

"Your dream, huh? Is that the one that ends with you being run out of town with pitchforks, or the one where you get burned at the stake in the village square?"

"Um."

"Exactly." He pauses, his silence heavy with meaning. "You

could move home, you know. There's always room for you on my couch. And now that you don't have to pay for Winnie's care anymore . . ."

Even though he can't see me, I shake my head. The three of us were—*are*—triplets, which means he's just as close to Winnie, genetically speaking, as me. But his relationship with her never went as deep.

How could it? *I* was the one who was in the car with her the night she entered a comatose state almost twelve years ago. *I* was the one who became a fake medium to pay for her long-term health care bills. *I* was the one who suddenly started hearing her talk to me right before she died last year.

And, you know, after.

Winnie's postmortem communication with me is neither regular nor predictable, but there's a pattern to it I can't deny. Most of the time, she comes only at night, her voice a cheerful backdrop that weaves in and out of my dreams. In other words, it could be written off as the natural nocturnal wanderings of the mind.

The only problem with that theory is that whenever I'm stressed or in trouble—or, it seems, investigating a murder—she adds daytime visits to her repertoire. It sounds crazy, I know, but I can tell when it's the real deal. Although Liam says he believes me when I tell him about some of the conversations Winnie and I have shared, I'm pretty sure he thinks I'm playing a few cards short of a full deck.

"It's nice of you to offer," I say with sincerity. Cynic though he may be, my brother does love me. That much I know is true. "But, no. I've chosen to live here, and I intend to see this thing through. I refuse to run away while my honor is at stake."

He laughs. "What honor?"

"My honor as a practitioner of the art of witchcraft, of course. Hang on a second, will you? I think there's someone at the door."

I'd hoped that in tying up my cell phone for a long chat with my brother in New York, I'd avoid any pesky calls from Inspector Piper or anyone else in the village who might be envisioning my head on the end of a pike. I'd forgotten, however, that in a small town like this one, people are just as likely to stop by as they are to provide a fair warning via phone first.

"Please enter," I call as I reach the bottom of the stairs. "My domain is always available to those in need." At Liam's snort, I add, in a lower voice for only his ears, "Don't be mean. What if it's a paying client? I have to give them a show."

The back door pushes open a fraction.

"No curse is so strong it can't be lifted, no problem so vast it can't be solved with the right approach," I add.

"Except for you running around town poisoning people," Liam says. "Don't forget to tell them about that part."

I hang up on him and hide the phone behind a potted fern just as a tentative head pokes through the opening in the door.

"Lenora!" I cry as soon as I recognize the small yet resolute face peering in at me. "How nice to see you."

I don't know that *nice* is the right word, but it's the only one I can think of on the spur of the moment. The MacDougal girl's braid is coming loose from its binding and she has a navy blue uniform jacket tied around her waist. With a backpack slung over her shoulder and a bike helmet in hand, the chances are high that she's stopping by on her way home from school.

"Do your parents know you're here?" I ask.

"No, of course not. They don't approve of you." She drops her backpack to the floor with a heavy thump. "Is it true you kidnap people's babies and trade them with demons?"

I bite back a laugh. "Not quite. You're thinking of changelings. The fairies are responsible for that."

She pauses in the middle of dropping her helmet to the floor along with her pack. "Fairies? But I thought they were nice."

"That's what they want you to think. Some of them are quite nasty. Is there, um, something you wanted? I'm not sure you need to take off your shoes. It's not that kind of house."

"Oh, can't I, please? They pinch my feet. I've been dreaming of taking them off all day."

The way she looks up at me, her little face so earnest and her eyes wide, makes it impossible for me to deny her request. Nor, apparently, am I able to stop her from continuing the sloughing off of the various items gathered about her. Shoes, the jangling contents of her pockets, the lanyard around her neck . . . I can only watch, bewildered, as she makes herself at home. She even goes so far as to put the kettle on and set about preparing an afternoon tea.

"You don't mind, do you?" she asks as she blithely continues setting items on a tray. "I'm always *starving* after school. One of the mums petitioned them last year to only serve vegetarian organics, so lunch is complete rubbish. My friend Meera smuggles in snack cakes most days, but she was out sick. Do you have any milk?"

I gesture toward the miniature fridge.

"Lovely. Now we can have a comfortable chat. Did you hear that Mrs. Blackthorne died last night? They took her to hospital, but she'd been poisoned, so there was no hope. I've never seen anyone get poisoned before. It was kind of gross, wasn't it?"

"It was very gross," I agree. And, because I'm ostensibly the grown-up in the room, I add, "Do you need to talk to someone about it? I'm sure it was very upsetting, seeing—"

"Oh, I'm all right—really I am. I was a little upset last night, but my brother, George, is always killing things like ants and flies and mice out in the fields behind our house. I see a lot of dead things."

"He kills mice?" I ask, somewhat alarmed. The ants and flies I can understand, but killing something with a pulse requires a whole different level of maliciousness. If there's a line to be drawn in the sand, a functioning circulatory system is where I'd put it.

"Well, he has to." She bites into a digestive biscuit. "Ever since our cat disappeared last month, it's his job to keep them from coming into the house. He's good at it, too. By the way, the kids at school are saying you poisoned Mrs. Blackthorne, but I told them that you're the good kind of witch, like Professor McGonagall. It's true, isn't it?"

I blink. "That I'm the good kind of witch, or that I didn't poison Mrs. Blackthorne?"

She waves an airy hand. "Either one."

"Um . . ." I strain to think of a polite—and kid-friendly—way to close this conversation. The best I can come up with is, "There's no such thing as a good or a bad witch. Just ones with ordinary human motives. And, no, of course I didn't poison that poor woman. Was there something you needed, Lenora? I don't mean to be rude, but—"

"I've come to apply to be your apprentice." She sets the completed tea in front of me with a flourish. For a girl who's never set foot in my kitchen before, she's done a decent job of it. There's even a miniature sugar spoon I can't recall seeing before. "It's a school thing. We're supposed to find a profession we're interested in and then job shadow for the rest of the semester. Oona wanted me to apply at her office, but I hate all those crying kids."

"Oona?" I echo.

"My mum—if you can call her that. So, can I?"

"Well, actually . . ."

"I'm a keen worker. You won't regret it." She blinks expectantly up at me. "You aren't drinking your tea."

"I'm sorry," I murmur. I obligingly lift the cup to my lips and sip. The tea is good—strong and rich, with just the right amount of milk to take the edge off.

"See? And I make a smashing cuppa." She leaps to her feet and drags her eight-ton backpack across the floor. After a brief struggle with the zipper, she reaches inside and extracts a piece of paper. "Aha! Here it is. The job-shadow form. You just fill in the top part, and then my parents have to sign at the bottom."

I see an easy out and latch on to it. "I'd love to have you, I really would, but I don't think your parents will agree to this plan. Or, to be fair, your school. My profession isn't exactly . . . academic."

"Oh, it doesn't have to be," she says, unperturbed. She pushes a pen toward me. "The Haldwell twins are going to shadow the guy who makes the cider for the pub, and he does it in his bathtub. Here."

When I hesitate once more, her voice adopts a wheedling note I find difficult to withstand.

"Please, Madame Eleanor? I think what you do is so neat. If you fill it out, I'll get my parents on board, I promise. I just know it'll help me develop my interests in botany and folklore."

Botany and folklore *are* important things for a girl to learn, I'll admit. They're science and literature wrapped up in one witchy package. At her age, I'd have loved to be able to ask questions of someone other than the overworked librarian, who was far too busy unjamming the copier to care about my queries into the underworld.

And to be honest, there's no way Lenora's parents will agree to this. Her mother loathes me and her father is the local schoolmaster. If anyone can halt a disastrous apprenticeship in its tracks, it's Dr. and Mr. MacDougal. With only a niggling pang of guilt, I begin to fill out my portion of the page.

Name of Profession: Dabbler in the Dark Arts.

Years in Profession: Either eleven or an eternity, depending on your constructs of time.

Education: School of Hard Knocks, twenty-nine years (see above on time).

Licensing and Insurance: None, whatsoever.

I sign and date the page with a flourish. If that doesn't get someone at the school to take this poor, deluded child under his or her wing and direct her toward a more respectable position, I don't know what will.

Lenora takes it from my hand and giggles as she reads it over.

"You're funny, Madame Eleanor. What do we learn first? Can I start this afternoon?"

As my primary plan for the rest of the day is to research the physiological effects of various poisons on the human system, I'm not sure it's a good idea to have a twelve-year-old sidekick whose parents may or may not be sending her to boarding school after this.

"Why don't we wait until your school gives the formal okay?" I suggest. At her crestfallen look, I add, "And for homework, you can, um, find out if there have been any changeling sightings in this part of England during the past hundred years."

She perks. "Ooh, can I? Would that sort of information be at the museum?"

I think of the small, underwhelming village museum that contains mostly Roman pottery shards and Hartford family history archives and laugh. "Sure. Why not? Write me up a five-page report on all the instances of the occult you can find."

From the beaming way she leaps to her feet, you'd think I just handed her an all-expenses-paid cruise to the Bahamas.

"I'm on it," she says with a salute. She also begins the laborious process of returning all her belongings to her pack. Only the form doesn't go back into the backpack—that she holds in her hands with a kind of reverence I'm starting to find worrisome. "I'll come by tomorrow about the same time, yeah? Unless you want to meet somewhere else?"

"How about the tea shop on the edge of the village?" I suggest. I don't usually work from a remote office, but it seems wise to meet Lenora somewhere highly public. That way, if her parents want to murder and/or arrest me for the corruption of their minor, they'll have to do it in front of an audience. "It'll be my treat."

"Deal." Lenora sticks out her hand and holds it there until I give it a perfunctory shake. It's a very businesslike way to conclude our transaction—a thing I appreciate and fear at the same time. "And thank you, Madame Eleanor. You aren't going to regret this."

A, Arsenic: Vivian's poison of choice and old lace accompaniment. Signs of poisoning include flu-like symptoms and dehydration. Tasteless. Can be purchased online.
B, Belladona: Great name for a plant or Bond villain. Signs of poisoning include hallucinations and dilated pupils. Sweet, mild taste. Grown in England and can be purchased online.
C, Chloroform: Ideal for kidnapping ladies in historical romances. Signs of poisoning include unconsciousness. Smells like, well, chloroform. Can be purchased online.

"Sheesh. You can buy just about anything online these days, can't you?" I turn away from my scribblings and address Beast, who sits curled at my feet. She likes to be near me whenever she's in the house, but it's rare that she comes close enough for me to pet her. She likes to keep the mystery alive that way. "Someone needs to take a serious look at what kinds of companies are shilling arsenic and chloroform to the masses. This can't be legal."

I scroll farther down the helpful website I've found, which is most likely being flagged and watched by several government information agencies.

D, Drip Drip: Seriously, Ellie. I think your bathroom is starting to flood.

The sound of my sister's voice doesn't, as it first used to, frighten me. Back when I wasn't sure who was speaking to me—or why—I'd had serious doubts about my mental state. Now that I know it's my sister keeping an ever-watchful eye on me, I feel delighted. Her visits aren't nearly as often as I'd like.

"I put a pot in there," I protest as I rise to my feet. "Two of them, actually. And you'd think the clawfoot tub would manage to catch the rest."

Winnie doesn't respond. Beast, however, does. With a mewl of protest at being dislodged from her comfortable position, she arches her back and leads the way to the tiny room next to mine that just manages to contain a toilet, a pedestal sink, and the aforementioned tub.

That's another thing I should probably mention—animals appear to be able to hear Winnie, too. Either that or my sister has taken on the form of my cat and intends to judge my life choices from her comfortable feline perch. I haven't been able to decide which option makes me sound less deranged, so I'm leaving them both open.

"Oh, no!" I cry as I enter the bathroom to find that the thatch has sprung not one, not two, but *three* more leaks. The subdued patter of rain overhead might sound like a soothing evening backdrop, but the way the water channels in and soaks through the plaster is anything but.

I dump my toothbrush out of its cup and place that vessel under the largest of the drips, but based on the rate of precipitation, it won't last long.

"There's nothing else to do," I say with a groan. "I'm going to have to dip into the last of my savings and have the roofer out. There's just enough in there to eke out a down payment."

And by *just enough*, I mean literally that. I'll have nothing left but the money Mr. Worthington paid me for Regina. Which means that unless the roof thatcher is willing to work for all-you-can-wear attraction elixirs, I'm going to need to seriously step up my investigation game around here.

Of course, you could always ask your boyfriend—

"Not you too, Winnie! You're supposed to be on my side, remember?" I cross my arms and glare in a general upward direction. All I get for my pains is a drop of cold rainwater in my eye and the sound of her laughter echoing until there's nothing left but silence.

I know, without quite understanding why, that she won't be back again tonight. I'd love a chance to brainstorm other financial options with her—taking on a roommate, perhaps, or starting an herbal medicine class for the locals—but her advice tends to be less than practical. I imagine it's because there's no need to earn a living where she is. She probably doesn't even have to eat.

"The only way this night could get any worse would be if the wind were to pick up and the entire roof blow away," I mutter. "Either that or if Mr. Worthington's pig runs away again and he comes back to demand a refund."

I'm not sure who I'm speaking to at this point, but no response is necessary. Now that the idea of a runaway pig stealing the last of my lunch money has taken hold, it's difficult to exorcise.

Fears are much harder to get rid of than ghosts that way.

Which is why, despite the pelting rain and the fact that it's nearing eight o'clock, I bundle myself up in a heavy mackintosh and head toward Mr. Worthington's farm. I grab my handy fence-fixing bag on the way as well as a few flax flowers I keep perennially growing in my garden. It wasn't just Mr. Worthington I sent to the evergreen crossroads; I make *all* my clients plant flax seeds in that location as part of their rituals. It totally freaks them out when they pass by to find fully grown flowers where they placed their seeds only a few days previously. Anyone with knowledge of horticulture would be able to tell that the soil is loose and the roots haven't yet taken hold, but that's a risk I'm willing to run.

Besides, it makes people happy. To see living proof of magic, to believe wholeheartedly in the power of something miraculous, is more therapeutic than a lot of so-called medical remedies these days.

The evergreen crossroads aren't located on an actual road,

but almost everyone who lives in the village knows where to find the crisscrossing footpaths that wind through the small forest thicket that borders several local farms. After dark, when the cold settles in and the moon slips behind a cloud, it's quite eerie out here.

As I expect, I arrive to find evidence that more than one person has been doing some impromptu gardening out here. I like to think that in a few months all those seeds I've caused to be sown will provide a beautiful—and fully natural—floral backdrop to anyone wishful of enjoying a picturesque sojourn through the woods. Right now, it mostly looks like an energetic puppy tried to hide a favorite bone.

I choose an area off to one side and set my bags down. Cold, rainy, nighttime gardening isn't my favorite activity, so I make short work of getting the flowers into the soil. The cheerful blue blooms look a little wilted after their brief journey, so I say a quick chant over them just to be sure.

"Keep them strong, will you, Winnie?" I add, since she's the only *real* magic I know.

She doesn't answer. However, a scuttle in the underbrush sounds to my right, so I divert my attention there. I half expect Beast to be sitting in attendance, watching me with her narrow-eyed look of judgment, but the creature moving around the foliage isn't a cat. It's a mouse—a *fast* mouse, which darts between my legs and runs off the other direction with such speed that I lose sight of it almost immediately.

Knowing what I do about Winnie and animals, I peer into the bushes and take a few steps that direction, unable to shake the feeling that it wants me to follow. It's a feeling that pans out a few feet later when I pick up on a trail of another kind.

"Oh, dear," I say, recognizing the splatter of blood over the leafy undergrowth in an instant. "This can't be good."

Considering my current position as a possible suspect in Sarah Blackthorne's murder, I'm careful not to touch or dis-

place the blood in any way. I can't help my footprints or the fact that I just did a little late-night gardening, however. Whether I like it or not, my presence here is now undeniable.

The trail extends some yards away, taking me past the tangle of ferns to a small clearing. As soon as I reach the outer edges, I stop. Not too far from where I'm standing lies a carcass—cracked open and bloodied, devoured as if from the inside out. My first feeling of relief at discovering it's an animal carcass rather than a human one is quickly replaced by a strong revulsion.

Revulsion and, unfortunately, recognition.

"Regina?" I draw forward with my hand pressed to my nose. The smell isn't one of decay—the pig hasn't been dead long enough for that—but the metallic tang of a bloodbath is strong.

Bloodbath, the only word I can think of to describe the scene. Whatever kind of predator killed Mr. Worthington's pig, it wasn't a small one. Chunks of the body have been ripped off and scattered all over the ground, the entrails leading off into the underbrush. I recognize a large intestine as the cause of the blood-spattered trail.

"Poor Mr. Worthington!" I cry as I back quickly from the scene. Then, in a more selfish turn of events, "Oh, no. He's going to want that refund for sure now."

I hesitate, unsure about the proper authorities to notify for farm animal's death. Inspector Piper pops to my mind only be immediately dismissed. I can already hear the questions his lips.

Do you ask all *your clients to plant flowers in this locati just the ones with a penchant for porcine company?*

Did the mouse talk to you before it led you to the scer

Would you like to bring in your own counsel or have appointed to you by the courts?

No thanks. I like to think I have a healthy respect but that respect doesn't extend to making my ow

able. There are also quite a few farms around these parts I could ask for assistance, but it's late enough that my visit isn't likely to be welcomed.

In the end, I cut in the direction of Mr. Worthington's house. It's probably too late to be calling on him, too, but the least I can do is notify him of what I found. And apologize in person, though I'm not looking forward to the task in the slightest. Although most of the people who seek my help are in emotional or spiritual distress of some kind, I don't deal with death directly.

Or, at least, I never used to. Ever since coming to this place, death seems to surround me at every turn. Just ask Inspector Piper.

I've developed rather hearty country-walking skills during my time here, so it doesn't take me long to turn up Mr. Worthington's drive. I inspect the lines of the fence as I do, searching for the telltale sign of Regina having eaten through the posts and escaped. After Sarah Blackthorne's death last night, I hadn't been in the mood to check on the grounds, so I expect to see all kinds of havoc wreaked in my absence.

But there's nothing. The wire I hung is still firmly in place, all the posts standing erect. Even the gate appears to be fully latched.

"You." Mr. Worthington bursts through the door with his finger outstretched. I flinch at the look of outrage and accusation in his gaze, but I don't back down. "How dare you show your face around here. What have you done with my Regina?"

Instead of jumping into my sorry news, I cast an anxious look at that fence. "How did she get out?"

"Your black magic, that's how. Where did you put her? Where has she gone?"

"You didn't accidentally leave the gate open?" I ask. "Or on purpose? The binding spell was strong, but physical barriers are also important. Maybe I should have made that part clear."

"Of course I didn't leave the gate open," he says with all the

air of one talking down to a child. "She was perfectly happy when I fed her breakfast this morning. I came out at lunchtime to find her missing, and she hasn't come home all evening. You were supposed to fix this. You promised!"

There's more anguish than accusation in his voice by this time, causing a flood of guilt to wash through me. Strange as it might seem for a man to be so enamored of what, to me, looked like a tasty side of bacon, Regina was very much his pet.

"Mr. Worthington, I'm afraid I have some bad news. Can I come in?"

He doesn't want to let me over the threshold, I can tell, but his good manners get me past the door and a cup of tea placed on a tray in front of me. The fortifying brew is welcome after my brisk walk and the horrors of the kill site, though I mostly just clutch the cup between my hands and absorb the warmth.

"What is it?" Mr. Worthington sits perched at the end of his chair, watching me warily. "What did you do?"

"I didn't *do* anything," I say as gently as I can. "But I was out for a walk and stumbled across something . . . unpleasant."

"Unpleasant?"

"Your pig. Regina. She's—" For what might be the first time in my life, I wish I'd gone straight to Inspector Piper with this one. "I'm, uh, afraid she's dead."

The blood drains from Mr. Worthington's face. He leans back in his chair, all of his gaunt angles collapsing in on themselves. Alarmed and still feeling horribly guilty, I crouch next to his chair and start plying him with tea and biscuits, taking his thin hand in mine and giving it a pat.

"She's in a better place," I promise. "She's at rest now. I can feel it."

At the mention of a world other than the one we inhabit, Mr. Worthington seems to regain some of his color. He bolts upright in his chair and snatches his hand from mine. "She's dead?" he cries. "You killed her?"

"No, not me. Someone, some*thing* . . ." I have no idea how

to finish. "A coyote, maybe? A wolf? I don't know what kind of predators are wandering about Sussex, but some sort of animal got to her. I'd take you there, but it's awfully gruesome."

"Get out." Mr. Worthington's command is low but strong.

"I'm sorry that the binding spell didn't work, but in a way, she'll always be with you now."

"Out," he says again, even firmer this time. There's nothing for it but for me to rise to my feet and heed his command. Grief affects everyone in different ways, and for a man as sensitive as this one, I'm not surprised to find that he's filled with nothing but loathing for the messenger.

Which is how I find myself standing outside his front door, still with the teacup in my hand. I place it on the doorstep and back carefully away, taking another moment to check the fence while I go. Everything is intact and upright, no sign of escape anywhere.

What I *can* see, however, is Mr. Worthington twitching the curtains and talking into a telephone handset. Since there's a good chance he's currently on the line with Inspector Piper or another member of the village police force, I decide it's a good time to retreat.

And if I take the long way back, avoiding those crossroads and the gory carcass that lies in wait there?

Hey. I'm only human, after all.

Chapter 4

"The lunch special is bacon pie. The pork chops are decent, too."

It's only through supreme force of will that I manage not to gag at this bounty of porcine splendor.

"I'll just have the soup, please." Turning to my companion, I add, "If you know what's good for you, you'll order the same thing. I can't be held responsible for my actions if anything pork-related wafts past me."

"With such an offer on the table, how can I refuse?" Nicholas smiles up at our waitress. Catherine is the only waitress in the only pub this village has, so it's important to stay on her good side. "I'll have the same. And I'll pay you five hundred pounds to throw the rest of your special out. When Madame Eleanor has a feeling about something . . ."

Catherine giggles. "I doubt the cook would throw it out for five thousand. You know how he gets about his special recipes. I'll be right back with your drinks."

I watch her happily carefree departure with a frown. "Drat. She must have thought you were kidding."

"That's because I *was* kidding. Was it really that bad?"

We're seated in the deepest, darkest corner of the village pub, the booth so poorly lit that it's difficult to make out all the features of Nicholas's face. The lines of him are there, though, familiar and deeply grooved and, in this instance at least, sympathetic. He has to fly out this afternoon to attend to some kind of important business meeting in Spain, which means this date has to serve as both a meal and a good-bye.

Once he leaves, I also intend it to be an opportunity to grill the local residents about Sarah Blackthorne, but that part goes without saying.

"In terms of all the horrible things I've seen in my life, no," I say. "In terms of things I'd like to eat for lunch ever again, yes. What are they going to do with her?"

"You mean, other than serve her at the local pub?" Nicholas takes his napkin from the table and spreads it in his lap. Even in this dingy atmosphere, where the tables are covered with the grease of centuries past and there's fireplace smoke permanently etched into the walls, he's one hundred percent refinement. "Take her to the rendering plant, I imagine. Poor Mr. Worthington. He's had that pig for years—too many, if you ask around. It's eaten most of every garden within walking distance."

"Don't look at me like that," I say. I don't need incandescent lighting to tell me I'm being judged. "I fixed the fence. *And* I checked it as I was leaving his house last night. It's still intact. There's no way she escaped on her own."

"Is this the part where I remind you that pigs can't fly?"

"No." I fight the juvenile act of sticking my tongue out at him. The main problem with dating a fancy millionaire is quelling my natural petty urges. "But something feels weird about this whole thing, especially so soon after Sarah's death. How did the pig get out? What killed her? And why did I find her in the one place where I've been sending my clients to plant flax seeds?"

"One might also ask why you're so obsessed with flax in the first place," Nicholas not so helpfully adds.

Catherine returns with both our drinks and our food, forestalling my sharp response. By the time I've lavishly buttered a roll and started in on a nice vegetable soup, I'm feeling much more conciliatory toward my lunch date.

"Did you know that there are thousands of naturally growing poisonous plants?" I ask by way of conversation. "Several hundred can be found in the United Kingdom alone."

"Why do I get the feeling you didn't ask me out for the simple joy of my company?"

"And most of them are just ordinary flowers," I say, blithely ignoring him. "*Flowers*, Nicholas—and I'm not just talking poinsettias, which everyone knows you aren't supposed to taste. Hydrangeas have cyanide in them. If bees make honey from rhododendrons and you eat it, you can throw up for days. And prolonged exposure to daffodils can actually cause headaches and nausea. I love daffodils. They're one of my favorite flowers."

"Is that a hint?"

I smother a laugh and lean in, doing my best not to let his charm through my defenses. I also drop my voice, since the last thing I need is the family in the next booth telling everyone they know about Madame Eleanor's preferred topics of lunch conversation.

"The wonder is that any of us are still alive," I say. "That number doesn't include chemical and pharmaceutical poisons, which are also alarmingly prevalent—not to mention ridiculously easy to get. In fact, I think I accidentally bought a dozen cases of elephant tranquilizers online last night. What am I going to do with that many elephant tranquilizers?"

His lips quiver until they reach something approaching a smile. "The real question is why you object more to the quantity you ordered than the fact you made a purchase at all."

My own lips are tugged in an answering upward direction. I hide the expression by patting my mouth primly with my napkin. "Yes, well, an attractive young woman living alone can never be too safe. Daffodil poisoning takes *hours.*"

"I shouldn't find that comforting, but I do." He shifts, his large, strong hands making their way under the table toward my knees. Since I'm dressed as I usually am, in a flowing, floaty shift dress layered over tights, he doesn't make direct contact with my skin. Still, there's reassurance in those hands. There's warmth. "Eleanor, I know you live in a strange world of your own making, but I promise you that people don't normally walk around poisoning their neighbors. In fact, most of us—"

I don't get to discover what most of the populace does because Nicholas cuts himself off with a grimace. I'm understandably alarmed at the sight, however discreet it might be. This is a man who can face down a waving gun with no more than a blink, a man who meets a fake psychic and thinks, *Huh, she seems my type.*

In other words, he's not the sort to ruffle easily.

"Hello, Lewis," he says, his normally urbane voice strained around the edges. He's also stiffer than usual as he rises to his feet and extends his hand to greet the man approaching our table. "I wish I could say I'm happy to see you again."

I stare at my beau, unable to hide the shock from my face. Although I pride myself at having been present at—and the cause of—those delightful occasions where passion drives his normally polite façade away, this hostility is something different, something ominous. Like a total eclipse, it's impossible not to feel the sudden plunge into darkness.

But the moment passes as quickly as it comes, and I'm forced to wonder if I imagined it.

"That would be inappropriate given the circumstances." He pauses and nods. "I'm sorry about your loss."

I stare again, this time at our guest. Although the pig's death is still forefront on my mind, I can only assume the loss Nicholas refers to is of the human variety. Sarah Blackthorne didn't have any immediate family—at least, none that I know of—so I'm understandably curious who the newcomer might be.

The man looks almost nothing like her. Sarah had been a robust woman, shaped by her love of a good Sunday roast and long, rambling walks through the countryside. This man isn't nearly as imposing a physical specimen. He's stockily built across the shoulders, but his stature is stunted—he's only about two inches taller than me, and I'm a dab of a woman at five feet three. He's also a tad on the hirsute side for my tastes. Not only does he sport a shaggy, unkempt head of brown locks, but his facial hair looks as though it could use a good trim. Neck beards are a difficult look for *any* man to pull off, let alone one wearing the loose, wrinkled suit this one has on.

"Hello," I say and leave it there. One of the many skills I've learned over the course of my career is reticence. Until I know who this man is and his relationship to Nicholas, I'm not committing myself to anything.

My patience is soon rewarded.

"Eleanor, please allow me to introduce you to Lewis King." Nicholas speaks with all the social grace I've come to expect of him. "Lewis is—*was*—Sarah Blackthorne's nephew."

"Of course, the nephew," I say, even though I have no more knowledge of Sarah's family tree than I do that of the Habsburgs. "What a terrible tragedy. You must have come down from London the moment you heard—and on the early train, too, poor man. Public transport can be such a trial when you've had a shock."

Nicholas's lips twitch in what I suspect is a smile, but he has enough control over himself to hide it. He knows as well as I do that Sarah never spoke to me if she could possibly help it, let alone discussed her nephews. But he also knows that I can read a person faster than I can a road sign. That beard? That suit?

Nothing screams a long, early morning commute in a railcar louder than that.

"Oh, d-did Aunt Sarah mention me?" Lewis stammers, somewhat bewildered.

Never one to lie if he can possibly help it, Nicholas coughs and changes the subject. "Eleanor moved to the village a few months ago. She bought the cottage on the west lane."

"The w-west lane, eh?" Lewis turns his head to examine me more closely. His stammering is less pronounced, but still evident. As neither man acknowledges it, I assume it's a condition of long standing. "That's interesting."

"Is it?" I ask.

Nicholas's own smile is tight. "Lewis is referring to the cottage's origins, of course. He's always been fascinated with that part of history."

I blink, confused at the animosity flowing from Nicholas toward the newcomer, who, from the look of it, is not only mild and unobtrusive, but a man in mourning. Especially since I've always understood the cottage to have been built and inhabited by a centuries-old family whose primary function was to tend to the Hartfords—first as servants, and later as general factotums.

Until I bought it, of course. Factoting has never been my strong suit.

All is explained when Lewis says, "It was b-built for the first Hartford's mistress, wasn't it?"

"Was it?" I ask, instantly diverted. General factotums are all well and good, but I'll take a seedy sex scandal over commonplace drudgery any day of the week. "That's a story I haven't heard before. I had no idea I lived next to such a sordid family. Tell me more."

Lewis opens his mouth—presumably to spill all the details—but he's prevented by a low cough and Nicholas's gentle but firm, "I really am sorry about your aunt, Lewis. Her death must have come as a blow, sudden as it was. I'm sure there's quite a bit of work to do making arrangements and so forth, so we won't keep you."

It's a testament to Nicholas's inborn autocracy that Lewis drops the subject of mistresses and love shacks as easily as he picked it up.

"Alas, you're right." Lewis nods his agreement. "Aunt Sarah was never great at k-keeping things in any kind of order. The last time she had me down to look things over, she had three decades' worth of t-tax receipts in a box. It'll take a few days to untangle everything. I've resigned myself to staying over the weekend."

I open my mouth to add that it could end up taking much longer than that if he wants to see justice done to her murderer, but Nicholas gives a curt shake of his head, so I close it again.

"At least the c-company has improved since my last visit," Lewis says with a polite nod at me. "Send my regards to your mother, won't you, Nicholas?"

"I will. If you find time, you should stop by for a visit. I'm sure she'd love to see you again."

Lewis finds nothing odd in this pronouncement, which leads me to believe he doesn't spend nearly as much time in these parts as his conversation suggests. Vivian doesn't love seeing anyone, let alone shaggy young men with little to recommend them.

I wait only until Lewis's disheveled head departs before turning to Nicholas with an accusing finger in the air. "I'm living in a den of iniquity, and you never once thought to mention it?"

Nicholas sighs. "Something tells me you aren't about to berate me for my ancestors' moral laxity, are you?"

I'm not. Not even close. "You know how much I love dens of iniquity. And scandals. You told me it was the gatekeeper's cottage, but we must have different ideas of what that job constitutes. Was the first Hartford a cad? Did he seduce an innocent maiden and install her there, or do the family tastes run more to runaway actresses? Oh! Are there dozens of illegitimate Hartfords roaming the countryside even to this day?"

Nicholas declines to answer my questions, which leads me to believe there's more to this story. In fact, the way he sighs and shakes his head makes me think there might even be illegitimate Hartfords numbering in the hundreds.

"And here I always thought you guys were pillars of the community," I say with a cluck of my tongue. "Oh, dear. What would my friend the vicar say?"

He struggles to suppress a smile. "*My* friend the vicar would tell you not to throw stones at glass houses, Madame Eleanor."

"Now, wait just a minute," I protest. "Is that meant to cast an aspersion on my profession, or my name?"

"Can't I asperse both?"

"You can," I allow. "But I'm not the one who just invited a grieving man to visit your mother. She'll probably make him bring his own tea and dance for his supper. Spill. Why don't you like him?"

He blinks. "Did I say that?"

"You didn't have to. I sensed it." I place a hand to my temple. "So much animosity . . . And at such a troubling time . . ."

He sighs again—and this time, there's real regret behind it. There's also a soft look in his eyes as he reaches for me.

"As much as I'd love to have you read my mind or my palm or any other part of my body you take a fancy to, I'm going to be late for my flight," he says. "No, don't bother pretending you're sad to see me go. You've been waiting all morning for me to leave so you can continue your investigation and make enemies of the villagers."

"I beg your pardon. Not everyone in this village is my enemy."

His response to that is a soft kiss pressed against the side of my neck. His breath is warm and his lips are delightful, but he stops himself before gently murmuring in my ear. "Not yet, Eleanor dear. But remember, you've only just moved here. Rome wasn't brought to ruin in a day."

He pulls away and drops a large bill to the table, pausing only to offer me a slight wave before disappearing through the door. Despite his blasé exit, I feel a pang at seeing him go. I need a Watson to my Sherlock, a Frank Hardy to my Nancy Drew. The great detectives always work in teams.

He's right, you know, Winnie says. *You have plenty of time to make enemies.*

"Don't you start with me," I mutter. It's bad enough having a gentleman suitor who thinks so little of my ability to be conciliatory. Winnie is supposed to love me unconditionally. That's how ghost sisters work. "You probably already know who did it. The least you could do is give me a clue."

As if on cue, a voice answers, "What's that, m'dear?"

I turn to find General von Cleve sitting on one of the bar stools, nursing a half-empty glass and watching me with interest. Never one to overlook a gift potentially sent from beyond, I say, "Oh, nothing. I was just talking to myself. My date abandoned me for the sunny shores of Spain. . . . Would you mind if I joined you instead?"

He gestures to the empty seats on either side of him. "I'd be delighted. Catherine, get this lady a cider, would you?"

I think of the Haldwell twins and the man with the bathtub distillery and politely decline. "More tea will be fine, thanks."

"Keeping up your energy, eh?" he asks. His smile, if he's wearing one, is hidden behind an elaborate, swooping mustache that would have looked at home during the British Raj. In fact, almost everything about him calls to mind the questionable imperialist ambitions of old. His short stature, puffed chest, and slightly bow-legged gait are out of place in this age of tanks and military satellites. "An enviable choice. Caffeine after noon always keeps me awake. If you want my advice, don't ever grow old. The body loses its tolerance for vice."

I'm pretty sure Vivian and her love of a good sherry—or twelve—would disagree with that, but I merely smile and say, "Oh, I rarely sleep when the moon is this close to full. There's so much work to be done."

"Well, now. Would that be the naked dancing I've been hearing so much about?"

I almost fall off the stool in my surprise. "Define *so much*."

He laughs and takes a sip of his cider. "It's a small village. Word gets around. Can't say I'd recommend it this time of year, though. A mite chilly once the sun goes down."

He can say that again. No way am I Lady Godiving around this place unless the thermostat is well into the seventies. "But, that's half the power of it," I say. "Human suffering is a potent force in our universe."

Partially to change the subject and partially because it seems as good a segue as any, I add, "How are you holding up after the other night, by the way? I understand that you and Mrs. Blackthorne were close."

Despite his benign appearance, the general is as sharp as they come. He casts me a shrewd look down the length of his nose. "Sure, you could say that. As close as a person could be to that old crow."

I choke on my tea. The current state of fear in the village is such that several people start up, fearful lest I fall into a paroxysm right there in the middle of the pub. Gaining control, I manage, "You didn't care for her?"

"Sarah Blackthorne was, without doubt, one of the most unpleasant people I've ever had the misfortune to meet. And I was a POW in the Korean War, so that's saying something."

I can't argue with that. "I had no idea so many people disliked her," I say. "I always assumed she was one of the staples around here, but Mrs. Hartford said something along similar lines yesterday."

The general snorts, sending the ends of his mustache billowing. "She would. Viv and Sarah were enemies for as long as the pair of them breathed the same air."

"Really?" My purpose in instigating this conversation was to gain insight into Sarah's death, but it seems I'm getting much more than that. I prop my chin on my hand in a show of casual interest. "But Vivian's such an easygoing woman. The whole family is—getting a reaction out of them about anything requires a crowbar and mountains of patience. I know she's not very hospitable, but that's part of her charm, don't you think?"

"If that's what you find charming about her, then you're stranger than most of the people around here suggest." Even though the general's words are gruff, his expression isn't at all unkind. "But, no. They never got along. There's only room in a village this size for one strong-willed and influential matriarch."

"Mrs. Hartford didn't kill her," I say with a certainty I have no claim to. The first rule of any investigation is to keep an open mind, but I hold on to that certainty all the same. The only way Vivian Hartford would ever poison another human being is by serving them a casserole ten days gone. "She'd never do anything that obvious. Her revenge would be subtle and years in the making."

"Who says it wasn't?" the general mutters. He contradicts himself two seconds later by adding, "But if you're looking for a sure thing, the fête planning committee's your horse. Everyone and anyone who held a grudge against that woman was there that night—it's half the reason I go every year."

"Because you also held a grudge against her?" I ask.

He laughs and returns his attention to the cider. "Because it's the only entertainment this blasted village has to offer. Last year, someone threw a knife at her head."

I blink, startled. How is it that no one thought to mention this before?

"It was a butter knife, but that doesn't matter. You'd be surprised how many body parts you can remove with cutlery. Even a spoon will do in a pinch."

I'm tempted to ask for details, but I have the feeling the general has a much stronger stomach for that kind of thing than I do. "Does Inspector Piper know?" I ask instead.

The general chuffs out a sound that's mostly annoyance. "Who can tell with that man? But I will say one thing, m'dear. Whoever killed that woman did the whole village a favor. If this thing doesn't end in a ticker tape parade and a public holiday, I'll eat my hat."

As he's wearing a tweed tam that looks as though it's been in use since the Jacobite rebellion, I can only assume he means what he says.

I also make a renewed vow to be part of that ticker tape parade through any means necessary. I can hardly take credit for killing the woman, but I *can* do these people the favor of finding out who did.

Parades, holidays, an appreciative village buying my elixirs in bulk . . .

Why not? Stranger things have happened. I mean, if people are losing limbs to spoons, as the general suggests, stranger things are happening all the time.

Chapter 5

"The fête must go on."

Annis pulls open the door to the vicarage with a wide smile, no element of surprise on her face. It says quite a bit about this woman that she finds nothing odd in having the village witch stop by for an afternoon chat.

"Hello to you, too, Ellie." She steps back to allow me inside, her gesture as warm as the smile. I think there must be a rule about vicars wherein they have to let you inside no matter who you are—it's like the opposite of vampires.

The vicarage is a huge, rambling home nestled next to the village church. Although the building is spacious, the rooms are small, dark, and cramped. From the look of it, the structure was built to house huge families in the days before birth control, all those dozens of happy kids crammed inside and lighting up the gloomy interior. As it is now, Annis makes do by hanging needlepoint and stacking pillows everywhere. Dark it may be, but there's no denying it's inviting.

So is Annis. She takes my shawl and hangs it on a nearby rack. "It's a cold one today," she says. "Not many people out and about, but I suspected you might stop by."

"Don't tell me you've gained the power of clairvoyance on top of everything else. I can barely pay my bills as it is."

"Not clairvoyance. Just a good guess." She leads me toward her office, the largest and grandest of all the rooms on the first floor. From the heavy wood wainscoting and butler's pantry off to one side, I assume it was once the dining room, but it works much better this way. There's a very confessional air about it. "You're here about Mrs. Blackthorne, aren't you?"

The problem with Annis is that she could, if she put her mind to it, run me out of business in three seconds flat. She does everything I do—reads people and offers comfort accordingly—but she does it for free. And without any of that dark magic stuff, either.

"Well, yes," I admit. "I *am* here about Mrs. Blackthorne. More to the point, I'm here about the fête. I think we should keep going with the plans. It was her pet project, wasn't it? She'd want us to finish what we started."

"That's a very kind and generous thing for you to say, seeing as how you barely knew the woman." Annis points to the leather club chair sitting opposite her desk. I obligingly take a seat as she parks herself on the corner of her desk, one of her legs swinging like a gentle pendulum.

"In other words, you don't believe a word of it?"

She laughs. "Well, no. Not really. But I'll admit the sentiment is in the right place."

"Even a broken psychic is right two times a day," I quip. Before she can kindly disagree with my self-deprecation—a thing I know from experience she'll do—I say, "The truth is, I'm sort of helping Inspector Piper with the investigation, and I think it'll be good to have everyone in one room again."

"Like a game of Clue? How exciting."

That's another thing about Annis—she has the disconcerting ability to make me feel like the most ridiculous person in the world. She does it by agreeing with everything I say, accepting my most outlandish requests with a perfectly calm smile. And she means it, too, that's the thing. Nicholas mocks me, Liam chides, and Rachel laughs outright . . . but Annis just earnestly accepts me as I am.

I'd hate her for it if I didn't love her so much.

"People didn't seem to care for Sarah much, did they?" I ask.

"No, they didn't. But then, you're not everyone's cup of tea either, are you? It's a good thing we all have different tastes."

"Touché. Do you ever say a bad word about anyone?"

"Not if I can possibly help it." She offers a serene smile and hops off her desk. "Annoying, aren't I? If it makes you feel any better, I used to be a real 'see you next Tuesday' about it. The only thing worse than a prig is a prig who prattles on about how good she is."

I choke.

"To be honest, I *would* like to continue planning the fête," she continues, blithely disregarding my attempts to recover my equanimity. "The last thing this community needs is to be derailed by another devastating loss. Keeping busy would be good for all of us. Perhaps we could choose a charity dear to Mrs. Blackthorne's heart and donate half the proceeds to it. That would be a nice gesture, don't you think?"

Since no one has ever solicited my opinion on this topic before, I'm not sure how to answer. I'm not exactly known for my generosity. "Yes?"

"We'll do that, then. Good thinking. Since it was your idea, I'll put you in charge of choosing the charity."

"Me?" I glance around, half expecting someone from the village to pop out and claim my unworthiness for such a heartfelt task. "But shouldn't you ask one of her friends? Or her nephew? Nicholas and I were having lunch earlier, and he introduced me to someone named Lewis King. Apparently, he came on the early train from London."

A moue purses her lips, a flash of distaste and nothing more.

As was the case with Nicholas, the expression is gone as quickly as it came, almost as though it exists only in my imagination. But that makes two very calm, very unruffled people who have reacted negatively to that man.

Once, and I'm willing to accept the hand of chance. Twice, and it's time to take note. In permanent ink.

"Okay, what's wrong with him?" I ask.

"With Lewis King?" Annis blinks at me, the picture of innocence. "Grief, I imagine."

A neat parry. I riposte. "Do you know him?"

"I used to. He spent a few summers here when we were kids."

"And?"

"And people change, thankfully. What a terrible world it would be if our childhood foibles were to be forever held up as judgment against us."

It's as good as a killing blow. Annis might look like the softest, sweetest woman in the world, but she's also taken the Seal of the Confessional. If she doesn't want to talk, she won't. I'd have a better chance of cracking open the vault containing the crown jewels.

"Maybe I'll stop by to see if he has any ideas about his aunt's preferences," I say, acknowledging defeat as gracefully as I can.

"What a lovely idea. I'm sure he'd welcome the company." She checks her watch with a gesture that's old as, well, time, and smiles once more. "Thank you for doing this, Ellie. It's very generous. I think the community will rally behind this idea. And behind you."

I doubt it, but I don't argue further. Anything that can help improve my public image is a thing to be embraced with both arms—and possibly a leg.

"Since the church basement is still taped off, we'll have to hold the meeting here instead," Annis adds as she walks me out. "Do you think Monday is too soon? Or should we wait until after the funeral?"

She keeps up a lighthearted flow of conversation, most of which involves the etiquette of planning a large, public celebration in the wake of a traumatic death. By the time we're at the door, I can't decide if she genuinely needs my insight on such a delicate subject or if she's being kind and pretending to solicit my advice. Either way, I find myself in perfect charity with her.

Until, of course, she lands one final thrust.

"Oh! I almost forgot to tell you how pleased I am that you're taking Lenora MacDougal under your wing." She clasps my hand in a warm gesture and holds it between her own. The action prevents me from falling over, which is my initial instinct. "To be fair, I'm also terribly jealous. I *had* hoped one of the kids would show an interest in the church, but, alas, every spring goes by and no one seems to want to help me pass out Bibles and replace candles. I can't imagine why. I suppose there's always next year."

I blink. "Is, um, Lenora your source of information?"

"Oh, no. Ian MacDougal and I had a nice chat about it last night. He was a little worried about the less traditional aspects of your vocation, but he came to see the benefits. When I told him how much of your training comes from literary influences, he became quite excited about it, actually."

I doubt he'd feel the same if he knew those literary influences were mostly gothic romances, magician handbooks, and a brief flirtation with Christopher Pike, but I focus on the more pressing issue at hand. "But surely Dr. MacDougal would never . . ."

At Annis's friendly wink, I falter. "Never say never, Ellie. I'll admit, Oona can be a bit stiff, but she's a reasonable woman underneath all that starch. You just have to give her some time to get used to the idea, that's all. I think you two could be friends."

"Why not?" I say with a laugh that's only partially forced. "With friends like Inspector Piper and Dr. MacDougal at my side, what use could I possibly have for an enemy?"

Chapter 6

"Werewolves."

As promised, Lenora is waiting for me outside the tea shop as soon as school lets out for the day. There's a slight mist in the air, which both I and my thatch roof know will turn to rain before long, but the girl doesn't seem to care. If anything, the damp is filling her with a buzzing, hopping energy.

"I hope I haven't kept you waiting long," I say.

"Well, you have, but it's all right. I don't mind." She pushes a stack of papers into my hand. "I didn't have enough time to write five whole pages on werewolves, but I did manage to get four."

"Did I, uh, ask you to write five pages on werewolves?"

"You asked for local instances of the occult, but there aren't any. Well, that's not true—there was one newspaper article about a woman from the sixties who said she was abducted by a UFO out by the cliffs, but you didn't say anything about aliens. And my grandma says *everyone* saw aliens in the sixties. LSD, you know."

"Oh, dear," I murmur. It's a nice, bland response that covers a variety of my feelings, not the least of which is alarm at my pupil's enthusiasm. And apparent knowledge of hippie drugs.

"When I didn't find anything yesterday, I asked the guy at the museum if I could come back before school this morning instead. He came early and let me in." She flicks the papers in my hand. "Which is when I found the werewolves."

"Benji did that?" I ask, suspicious. The young man who works at the museum could hardly be called conciliatory, especially where I'm concerned. I *may* have once manipulated his boyish crush on Rachel Hartford in order to access some important information for a case. The results were worth it in the end, but I'll admit my methods lacked finesse. "Just for kicks? Out of the kindness of his heart?"

She shifts her attention to the strap of her backpack. "Well . . . I did tell him it was a special assignment for you. And . . . I maybe hinted that you'd make it worth his while."

I groan. "How much?"

"I wouldn't have done it, but you said you needed five pages by today."

"How much?"

"Twenty quid?" she says and immediately perks. "But I didn't tell him when. Maybe I can dip into next week's allowance."

The damp is really starting to seep in by now, so I push the door open and usher Lenora inside. She's once again carrying the eight-ton backpack, and once again starts shedding her layers the second she walks through the door. I'm ready for it this go-around. By the time we make it to a cozy table near the back, I've gathered an armful of scarves and gloves and baggage. I stow them at our feet.

"You don't have to spend your allowance, Lenora," I say, though I'm not so flush with cash that I don't *consider* the offer. Just a little. "I'll go see him in a few days. But let's keep the bribes to a minimum from here on out, yeah?"

"Sure thing, boss."

"And maybe don't call me boss."

She perks. "Speaking of, I'm supposed to have you sign this time card before we get started. My dad also wanted you to walk me home today, if that's all right. You won't have to all the time, but he wanted to thank you in person for taking me on as your apprentice. This is so exciting, isn't it?"

She shoves another paper in front of me. This one is an official-looking log with her school's logo stamped on the top, providing ample space for me to keep track of the hours she works and my satisfaction with her performance. Since I'm not so cruel I'm willing to depress her youthful fervor—and because I *did* promise I'd help if her parents approved—I fill it out.

While I'm busy trying to determine what industry I'd call my business, the waitress comes by to take our orders—a scone for me and what amounts to a full high tea for Lenora. It's a good thing this apprenticeship is an unpaid position, because at this rate, I'm barely going to be able to afford anything except her bribes and meals.

"So," she says as soon as the waitress departs. "Don't you want to know what I discovered about werewolves?"

To be perfectly honest, I *do* want to know—and not just because I can't believe the museum had something as fun as werewolf lore and I never noticed. It's starting to sound as though this girl is something of a genius. "Sure. Why not? Hit me with your official report, oh apprentice."

She giggles obligingly. "Right, so there used to be all kinds of wolves in England, yeah?"

"Did there?"

"Oodles. We learned about it in history class. Only the Henrys hunted them so much, they all died out."

"The Henrys?"

She waves a hand at me. "Number six, number seven—that whole lot." At my look of confusion, she adds, "They ruled in the fifteenth century or so. It's all in my report."

I nod as though I have the slightest clue what she's talking about. My knowledge of history is decent—or so I've always thought—but the hunting habits of British royalty never figured on the list.

"The ones they didn't hunt, they trapped. And they were so good at it, bam! The wolves got wiped out. Extinct." She punctuates her words with a wide, toothy grin. "And that's why there are so many werewolves around nowadays."

"It is?" I ask, confused. "I'm not sure I follow."

"It's pretty obvious, isn't it? They're getting revenge."

I hold up a hand. I *might* have been willing to play along for the wolf-murdering Henrys, but that last part can't possibly be true. "Wait a minute—you're telling me there are werewolves wandering around England as part of a centuries-old vigilante quest? What on earth did you find in that museum?"

She giggles again. "I know, right? It was this cool old book from the Castle Hartford collection. Anyway, the werewolves are crazy mad about all their cousins being murdered, which is why they keep popping up every few decades. I would be, too, wouldn't you?"

"Furious," I agree, since it's no more than the truth. I've gone to rather extreme lengths to take care of my sister, so I can hardly judge all of werewolfkind for doing the same. However, I *am* a rational adult who doesn't believe in shapeshifters, so I add, "But are you sure this wasn't a young adult novel you mistook for folklore?"

The way her face crumples in on itself is all I need to tell me I've taken a misstep. This child is obviously possessed of a keen mind, and even more obviously given rare chances to wheel it out and see what it can do. I've met her parents. They're hardly the types to indulge in paranormal pursuits.

"How silly of me. Of course it wasn't." I tap my forefinger on my chin. "The Hartfords would never have sent anything like that to the museum. Vivian keeps all the juicy stuff for herself. Keep going, if you please. This is starting to get interesting. What else can you tell me about werewolves?"

"Oh, lots of things," she says, her voice caught on a breath. It quickly pries loose. "They don't eat humans, since they're human, too, but they will bite someone to protect themselves or if they want to turn them. To find a mate, yeah?"

If I were a werewolf, I could see how that might be a rational way to get dates. I nod my encouragement.

"Which means they prefer to eat game—stuff like deer and rabbits—but they'll settle for almost any kind of meat. And always the heart. The heart is their favorite part. They'll even leave everything else behind in their rush to get at it. Let's see . . . Oh! You can only kill them with a silver bullet, although that one might not actually be true. Lots of people think you can hunt them the same way you can any old wolf."

"Wait a second." I hold up a hand to halt the overflow of information headed my way. "Go back to that bit about the heart."

"Cool, isn't it? They claw right in through the rib cage and grab it. It's a good source of iron. Oona makes me drink these horrible beet and spinach smoothies to get my vitamins, but I think I'd rather do it the werewolf way."

I close my eyes and try to conjure up the image of Regina's slain form. I didn't stare long enough to make a survey of all the organs, but something about the way the pig's body had been left, all torn open and exposed, causes me a momentary pang.

But it's only momentary. After all, I *don't* believe in stuff like this—that's the cornerstone of my entire worldview. Those who can't do teach. And those who don't believe make a pretty convincing show of it for cash.

"If it's okay with you, I'll take the report home and read it over on my own time," I say. "But thank you for this. You've been very . . . thorough."

"Cool. What should I research next? Vampires? Loch Ness? I should probably warn you that I did a report on Nessie last year, and I'm pretty sure the whole thing was a hoax. I re-created the picture in my bathtub using my dad's old Nikon."

I mentally survey my index of witchcraft and psychic lore for a topic that isn't so far-fetched it will get me kicked off this apprenticeship gig before it gets started. Nothing pops up right away, so it's fortunate that we're interrupted by another ravenous teenager come to drain my purse and the tea shop's display case.

"Rachel!" I cry, grateful for the distraction the newcomer provides. "It's good to see you. Want to join us?"

"Of course I do. Why do you think I came all this way?" She turns to my companion with a look of polite inquiry. "It's Lenora MacDougal, right? Your mum's my doctor."

"She's everyone's doctor," Lenora says. "And you're Rachel Hartford."

"The one and only." Rachel gives a mock bow, which means she misses the look of rapture the younger girl gives her. Since Rachel grew up isolated among the splendid decay of her ancestral home and all its riches, she has no idea how valuable it—and she—are in the eyes of the rest of the world.

Lenora knows, though. That glowing adulation in her eyes leaves no room for doubt.

"I hope you ordered something grand," Rachel says as she scoots into the chair next to Lenora. She's so busy settling in that the magnanimity of that, too, is lost on her. Lenora looks as though she's about to pass out from the ecstasy of it all. "Since Uncle Nicholas left, there isn't a lick of food in the house. Not anything I'm willing to eat, anyway."

The waitress comes by then with a three-tiered monstrosity of cream cakes, tarts, scones, and an array of puff pastries. The two girls lose no time demolishing the bulk of it. Even though there are more than five years between them, the bonds of clotted cream and jam are unbreakable. They're fast friends before the final bite has been cleaned from the plate.

They've also begun an in-depth argument over the merits of heart consumption for iron intake and werewolf transformation abilities, which means I've lost this battle long before it's even begun.

"Why didn't you tell me you wanted an assistant, Ellie?" Rachel demands, a frown shadowing across her face. "My gallery internship is only part-time. If you need help, you know I'd be happy to step in."

"She's not really my assistant," I say, the words automatic. But that just means the hurt look transfers to the younger of the two, and I realize I'm trapped. "Um, she's more like an apprentice. Because I don't pay her anything."

"Oh. That makes sense." Rachel pauses and licks a crumb from the side of her mouth. "So if I said I'd work for free, you'd let me be part of your team?"

"Well . . ." I begin.

I'm cut short by Lenora's gasp of excitement. "That would be so amazing! We could be like a team. Potions R Us."

I might balk with every fiber of my being, but Rachel finds nothing odd in this idea. "Ooh, or Paranormal Investigators Incorporated."

"The Werewolf Hunters."

"Werewolf Hunt*resses*, you mean," Rachel corrects her.

"Yes! That's it."

I'm lost before I ever get started. "You guys, we don't know for sure that there even are werewolves." Since I now have not just one, but *two* sets of beseeching eyes thrown at me, I adopt an academic tone and add, "What I mean is, one source document isn't enough to prove anything conclusively. You need more evidence to corroborate it."

"You mean, like pictures?" Lenora reaches for the ubiquitous backpack, where I'm fairly certain her father's Nikon is being secreted for yet another round of cryptozoological studies.

"Witness accounts." Rachel nods and starts scribbling notes on her napkin. "Ooh, or other werewolf books that back up the same theories. Was there a resource page in the one you read already?"

With that, there's nothing left for me to do. Whether I like it or not, I'm now the proud employer of two unpaid young ladies who are *far* too good at this for my peace of mind.

"So, which one of those things do you want us to do next, Madame Eleanor?" Lenora asks, leaning eagerly over the table. "Do we set a trap? A stakeout? How do you lure a werewolf out into the open?"

Both girls look at me with an expectant air, fully confident not only that I have an answer to that question, but also that I'm willing to share it with them.

"I'm not sure luring a werewolf anywhere is a good idea," I say and am confronted with two crestfallen faces. Quickly amending my plan, I add, "I guess it wouldn't hurt if you poked around a little—academically-speaking, I mean. Let's leave the stakeouts for later, once we have an idea of what we're dealing with."

The more I think about it, the better I like this plan. Even with their enthusiasm, I doubt they'll find anything else worth note, and this will keep them indoors and out of trouble. Plus, research. That's educational, isn't it?

"Go back to the village museum and look for historical records of animal attacks—it doesn't matter how long ago," I add. "Anything that went unexplained or unsolved will be of particular note."

"The village museum?" Rachel strives to hide her interest.

"It's as good a place as any," I say, hiding my sudden smile. Maybe I won't have to resort to giving Benji that twenty quid after all. With my strong powers of divination, I'm starting to suspect his crush might be mutual. "You can also try the library, but I doubt it will be as helpful."

"And when do we report back?" Lenora asks, her pen poised over a notepad and a look of eager inquiry in her eye. One thing I can see about the future: whatever this girl ends up doing as a profession, she's going to be amazing at it.

"Is your mother still making you go to the fête committee meetings?" I ask.

She nods.

"Then let's meet there on Monday. Since it's only Friday, that'll give you all weekend to work. We can make Rachel come to the meetings with us."

Rachel agrees with her customary good humor. I don't tell the girls that their presence at the meeting will also serve another purpose—to help me sort through the attendees to find the person most likely to have done in Sarah Blackthorne. After all, I'm supposed to be setting a good example here. Clandestinely recruiting them to help me solve a murder is hardly what I'd call *good*.

Then again, it can hardly be worse than sending them on the trail of a mythical beast who howls at the moon.

Right?

The MacDougal residence is one of the grander homes in the village. It's also one of the more isolated, a gorgeous brick house surrounded by rising hills and farmland in all directions. I'm not sure what led the original builders to place the house at the bottom of those farms instead of the top, but it gives the feeling of being cupped inside a warm green hand.

"It's just down this path," Lenora says as she trots along the lane alongside me. "And don't mind the empty flower beds. My parents are keen gardeners, but George lopped all the heads off last week."

"George sounds an awful lot like he's treading a firm path to juvenile delinquency," I say as we near the residence. The two stories are perfectly symmetrical, offset on either side with twin carriage houses.

Lenora giggles. "I've never met anybody who talks like you, Madame Eleanor. You always sound so fancy."

"An occupational hazard," I say, not altogether untruthfully.

Most of my vocabulary was gleaned from the gothic romances of my youth. "Spell books have a tendency to be written in archaic language. Is your brother here now?"

"Probably not." Lenora pauses at the end of her drive to check the mailbox. She shoves a parcel of letters under her arm and continues skipping up the drive. "He always goes out with his mates after school. He doesn't like to be here when—"

I don't need her to finish. The sounds of an argument assail our ears before we make it to the front porch. The voices aren't outright yelling, but there's an angry vibrato to the female side that's unmistakable. Similar sounds have been directed at me far too many times for me to pretend otherwise.

"How could you do that when you know how I feel about—?"

I mentally fill in the rest: *Madame Eleanor. Witchcraft. Americans.* Take your pick, they all fit the bill.

"Oh, right. This is my fault. As if I'm the one who—"

Handed Lenora over to an unstable, untrustworthy practitioner of the dark arts.

"This was not the arrangement we made. You promised, Ian. You said we'd start—"

"Uh, Lenora, I think I might have seen a werewolf track back there. Maybe we should double-check just to be safe."

"No you didn't," she replies with a frankness I find disconcerting. "You're just afraid of interrupting their row. Don't worry. They'll stop the second they know we're here. Hello? Is anybody home?"

She calls loudly enough to stop the next remark from cutting through the air. There's a careful nonchalance to the way she does it, as though she's had to learn the hard way how to make her presence known in a way that's unobtrusive and unoffending.

It breaks my heart a little, to be honest. That's an awful lot of adult wisdom to heap on such tiny shoulders.

"Oh, Lenora—you're home." Dr. MacDougal appears at the door, her normally neat exterior flushed, but only slightly. If I hadn't been looking for it, I might have missed it. "And Madame Eleanor. I see she managed to capture you."

Mr. MacDougal appears next to her. Whereas his wife is all sharp angles and clean, chic lines, he's the quintessential British schoolmaster. His hair must have once been as frothy and gingery as Lenora's, but it's since faded away to match the pale ashen hue of his skin. His shirt collar is wilted and droopy, and his shoulders are hunched in a way that signals defeat.

"Actually, I think I'm the one who captured her," I say with a smile. If everyone else is going to pretend I didn't just walk onto a scene of domestic dispute, then the least I can do is play along. "I've never had an apprentice before, but I get the feeling I landed on a gold mine with this one. Thank you for letting me have her."

Dr. MacDougal's smile is thin. "Of course. If you'll excuse me, I need to get back to the office. There are a few more patients coming in before the end of day." She leans over and gives her husband a chaste peck on the cheek. She almost does the same with Lenora, but something about the way the girl holds herself off gives her pause. "I'll pick up a takeout pizza on my way home. You'd like that, Lenora, wouldn't you? With extra olives?"

"Yes, thank you," the girl says. She's perfectly polite, but there's no denying the response lacks warmth.

Her mother opens her mouth as if to say more, but she must realize how close I'm watching because she presses her lips tightly together and continues on her way.

"She's been under a terrible amount of stress lately," Mr. MacDougal apologizes.

I wave him off. "I imagine it's difficult, losing a patient the way she did."

He blinks, as if unsure what I'm talking about. "Oh. Oh, yes. Sarah Blackthorne. A real tragedy. She'll be greatly missed."

Like most of the people I've talked to since Sarah's passing,

Mr. MacDougal's lack of sincerity wouldn't convince a baby to hand over its candy. But I know my role, so I nod and murmur something sympathetic.

"A horrible way to go," he adds thoughtfully.

He's prevented from adding more by the arrival of the infamous George, who comes barreling down one of the hills as though shot from a cannon. He looks to be about Lenora's age—maybe a year or so younger—with the same wide grin and exuberance of youth. I like him on sight.

He comes to a stop, mouth agape, when he sees me standing there. "Cor, Lenora," he says, a whistle squeaking out between the gap in his two front teeth. "You brought the witch home to see Mum? And you didn't wait for me? Oh, boy, I'd have loved to see her face." To me, he adds a wide-eyed, "Is it true that you float in water and can't be drowned?"

I catch the pained glance on his father's face and smother a laugh.

"Alas, I've never been very good at swimming," I confess. "I think you could drown me pretty easily."

George accepts this with a nod. He also tilts his head and looks me over, his eyes skimming over all the parts of my skin that are showing. "And have you got a witch's mark? Where the devil made you one of his own? Or what's t'other one—the witch's teat?"

"George Marshall MacDougal, that is quite enough out of you," his father commands in what I can only assume is his best schoolmaster voice. It's surprisingly authoritative; even I give a startled jump.

"What? I said teat. T-e-a-t. That's a real thing, isn't it, Madame Eleanor? Where the devil goes when he's hungry and you feed him—?"

Mr. MacDougal swoops down and grabs his son by the collar. "I'm so sorry," he says, his face suffused with red. "I honestly don't know where they get it."

"Don't worry about it," I say with a wink. "It happens all the time."

Mr. MacDougal doesn't loosen his grip, instead starts dragging his son into the house and away from any further embarrassing questions. As his attention is fixed elsewhere, I take a moment to pull the long sleeve of my dress back from my wrist. There's a pair of pin-site scars on my forearm from a long-ago broken bone, which, in the right light, look exactly like I was bitten by a vampire's fangs.

I flash the scars long enough for George to see them before lifting a finger to my lips in a gesture of silence. Both he and Lenora share a wide-eyed start of delight, their joy at having their theories confirmed a palpable thing. I ought to be ashamed of myself for indulging them, but shame is one of those things I lost touch with a long time ago.

I draw the line at showing them anything resembling a teat, however. Even a witch like me is allowed *some* decency in this world.

Chapter 7

I'm disproportionately disappointed to find that few people in the village have heard about Lewis King's arrival in town.

When I show up on Sarah Blackthorne's doorstep as early on Saturday morning as decency will allow, it's with the full expectation of finding myself part of a long line of callers waiting to get inside. More specifically, it's with the full expectation of finding that Penny Dautry has already come and gone.

I don't know Penny well, but she's well liked in these parts—mostly because of the incredible chocolate cake she makes whenever someone dies. It sounds macabre, I know, but she's something of a legend. No funeral is complete without her famous chocolate cake, dark and rich and so delicious I sometimes dream about it in my sleep.

I'm not saying people would murder someone just to get a taste of it, but . . .

"G-good morning. It's Eleanor, right?" Lewis pulls open the door in a sleep-rumpled state that indicates I'm the first to arrive bearing gifts. I don't have much—just an elderberry cordial I like to make when my kitchen isn't bubbling with elixirs—but

I've learned that one doesn't pay these kinds of visits empty-handed.

"Oh, dear. Did I wake you?" I take a step back, almost falling off the doorstep in the process. Sarah Blackthorne's home is one of half a dozen row houses situated just outside the village center. They're neither large nor imposing, but their tidy upkeep indicates they're well loved by those who live in them. "I wouldn't have come so early, only . . ."

Only I wanted to make sure I got a piece of Penny's cake doesn't sound very sympathetic, so I let my words trail off. As I hope, he takes the hint and picks up the thread for me.

"It's no bother." He pulls the door open and gestures for me to come inside. "To be honest, I haven't been sleeping well lately."

His comment leaves me feeling like a callous jerk, especially when coupled with his unkempt appearance, which hasn't improved since our meeting at the pub yesterday. His neck beard hasn't been trimmed in the slightest, and his flannel pajamas look as though they've been balled up in the bottom of his suitcase for decades. There are also heavy shadows under his eyes, which shine strangely yellow in the full light of day.

In other words, he looks like a man who recently lost his aunt.

"It might be easier if you stayed at the local B&B," I say with a cluck of genuine sympathy. I step through the threshold into the house, which bears a musky scent I can't quite place.

He blinks. "The local B&B?"

"Yes. I've heard Mrs. Brennigan does a mean fry-up. And I'm sure she'd offer you a discount, given the circumstances."

"Oh! You mean because of Aunt Sarah?" A conscious-stricken look crosses his face, and he clears his throat. "Of c-course. The local B&B—what a good idea. Is that for me?"

He indicates the bottle in my hand in a clear attempt to change the subject. Since I'm supposed to be here on a condolence visit, I allow our path to veer. "Yes. It's not much, just a cordial I make. It seemed the least I could do."

"Is it alcoholic?"

"Yes."

"P-perfect. Grab a couple of glasses, will you? There should be some clean ones in the cupboard."

Drinking the syrupy sweet liquor at nine o'clock in the morning had hardly been my intention in coming over here, but I'm not one to judge. Nor am I going to cavil at the opportunity to learn more about Sarah Blackthorne. From what I can tell so far, her home is a fairly typical residence around these parts—a little dark and cramped, perhaps, but at least there aren't buckets of rainwater everywhere. Whatever else her troubles, she obviously didn't have trouble paying for roof upkeep.

I open a few cupboards as I ostensibly search for glasses, taking a moment to examine each shelf as I go. They're mostly barren and a little sad. A few stacks of functional dishware, one or two tins of soup, a box of biscuits that looks to have been there since the seventies . . . *Ooh.* The one above the stove appears to hold various household cleaners. I'm not entirely sure, but there's a cylindrical container near the back that looks an awful lot like rat poison.

People don't keep rat poison strong enough to kill humans in their kitchens, Ellie. This isn't a BBC miniseries.

"D-did you say something?" Lewis asks.

I whirl, a pair of glasses in my hand, to stare at my host. His position in front of a large picture window casts him into a shadowy illumination, his form dark with rays of sunlight breaking around him. Tufts of his hair stand up on either side of his head, and he stands hunched, those broad shoulders braced as if to pounce.

But then he moves a little to the right, and the ominous image of him disappears as quickly as it came. He's nothing more than a short man in baggy pajama pants, looking as though he could use a stiff drink.

"No. No, I didn't say anything." I hold out the glasses and wait for him to take them. "Did you?"

"It must have b-been my imagination." With a half shrug, he uncorks the cordial and pours a liberal dose into each glass. "Like I said, I haven't been sleeping, and Aunt Sarah doesn't have anything stronger than cough syrup. She never drank."

"Good for her," I say politely.

"She never smoked, either. Or gambled."

No vices of any kind. Point taken. "What sorts of things *did* she do for fun?" I ask. I cross my fingers and hope he doesn't mention the drowned kittens.

It takes him a few seconds to come up with an answer. "She liked knitting. And crossword puzzles."

That seems like a woefully inadequate summation of a woman's entire life, and a pang I can't quite place floods through me. A small part of it is sympathy for this man and the aunt he lost, but the rest feels an awful lot like self-pity. As a woman living alone in a village like this one, I see much more of myself inside this house than I'm comfortable admitting.

I must not be the only one undergoing a contradictory mix of emotions, because Lewis lifts his glass in a half salute and kicks the entire contents back.

"This is really more of a *sipping* drink," I warn, but he doesn't so much as grimace at the sickly sweet taste.

With that, I decide to join him. Not only am I determined *not* to become as stiff and unpleasant as Sarah Blackthorne, but day drinking is a great way to bring down walls and make friends. It doesn't take a fake psychic to know that.

"Well, then. Bottoms up." I'm not quite as nonchalant as Lewis as the cordial coats my mouth and tongue, slipping in a warm trail down my throat, but I accept the refill he offers. "Those papers must have been in worse order than you thought," I add as he drains another.

He sighs and takes a seat, careful to keep the bottle close to his hand. "I have n-no idea. I haven't found them yet. I looked everywhere."

"Oh, really?" I feign disinterest as I take a seat across from him, but he makes a pointed look at my glass. My stomach revolts at the thought of another draught so soon after the last one, but I pick up the drink anyway. The next batch I make is definitely going to have less sugar. "That's odd. Maybe she took them to a professional to sort out."

He chuffs on a laugh. "That w-would be the first time. Aunt Sarah didn't trust very many people."

"She trusted you."

The glance he gives me over the top of his glass is sharp. "How d-do you know that?"

I don't. But as far as I can tell, either Lewis is the only relative Sarah Blackthorne had, or he's the only one close enough to her to drop everything upon hearing the news of her death. That means something.

"What have you heard about me, Lewis?" I ask. I run my finger around the rim of my glass to avoid his filling it again. The deep purple liquid matches my fingernail polish almost exactly.

He shifts in his chair. "J-just what Nicholas said at the pub, that you'd moved into the mistress's keep."

The mistress's keep—great. Exactly the image I want to project to these people.

"And?" I prod.

"That you helped get rid of a ghost up at the castle."

"And?"

His gaze snaps up to meet mine. "You're a w-witch, right? A psychic?"

I neither confirm nor deny the claim, opting instead to tilt my head and adopt a mysterious air.

"So it's true," he says on a long, slow exhalation. "You can talk to ghosts? You can see the other side?"

"If you find yourself in need of support during this difficult time, I hope you'll come to me," I say. Lest he think I'm the sort who preys on the newly bereaved, I add, "Free of charge. I only want to help you and your aunt find peace."

As I hope, the first tendrils of sympathy have the effect of loosening Lewis's tongue. Either that, or the third glass of cordial he tilts down his gullet pries the last of his reserve away. His stammering is already less profound, his posture less rigid and uncomfortable than before. He leans across the table, sending a waft of the musky scent in the house my way. "Eleanor, I have to confess some—"

A heavy knock at the door startles us both. I could curse the bad timing, but at least the foundation has been laid. Lewis King now knows who—and what—I am. And unless I'm very much mistaken, he'll come seeking my services before too much time has passed.

"With any luck, that'll be Penny," I say.

"P-Penny?" he echoes as he goes to open the door.

"Dautry. With the cake."

I call upon all my powers to make it so. Not only would having Penny show up with her chocolate masterpiece boost my image as a seer of things from beyond, but I need something to sop up all this alcohol.

But my powers, alas, are lacking. *Severely* lacking.

"Ms. Wilde. What a delight."

Standing on the doorstep is none other than Inspector Piper, who looks not the least bit delighted to find me installed inside Sarah Blackthorne's home with a glass of viscous purple liquid in hand.

"Inspector," I reply with a tight nod. "Just the man I was hoping to see."

Then, before Lewis can turn around and put up a protest, I toss the contents of my cup into a potted plant behind me. The action doesn't reach Lewis's eyes, but Inspector Piper definitely notices. His nose twitches as he makes note of possible poisons in the soil.

"Am I? Now that *is* a delight." He turns his attention to Lewis, his sharp expression softening to something approaching humanity. "If I could have a few minutes of your time, Mr. King? I have a few follow-up questions I'd like to go over with you regarding our conversation yesterday. But I can come back when you don't have, uh, company."

"Who? Eleanor? I don't m-mind if she's here. She already knows most of it, anyway. Did you know she sees things? *Mystical* things?"

Inspector Piper coughs. "I've heard something to that effect, yes."

"Right." Lewis hooks a thumb over his shoulder. "If you don't mind, I'd l-like to get dressed and have a quick shave first. Will you . . .?"

"I'll entertain the inspector," I promise. "Take your time."

Lewis lopes obligingly up the stairs, leaving a wake of that same heavy scent behind him. It's not an unpleasant smell—not precisely—but it's not one I'd like to linger over, either. There's something almost loamy about it, like he rolled around in the dirt before answering the door.

Reading my mind like the psychic I know he isn't, Inspector Piper pulls a small bag from the pocket of his overcoat. I watch, amused, as he approaches the potted plant and starts spooning some of the dirt in.

"You don't object, do you?" he asks as casually as if we're discussing the weather.

"On the contrary, help yourself." I step back and allow him to do his work. "But it's just my elderberry cordial. If your office is as strapped for cash as you say it is, I can save you the trouble and write down the list of ingredients."

"Let me guess—elderberries and vodka?"

He's not too far off. There's also a vast quantity of sugar and a few cloves thrown in for fun, but I doubt he'd appreciate the difference.

He finishes his task with a neat efficiency I can't help but admire. He also tucks the bag of dirt carefully in his pocket, which doesn't bode well for the conversation to follow. Nor does the fact that he remains standing perfectly still. My own inclination is to start rummaging in as many drawers as I can while Lewis is occupied upstairs. This kind of preternatural calm can only signal an incoming storm.

It does.

"It's just as well that you're here," the inspector says after a lengthy pause. "It saves me the trouble of tracking you down for questioning."

"Questioning?" I ask, all politeness.

"Yes. Mr. Worthington filed a rather . . . interesting police report yesterday."

I groan and pass a hand over my eyes. "Why am I not surprised?"

"I imagine it's those psychic abilities kicking in."

The inspector's rare show of humor startles me into a laugh. The feeling it evokes—of having the ground pulled out from under me—doesn't go away when he relaxes enough to reach in his pocket once again. This time, he extracts a red lollipop that crinkles as he takes it out of its cellophane wrapper.

"Geez. How deep does that pocket go?" I ask as he sticks the lollipop in his mouth. It pushes one of his cheeks out like a squirrel hoarding walnuts.

"Not nearly deep enough. I only have one more, so let's make this quick, shall we?"

Understanding creeps over me, and with it, a smile. "Did you know that the average person gains between six and ten pounds after quitting smoking?" I ask.

He doesn't miss a beat. "Did you know that before the police used fingerprints to catalog criminals, they used a system of facial measurements?"

I did know that, actually, but only because I went through a phrenology phase during my early paranormal studies. "Well, did you know there's a disproportionate number of clinical psychopaths who enter the law enforcement field?"

In true psychopath style, that factoid doesn't garner me so much as a blink. "Did you know that pig carcasses and human carcasses decompose in almost the exact same way?"

"Okay. You win." I fall into the same kitchen chair I was seated in before. "That's really gross, by the way. How do you know that?"

Instead of sitting down, he leans on the edge of the table. "They use pigs in forensic studies all the time. They're easier to get hold of than human remains. Cheaper too."

"Poor Mr. Worthington. What did they end up doing with Regina?"

"Right now, she's being held in the morgue pending further investigation."

"Really?" I shoot up in my seat. "Why? Did you find something?"

"You mean other than the badly mauled remains of an animal in the exact location where you've been sending your clients to plant flax seeds?" He shakes his head. "No. Not yet. Tell me about this spell you put on the pig."

I groan and slink back down. I should have known better—it was only a matter of time before he figured out that bit about the crossroads.

"I didn't put the spell on *Regina*," I protest. "I put it on Mr. Worthington."

When Inspector Piper's brows raise, I rush to add, "And it wasn't really a spell. I gave him some, uh, artisanal water to drink and said a chant. I also repaired his fence in all the broken places. You could say that was where the real magic happened."

He swishes his lollipop to the other cheek and blinks at me. "That shows how little you know. That pig has been eating—"

"Yes, yes. I know. She's been eating her way through that

fence for years." Why hadn't anyone seen fit to tell me about Regina's taste for fence posts *before* I took on that sorry job? "But that wasn't how she escaped this time. You can check for yourself. The fence is still fully intact."

"Hmm," he says. Just that, just *hmm*.

"What kind of animal could have done that to her?" I ask.

"A tiger would be my first guess."

I laugh. "A tiger? Roaming around Sussex? Are there any circuses traveling through the area I haven't heard about?"

He doesn't answer my question. Instead, he crunches on the last of his lollipop and tosses the empty stick on the table. I can't decide if it's better or worse than when he used to fling his cigarette ashes everywhere. "Is there a reason you're paying a visit to Lewis King less than twenty-four hours after he arrived in the village?"

Here, at least, I'm standing on firm ground. "Actually, there is. I've been sent as envoy."

"Oh?"

"Yes. Annis asked me to."

His "Oh?" this time is much more genuine. Everyone loves Annis.

"She's decided to give half the proceeds from the spring fête to a charity in Mrs. Blackthorne's name. She wasn't sure which charity to choose, so she put me in charge of finding the best one to honor her."

Inspector Piper closes one wary eye.

"I know. It sounds ridiculous to me, too. But it was her idea."

"Of all the people in her parish, she felt *you* were the best candidate for the job?"

I shrug. "I thought it was a strange request, but what can I say? She sees the potential in me. I figured talking to Lewis was the best way to go about it."

He doesn't buy any of it. "We've already made a thorough

search of the place," he warns. "So if you're hoping to find bottles of poison in the bathroom cupboard . . ."

I think of that canister of rat poison above the sink and sigh. It seems Winnie was right. "You already confiscated them. Got it."

"Did Eleanor offer you some of her c-cordial?" Lewis appears at the entrance to the kitchen in much more presentable form. His clothes still don't look as though they've recently seen an iron, but at least he's washed and freshly shaved. All signs of the beard—neck or otherwise—have disappeared, leaving a slightly cherubic visage I'm not sure I'd have recognized if it weren't for those topaz eyes. "I think there's a tin of Nescafe somewhere around here, but I can't vouch for how old it is."

Inspector Piper shakes his head. "I'm good, thanks. I only came by to ask if your aunt has a garden out back."

"A g-garden?" Lewis looks a question at me. His faith in my understanding of the local police force and/or his aunt's horticultural tendencies is touching but misplaced. "Not really, no. N-none of the houses in this row have much of a yard. There's only enough room out back for the rubbish bin and a few old cement blocks."

"Mind if I take a look anyway?" Inspector Piper doesn't wait for a response. "You can lend me a hand, Ms. Wilde. I assume you're familiar enough with the aconitum plant to recognize it on sight?"

I start, my head in a sudden whirl. "Excuse me?"

"*Aconitum napellus*," he echoes as one reciting a prayer. "Aconite. Monkshood. Devil's helmet. Queen of poisons. Let me think . . . I'm missing a few."

I don't need him to keep reciting the plant's common names. I already know the most important one. "Wolfsbane," I say.

He snaps his fingers. "That's the one. So you *are* familiar with it?"

Only in the sense that it's one of the most dangerous poisons known to mankind, and no witch worth her salt would be unaware of its powers. Even accidentally brushing against the plant can cause death within a few hours. By all accounts, the death isn't a pleasant one. In fact, it might look a little something like a woman having a violent, heaving heart attack on the floor of a church basement.

"I've come across it in my studies a few times," I say carefully. "Is that what . . . ?"

"*Aconitum* poisoning." Inspector Piper nods once and turns his attention to Lewis. "Administered sometime in the hour preceding her attack. That's what we're writing as your aunt's official cause of death. I'm very sorry."

"Oh. Er. Right." Lewis casts another one of those wary looks around the kitchen, eventually landing it on me. "It grows in backyard gardens?"

I'm not sure how wise it is for me to start spouting off everything I know about aconitum while the inspector is watching to see what I give away, but I've never been able to resist a chance to show off. Besides, I'm practically thrumming over here.

Wolfsbane. A poison commonly associated with—you guessed it—wolves, werewolves, and other creatures known to howl at the moon. Some legends say it's the only way, short of the ubiquitous silver bullet, to kill a werewolf.

Lenora and Rachel are going to freak out.

"It's not really native to these parts, no," I say. "It *can* grow in this climate, but it's rare to find it in the wild, since most of it has been eradicated for safety's sake."

A noise escapes Inspector Piper's throat. It sounds like admiration. Well, either that, or he's disappointed that he didn't think to grab a tape recorder ahead of time. This does sound an awful lot like a confession.

"It's most common name—monkshood—tells you pretty much everything you need to know about what it looks like," I add. "It's purple and weirdly lumpy and looks like, well, a monk's hood. If we're going to search for it out back, we should probably wear gloves. You don't want to mess around with this stuff. It's very potent."

Lewis takes me at my word. He grabs a pair of yellow rubber gloves from the sink and pulls them over his hands. I opt to tuck my bare limbs inside my shawl, but Inspector Piper doesn't take any precautions other than to fish the last lollipop from his pocket and stick it in his mouth.

"Lead the way," he says to me. "Seeing as how you're our resident expert."

Having never been in Sarah Blackthorne's backyard before, I'm not sure what I expect when I push open the door and step out. True to Lewis's suggestion, we find ourselves in a small patch of a yard that's barely big enough to hold the three of us. There aren't any cement blocks, but it's easy to imagine them stacked and crumbling. A garbage can tipped over on its side and a rusted bicycle leaning against the back of the house set the tone for a space that's as different from the tidy house front as you could possibly get. Plant life, if you can call it that, is limited to a few patches of grass and dandelion weeds nodding at us from a crack in the house's foundation.

"Aunt Sarah never came back here much," Lewis says by way of apology.

Inspector Piper crouches by the garbage can and begins poking at the contents with the end of a pen. I'm not sure what he hopes to find—all I can see from where I'm standing is an awful lot of microwavable dinner packages for one.

"I'm no botanist, but I don't think you're going to encounter any aconitum back here," is my contribution.

Sighing, Inspector Piper rises to his feet. "No, it appears not. I don't suppose you have any growing in *your* garden, do you?"

I take a wide step back, stumbling against Lewis as I do. His hands come up to steady me, and I'm struck by how strong he seems. The quick press of his muscles is enough to convince me that despite his short stature and cherubic face, there's more to him than meets the eye.

"My garden? Uh, no. I have quite a few herbs out there, but nothing poisonous." At least, not to my knowledge. I'm going to have to give that well-tended patch a good going-over when I get home. "I have a cat. I wouldn't want her to get into anything dangerous."

"Ah, yes. A cat."

"You can come look, if you want," I offer. "I'll give you the grand tour."

"I'll do that, thanks."

I can't decide if it's a promise or a threat, but Inspector Piper takes his leave shortly thereafter. I'd like to stay and talk to Lewis some more, especially since I haven't yet broached the subject of his aunt's favorite charities, but he, too, appears to be disinclined to continue enjoying my company.

"It's t-true, isn't it?" he asks as he escorts me to the door. We can still see Inspector Piper walking off down the street, pausing every few steps to examine the plant life at his feet. "She was murdered? Someone k-killed her?"

My heart goes out to the poor guy. It doesn't appear that Lewis is unduly wracked with grief at his aunt's passing, but no one likes to hear that their relative was done off on purpose. That's the sort of taint that never goes away.

"It could have been an accident," I say. "It's potent stuff, wolfsbane. One touch is sometimes all it takes."

He pulls the rubber gloves more firmly over his hands. "I'll b-bear that in mind, thanks. And thank you for the cordial. I have the feeling I'm going to need it."

"Don't worry—any minute now, you're going to be bombarded with villagers come to pay their respects. And none of them pay their respects empty-handed."

Even as I say the words, I'm struck by how eerily empty the front porch seems. I'm not kidding about the usual deluge of villagers—these are people who will roll out any excuse to share baked goods, homemade liquors, and hours of gossip. Last month, the tailor's wife was diagnosed with gout, and they raked in enough casseroles to last them through Easter.

"They're probably just waiting until a more polite hour of the day," I add.

"I'm s-sure you're right," Lewis agrees, but I can tell he doesn't believe me. For whatever reason, people are avoiding both this house and the man inside it.

Remembering what the general said about Sarah Blackthorne, I can't help but wonder if the community dislike of her really runs that deep. Or, I think, recalling all too clearly the reaction both Nicholas and Annis had to Lewis's appearance on the scene, perhaps it's the nephew they're avoiding?

Either way, this isn't a family anyone will miss.

The thought is more depressing than I'd like to admit. If there's one thing I've learned over the past few months, it's that gaining a foothold in this community isn't an easy task. If a woman who lived here her entire life couldn't manage it, what chance is there of someone like me making it work?

Chapter 8

No one assembled inside the vicarage for Monday's fête planning committee looks capable of murder.

To be fair, murderers, like beauty, come in all shapes and sizes. There's no reason why the gentle widow with the fluffy white perm and a Pomeranian in her purse couldn't slip some wolfsbane into a cup of tea and serve it out of her great-grandmother's china. In fact, from the way she keeps trying to tuck the purse—and the puppy—underneath her chair, she seems rather hard hearted as a whole.

The same could be said of the rest of the villagers gathered in the dark semicircle of Annis's living room. The ceiling is low and the lights are dim. The throw pillows, which usually make everything seem so much cheerier, are squashed under bottoms and behind backs. And everyone, from the respectable, upright MacDougals to the general, watching everything through his half-closed eyes, bears a look of mistrust.

They can't help it. Like me, they're all thinking the same thing: Someone in this room may have killed Sarah Blackthorne. Someone in this room may be willing to do it again.

The silent, accusing air is broken by what has to be the worst opening sentence known to man- and witchkind.

"I'd like to start today's meeting by giving the floor over to Eleanor." Annis speaks with the calm cheer that never seems to fail her. Although no one goes so far as to gasp their outrage, there is a low hum of discontent. "She's come up with the fantastic idea to donate half the fête proceeds to a charity in Sarah's name. Isn't that right, Ellie?"

I can hardly refute the beloved local vicar to her face, so I plaster a fake smile and adopt the air of the magnanimous benefactor she's making me out to be. It becomes easier when the hum of discontent transforms to a low-murmured approval. The sound is rather melodious, if I do say so myself.

"Well done," the general says with a liberal wink in my direction.

"Oh, what a lovely idea," says the Pomeranian-wielding widow.

"I told you what a boon she's been to the community," Mrs. Brennigan puts in.

Even Oona MacDougal seems to relax a touch. She doesn't go so far as to smile at me, but she does release the ironclad grip she's had on her daughter's arm since they walked in. Lenora takes immediate advantage and bounds across the room. She plops herself at my feet, where Rachel has already made herself comfortable on several of those now-squashed throw pillows.

I half expect Dr. MacDougal to raise a protest at her daughter's defection, but she merely watches Lenora settle next to Rachel with a small, tight smile. I watch, too, but I don't smile. Instead, a heavy feeling settles in the pit of my stomach.

The MacDougals' sudden acceptance of me is starting to make sense. The only wonder is that I didn't see it before. Naturally, they never wanted me to educate their daughter in the ways of witchcraft; what rational parent would? That would be like sending Hansel and Gretel into the woods with a basting brush and a favorite family recipe.

This story is much more predictable—and a lot less fun to tell. The Hartfords might not be nobility in the true sense of the word, but they're the closest thing to it in these parts. They have land, they have prestige, and they have money. They also have a tendency to keep to themselves, with the sole exception of the woman currently residing in a cottage about halfway between the castle and the village. A woman, as it were, with a foot on both sides of the tracks.

Oh, dear. What are you getting yourself into now, Ellie?

I wish I could give Winnie a concrete answer. Trouble, obviously, but I suspect there's more to it than that.

"On that subject, what charity did you end up deciding on?" Annis turns to me with an expectant blink. From those wide, guileless brown eyes, one would assume there's nothing but purity and innocence in her heart, but I know better. Both of those things *are* in her heart, but they're cushioned in a sense of humor that's enjoying my discomfiture far more than a vicar should.

"I didn't," I say with perfect honesty. "After talking with Mrs. Blackthorne's family and paying a few visits, I realized she wouldn't have wanted us to spend a single red cent on this village."

I allow the outburst to settle before I turn to address the assembled group, confident in my chosen path. Mostly because that outburst isn't filled with outrage or incriminations at *me*. It's all internalized—the way no one is quite meeting my eye, suddenly taken up with the state of their own fingernails, is a clear sign.

So are all the other things I've gathered about Sarah Blackthorne's life over the past few days. What I'm facing isn't a community in mourning; it's a community in shock, plain and simple. The spectacle of Sarah's attack was alarming, yes, and the loss of *anyone* to a violent death is unpleasant, but that's as far as these people's sympathy goes.

No one here misses her or her accusations of the evil eye any more than I do—I'm as sure of that as a woman in my position can be. Kittens are rejoicing. Penny hasn't baked a chocolate cake in weeks. Even her nephew can't muster up a convincing show of regret at her loss.

"Sarah was a solitary woman and a joyless one," I say. "She didn't have many visitors. She didn't have many friends. She didn't even have a pet."

All those meals for one, the fact that her house didn't contain a single bottle of gin hidden in the depths of the freezer—that's not how someone who finds delight in the small things lives. Or someone who routinely has guests.

"To pretend that any of you are mourning her passing would be disingenuous to her memory. You didn't like her when she was living, and to pretend that death suddenly makes her worth commemorating is a sham."

For a moment, I fear I've taken things too far. These are good people, *decent* people, and even Rachel is starting to look alarmed at my speech. But I press on, determined to see this thing through to the end. If there's one thing I've never lacked in my life, it's nerve.

"Let's keep the money here," I say in a gentler tone. "Let's spend it on community outreach and local celebrations. Let's enjoy it while we can. That might not be what Sarah Blackthorne would have wanted us to do with it, but I think we can all agree it would have done her a world of good to get out every now and then and take pride in the place she calls home."

The sound of slow clapping rises from the far side of the room. Glancing over, I expect to find Nicholas leaning in his languid way against the door frame, his familiar mocking smile in place. Instead, I'm greeted with the vision of a stranger.

No—not quite a stranger. That round, cherubic face and those yellow-tinted eyes are familiar, even if the man's taller frame and too tight, too bright clothes aren't.

"Richard!" Oona MacDougal leaps up out of her seat, showing more enthusiasm at the sight of our guest than I've ever seen from her before. The sudden burst of energy does much to soften her sharp angles, her lips lifting in what I suspect is a smile. "You came. You're here."

The man's face creases in an answering smile. "Of course I'm here. The prodigal nephew always returns—or didn't you know? Hullo, Annis. Mrs. Brennigan. Ah, General von Cleve—glad to see you're still alive and kicking."

"It'll take a lot more than old age to knock me down," the general replies. He also rises to his feet, though with a much more dignified air. He crosses the room with his hand outstretched. "I'm sorry about your aunt, Rich. I didn't like her, never did, but I know you were close to the old girl."

Richard's smile loses some of its wattage. "Yes, well. As this young woman was saying before I interrupted, Aunt Sarah could have sucked the joy out of a royal wedding on Valentine's Day. She was always good to me, though. Me and Lewis both." He paused to peer around the room. "He's not here yet?"

"I invited him to come to the meeting today, but he was busy with your aunt's affairs." Annis, too, crosses the room to greet her guest, offering first one cheek and then the other for the man to kiss. Her warm acceptance of this nephew's arrival is as far removed from her reaction to Lewis's as it's possible for a kindhearted vicar to be. "Eleanor here was just, uh, helping us decide how to best memorialize . . ."

A better woman than I would have had the decency to blush, but I catch a gleam in Richard's yellow eyes and realize there's no need. If ever a man was willing to overlook the near-slanderous aspersions cast on his dead relative's name, it's this one.

"She was absolutely correct," Richard says with a smile my way. "Aunt Sarah was a bitter old miser, and the last thing she'd have wanted was for any of you to experience joy at her expense. I say you take that money and throw the biggest party this village has ever seen. I'll bring the champagne."

"Well, I didn't mean a party so much as a new park or a commemorative bench under a tree," I say, "but—"

My belated attempts at recovering my image fall into the sudden cacophony that bursts out. Not since the mythical vicar and his twelve mythical children has this room seen so much energy, so much verve.

Well, that didn't go quite as you planned, did it? Winnie asks.

No, it most decidedly did not, but at least one of my more pressing questions appears to have been answered. From the easy way everyone in attendance suddenly lights up with delight, it appears I have quite a few potential murderers in my midst—all of them cheerfully throwing Sarah Blackthorne under the figurative bus. Only the general and Annis appear concerned at the party atmosphere; the general with a worried pucker to his brow, and Annis with a slightly bemused glance at me.

I mouth a quick apology at her, but all she does is shrug helplessly. She could, I know, quiet this room with a soft-spoken word and her usual air of dignity, but she allows her flock to gather around Richard with halfhearted apologies for his loss and wholehearted enthusiasm for his return. Even Rachel and Lenora, still at my feet, are whispering excitedly to one another.

"—but did you see the one—?"

"—exclusive interview, I swear on my—"

"—broke up with that model—"

"Okay, out with it," I say to the two girls. "What's going on, and why is everyone in this room acting as though they've gone stark raving mad?"

"Because they *have* gone stark raving mad, Ellie." Rachel clasps her hands to her chest and sighs. "Don't you know who that is?"

"Sarah Blackthorne's favorite nephew," I say, hazarding a fairly good guess. "And Lewis King's least favorite brother."

The two girls shake their heads at me as though I've recently landed from an alternative universe. In the normal way of things, that's exactly the impression I want to give—my dark heels, dark lipstick, and floaty purple dress demand it—but perhaps not a universe quite as removed as what they have in mind.

"That's Rich *King*."

"Yes, I gathered as much."

"*Rich* King."

"I don't see how emphasizing a different part of his name is going to help me."

Rachel is the first to give in to my ignorance. "The famous celebrity host? *Red Couch Diaries*? Ellie, you've lived in England for almost four months. How can you not have seen him on the tellie?"

For starters, I don't *have* a television. The cottage came with one of those huge, flat, oversized ones, but it was the first thing I got rid of. The cozy atmosphere and AGA stove I can sell, but Eleanor Wilde brewing potions by night and watching game shows by day isn't part of the image I'm trying to project around here.

Secondly, I resent the implication that living alone with only a cat for company means I have nothing better to do than bulk up on British dailies. Yes, Sarah Blackthorne might have been cooking microwavable meals for one most of the time, but I have friends. I have visitors. People love me.

They tolerate you, anyway.

I flap my hand in a gesture designed to quiet my sister, but Lenora assumes it's meant for her.

"Madame Eleanor is too important to bother with things like television," she says with all the confidence of a twelve-year-old who's seen almost nothing of the world.

"Is that a fact?" As if drawn by the mention of fame, Rich *King*—no, excuse me, *Rich* King—draws close.

His smile is even more disarming from close up, though I find the glittery sheen of his canary yellow shirt a bit much for anywhere outside of a nightclub. He's also older than I at first assumed. His hair is thick but far too uniform in color not to have come from a box, his healthy tan extending to a line at the top of his neck where the makeup stops. He's not a bad-looking man, but he's hardly the spring chicken he'd like everyone to believe him to be.

"Then what, may I ask, does Madame Eleanor consider worthwhile?" he asks, still smiling. "Village fêtes, obviously, but that part goes without saying."

His words snag on my conscience. "I'm sorry you walked in when you did. I know it must have sounded harsh, those things I was saying about your aunt, but all I meant was—"

"Oh, I know what you meant, and I'm glad someone around here finally had the stones to say it." He laughs, showcasing a row of pearly white veneers up top and a crooked lineup of yellowing teeth on the bottom. "She was a tough old bag, Aunt Sarah, but not a bad sort, when all was said and done. A little fun would have done her a world of a good. It's a shame you didn't arrive in this village earlier. You two could have been good friends—you have a lot in common."

Every part of me balks at that implication, but Richard is drawn away by a pair of sharp-eyed matrons I know for a fact have daughters of a marriageable age. Since they've both bought several bottles of my attraction elixir and neither one appears to be cloaked in lavender, I assume those daughters won't remain marriageable for long. . . . Not if they have anything to say about it, anyway.

Rachel bounds after them without a single backward glance, but Lenora has the decency to wait until I wave her off before she, too, departs.

"Alas, poor Madame Eleanor." Oona MacDougal sidles up to replace my entourage, watching as the entire room crowds around Richard to offer condolences, ask about his television show, and, in one case, brandish a pen for an autograph on an impressive display of cleavage. "Your shining star is about to be replaced."

"I beg your pardon?" I ask, trying to sound less affronted than I feel.

"If it's any consolation, he won't stay long. He never does. He flits in and out with the seasons. You'll be back to being the village oddity in no time."

"I'm not jealous."

"Of course not."

"I'd never even heard of the guy before today."

"Why would you?"

I strongly suspect Dr. MacDougal to be laughing at me. The knowledge doesn't, as expected, make me want to retreat. If anything, I like her all the more for it. A sense of humor—even at my expense—is always a good thing.

"Anything he does to take the pressure off me is welcome," I say in what I hope is an accurate summary of my feelings. "By the way, you rushed off so suddenly the other day, I didn't get a chance to talk to you about Lenora's apprenticeship. I wanted to assure you that—"

Oona raises a hand to silence me. It's just as well, since I'm not sure what sort of reassurances I have to offer a woman as steeped in the sciences and medical community as she is. "I make it a rule never to squabble in public, Madame Eleanor, so the less we say on the subject, the better."

I, however, would much prefer to have our squabble deep in the public eye. There's a much better chance of me walking away with my dignity—and body parts—intact that way.

"I know it's not your ideal placement for her, but I'm doing my best to keep it educational," I say.

"Oh?" she asks with careful civility. "Is that what you'd call werewolf studies?"

My heart sinks. I thought I'd have at least a week or two before Oona took too much of an interest in her daughter's work, but I obviously hadn't counted on the influence of someone as important in the neighborhood as Rachel Hartford. I have the feeling this woman is going to take a much keener interest in this project than I'd prefer.

"She wrote four pages on the subject. Four *good* pages, actually. Do you want to read them?"

Oona's sharp brows raise, and she watches me with a kind of attentive wariness I know from experience is that of a skeptic trying to decide if my intentions are pure. Since they are—in this case, at least—I double down.

"I'm not grading it or anything like that, but she has a solid grasp for how to present evidence in a way that's both convincing and entertaining. You might have a scholar on your hands."

"What I have, Madame Eleanor," she says dryly, "is a child with an overactive imagination and far too liberal an upbringing. I wanted to send her to boarding school, but her father wouldn't hear of it. The English countryside is as good as any unyielding Swiss matron, he said. Nature will fill in what traditional learning can't, he promised."

That sounds like pretty solid advice to me, and I'm about to say as much, but Oona prevents me from being able to form any words at all.

"Speaking of evidence, I assume you've had a chance to read the report on Mr. Worthington's pig?"

I blink, unsure at first if Winnie is playing tricks on me by speaking aloud at the worst possible moment. It wouldn't be the first instance—she once reminded me to take out the garbage while Nicholas was kissing me good-bye outside my gate—but there's an expectant purse to Oona's lips that indicates she's waiting for an answer.

"I didn't know there was a report on Mr. Worthington's pig," I say in the breezy, neutral tone I always adopt when I'm unsure of my ground but unwilling to let it show. "I was under the impression that Inspector Piper was waiting for an authority to take a look at the remains."

"He was. And I did."

Not even the most consummate professional would have been able to hide her surprise at that one. "*You're* his authority on pig corpses? But—"

"But I'm a family practitioner? Tsk, tsk, Madame Eleanor. Can't a woman have more than one accomplishment in this world? I wasn't born a doctor, you know. Once upon a time, I was just a pig farmer's daughter."

"That's how you got interested in medicine in the first place," I say with a nod. Unless I'm very much mistaken, it's also why she's so keen on throwing her daughter into Rachel Hartford's path. Some things are difficult to shake no matter how much education you manage to secure. A childhood spent wading through pig slop is one of them. "Your son likes to dissect things, too. Of your two children, he's the most likely to follow in your footsteps. You should cultivate that."

At my quick—and I hope accurate—assessment of her family situation, Oona relaxes a little. "Yes, well. If you haven't been granted access to that report yet, you'll hear the details soon enough. I'm not sure what sort of line of reasoning you're following with this werewolf nonsense, but I'd appreciate it if you didn't go planting ideas in my daughter's head."

"Oh, the werewolf wasn't my theory—"

"She's young, she's impressionable, and she thinks the sun rises and sets on your shoulders. And while I will admit that it was strange to find the heart removed from that poor pig, there are a number of predators that will do that to their prey."

It takes me a moment to process everything she's telling me. "I'm sorry. Did you just say the pig's heart is *missing*? As in, all the way gone?"

"They found pieces of the entrails scattered for half a kilometer in all directions, so it doesn't necessarily mean anything." When I don't respond right away, she adds, somewhat testily, "Birds, Madame Eleanor. They most likely picked up bits and pieces before the pig's body was fully recovered."

"A bird couldn't have picked up a whole heart," I protest, even though I'm not fully conversant in the intricacies of pig anatomy. How much could it weigh? Two pounds? Three? "Did it look like something had . . . eaten it out?"

She sighs. "Not necessarily *eaten*, but the extraction was a violent one. Far too violent for a twelve-year-old to hear about, at any rate. Which is why I'd appreciate it if you'd avoid making the connection shining so clearly in your eyes."

As much as I wish I could control the sheen of my eyeballs, I can't. Especially not in this situation.

A pig murdered in the wilderness, its heart eaten on site? A woman poisoned by wolfsbane a mere twenty-four hours earlier? I don't care what your spiritual leanings are—that's a mightily interesting connection.

"Of course I won't tell Lenora anything she can't handle," I say, but it's too late. As if drawn by the mere mention of werewolves, the girl in question bounds across the room. This time, Rachel isn't with her. She and the woman with the impressive—and now signed—cleavage are the last two holdouts doing their best to keep Richard King entertained on the other side of the room.

"What can't I handle?" Lenora asks. "What have you been telling Eleanor? You *promised* you wouldn't get in the way."

"I'm not getting in the way. I merely—"

Lenora turns to me with her hands clasped tightly in front of her chest. "Don't let Oona scare you. She can't tell me what to do."

"Now, Lenora. You don't mean that."

"Yes I do. You know she's not my real mother, right?"

I didn't know that, not officially, but the news doesn't come as a surprise. The strained relationship between them, the desire to ship Lenora away to boarding school, the fact that Mr. MacDougal had the final say about the apprenticeship . . . Nothing says wicked stepmother quite as clearly.

"Relationships are rarely as cut and dried as we like to believe they are," I say. "Does she feed you?"

"Well, yes, but—"

"Does she clothe you?"

"Of course, but that's not—"

"Does she sign your permission slips?"

"Madame Eleanor, that's not fair! She only does all those things because that was the deal when she married my dad. I was only a year old, so I didn't get a say."

I catch sight of Oona's tightly drawn face and feel a pang for the other woman. She's trying to hide it, I can tell, but Lenora's words sting. Her job raising someone else's preteen can't be an easy one.

"Part of being a responsible witch is respecting the bonds of female companionship, no matter what form they take," I inform her.

Lenora opens her mouth as if to argue before closing it again just as quickly. For a brief, triumphant moment, I think I've managed to get through to her, but I catch sight of Rachel coming toward us and realize she doesn't want to discuss this in front of her idol. Nor does Oona appear to be grateful for my intervention. Her look of pain has been replaced by one of irritation.

"Guess what?" Rachel says, her violet eyes wide with excitement. Apparently, she's picked up on none of the subtext surrounding us. "I just heard from Penny Dautry that the pig Ellie found slaughtered in the woods had its heart eaten out."

"No way," Lenora breathes.

"Yes way." Rachel takes the younger girl's hands and squeezes them. "Are you thinking what I'm thinking?"

Unfortunately for me, she is.

"Werewolf!" Lenora cries, unaware of her stepmother doing her best to glare me into a puddle. Any integrity I might have left vanishes when Lenora dances a jig right there in the middle of the vicarage. "Oh, boy. Werewolves, witches, and bloody, ripped-out hearts. This is going to be the best apprenticeship ever. Aren't you so glad you took us on, Madame Eleanor?"

As my answer to that question is one she probably doesn't want to hear, I merely offer a tight smile in reply. *And* do my best not to be left alone with Oona MacDougal for the rest of the afternoon. Some risks are too big, even for a woman as well versed with the shady side of the law as me.

"Is he tall? He always seems so tall. Please tell me he's tall."

"Um, okay. He's tall. It's as though he's walking on stilts. I have to crane my neck to look up at him. Earlier today, it was snowing on his head since it's being carried at a such a high elevation."

Liam accepts this barrage of nonsense with a happy sigh. "And when he talks, does it sound like chocolate is oozing out of his mouth?"

"I'm in England, Liam. Everyone talks like that. It's like living in a fondue pot over here."

"Indulge me. Describe his voice."

I tap my finger on my chin and think. As the man under discussion is currently walking in my direction, the thinking has to happen quickly. *Too* quickly. I've been waiting outside the vicarage in hopes of snagging a chance to talk with Richard King before he leaves, but my brother's fanboy demands are going to make me miss my opportunity.

"Could you do me a favor?" I ask Richard as I pull the phone away from my ear and hold it out. "Will you say something to my brother that makes it sound like you're ten feet tall and your saliva is made of chocolate?"

Richard cements himself in my heart by accepting this request without so much as a blink. "Good evening," he says in a voice that does, admittedly, reek of rich indulgence. "You're on with Rich King of the *Red Couch Diaries*—and looking quite dapper, if you don't mind my saying. Is that Burberry you're wearing?"

The tinny sound of my brother's squeal through the phone is audible even from my distance. I can only assume that the designer question is something Richard regularly asks the celebrity guests on his show, because my brother has not now, nor will he ever, spend that kind of money on clothes. He shops at Target.

Richard chuckles at something Liam says. "That's a wrap. Good night, and remember not to do anything I wouldn't do. If there is such a thing."

He hands the phone back to me. I mouth my thanks and prepare to resume my call with my brother, but Liam has already hung up. "Well, that was rude," I say as I drop the phone into my bag. "I think you broke him."

"I've been known to have that effect on people," Richard replies. His easy laugh robs the words of any conceit. So does his makeup. Out here in the daylight, the line where his foundation meets his skin is even more pronounced. Liam might falter in the presence of celebrity, but as a man, Richard leaves me largely unimpressed. "Were you waiting for me?"

"Yes, actually. I wanted to apologize again for earlier. I'm not normally—"

He holds up a hand that stops me midsentence. "Please don't. I hate apologies, both getting them and giving them. Put that one in the bank and save it for when I owe you."

I like his approach. I also want to discuss his aunt away from the madding crowd, so I tilt my head toward the road. "Would you mind terribly if I walked you back to Mrs. Brennigan's? I have a few questions I'd like to ask you." Then, lest he fear I'm going to foist my brother on him again, I add, "Not about your TV show or fashion designers or anything."

He hesitates. I'm afraid he's going to tell me exactly where I can stick my interference, but all he does is blink and ask, "How did you know I'm staying at Mrs. Brennigan's?"

It's not rocket science. There are no hotels—luxury or otherwise—anywhere in the immediate vicinity, and he already admitted he hasn't seen his brother yet, which means he's not staying at his aunt's. Unless he somehow scored an invitation to Castle Hartford behind my back, the only other place with vacant rooms worthy of a man of his repute is the Brennigan B&B. One of the rooms in their house was once used by a member of the royal family.

"I have my ways," I say with a serene smile.

"Then how can I refuse?"

Mrs. Brennigan doesn't live far from the vicarage, so I have to make good use of the time I have. I'm prevented from asking anything, however, by Richard's own, "Are you close, you and your brother?"

I think of Liam, who is probably on the phone right now telling all his friends about his brush with fame, and sigh. "We try to be," I say. "But we don't have a lot in common, so it can be difficult sometimes."

"You don't share his love of talk show hosts, I take it?"

"You seem very nice," is my polite reply.

Richard laughs out loud. "That's put me in my place, hasn't it? And before you ask, no, my brother and I aren't close, either. We never were, even as boys."

"It's just the two of you?" I ask.

"It is now," he says, a note of bitterness in his voice. At the introduction of Lewis King into the conversation, that same creeping antagonism I saw on Nicholas's and Annis's faces washes over him. "I'm sorry. I shouldn't be burdening you with our family troubles. What did you want to ask me? Is it about

Aunt Sarah's death? I can't tell you much, I'm afraid. I don't know who could have poisoned her, or why. I'm ashamed to admit it, but I haven't been down to see her in over a year. I *had* been planning to visit sometime in early summer, but . . ."

He looks off into the distance, his forehead knit in a way that reminds me of his aunt's heavy beetle brows.

"I understand from Annis that you and your brother used to spend your summers here," I prod.

He nods and returns his attention to me. "Our parents were in the diplomatic service, so we spent most of the year at school and our breaks with Aunt Sarah. She hated having us, said we cut up her peace until she was ready to throw us off the cliffs, but we didn't have anywhere else to go."

"Oh," I murmur, thrown for a temporary loop. At this point, I hardly expect to get a glowing report of Sarah Blackthorne out of anyone, but come on. The woman wouldn't even open her heart or her home to her *nephews*?

He notices my reaction and laughs. "I warned you about her. I warned the police inspector, too, when he called. To be honest, I'm surprised it took this long for someone to do away with her."

"You've spoken with Inspector Piper?"

"Yes. He wanted to know who the beneficiary of Aunt Sarah's will and life insurance policy is."

I can hardly believe my luck. My breath catches. "And?"

He laughs again. "The Tennis Foundation, I'm afraid."

By this time, we've reached the Brennigan B&B. The only concession to the service industry the historic home displays is a hand-painted sign hanging above a picture window. Otherwise, the house looks exactly like what it is—a gentleman's residence that's been painstakingly kept up over the years. I'm not quite ready to end this conversation, so I pause at the end of the walkway.

"The Tennis Foundation?" I echo. "As in, love-thirty and lobs and all that? Did your aunt play?"

"Not a single day of her life. I doubt she ever watched a match, either."

"Then . . ."

"She did it because she knew it was the worst possible place she could leave it. Poor Lewis. This may well be the end of the road for him." Richard glances at the oversized gold watch on his wrist and offers me his hand, signaling dismissal. "Thank you for the company and for doing your part to send my aunt off with good grace. As you can see, it's not going to be an easy task."

"Maybe I can convince the community to put up some tennis courts with the money we earn," I suggest as I give his hand a shake. "To keep to the theme."

He grins, showcasing that strange juxtaposition of perfect falsity along his top row of teeth and ordinary humanity on the bottom. "Well, Madame Eleanor, that's a wrap. Good night, and remember not to do anything I wouldn't do." He winks and heads toward the house. "If there is such a thing."

Chapter 9

"Fact number one: Werewolves are susceptible to silver. Especially in bullet form."

"False. Anything that can kill a bear can also kill a werewolf. You just need something strong enough to pierce their hide. Next?"

"Um . . ." Rachel glances down at the sheet of paper in her lap, which is covered in her long, sloping handwriting and even more of her long, sloping drawings. She's sitting cross-legged on my living room floor, surrounded by dozens of similar sheets. "Fact number two: Werewolves only appear during a full moon."

"Also false." Across from her, Lenora consults the leather-bound book in her lap. "They just need eighty percent of a full moon in order to transform from human to beast. But it says here that their wolf form is more powerful when the moon is all the way full."

Rachel looks up and pushes back a lock of her dark blond hair. "Oh, that's cool. How full is the moon right now?"

They both look to me for an answer. I'm not curled on the floor—mostly because I'm not a teenager and I have bones that protest that sort of thing—but I am overseeing things from my perch on the couch. "It'll be full on Friday, so three days from now."

Both of the girls perk up. "That's definitely close enough to count," Lenora says.

I hold back a sigh at their obvious show of enthusiasm. I'd hoped that by inviting the girls over to my house for this afternoon's educational session, we could keep things fairly werewolf-free. In anticipation, I'd emptied a huge pot from the backyard that used to contain geraniums, painted it black, and lugged it inside to emulate a cauldron. Alas, not even my handcrafted bottles labeled EYE OF NEWT and TOE OF FROG elicited much more than a few giggles and a reiteration that I am, apparently, hilarious.

"Hey, Ellie—can you push that cauldron a little closer?" Rachel asks now.

"Of course," I say, suddenly seeing a way out of this project. "Why? Did you decide to try the eye of newt after all?"

"No." A huge splash of water falls from the ceiling and lands in the middle of the paper, rendering the words into a dark impressionist piece. "But I need something to catch this drip running through the ceiling. Did you leave the tap on upstairs or something?"

I mutter a curse that includes not just the newt's eye, but all his mobile body parts. "No. The bucket upstairs must have filled up, that's all. It's getting worse."

"The roof?" she asks with a sympathetic cluck. "I'm not surprised. Thomas used to spend hours up there replacing the soggy bits."

"Yes, well, it's all soggy bits at this point." I hoist myself to my feet and begin dragging the fifty-pound pot closer to where the girls are seated. "We'll be lucky if the whole thing doesn't collapse on us."

Lenora doesn't seem to find this prospect the least bit alarming. "That would be so cool."

Rachel is less impressed. "You should have someone out to replace it. I think Grandmother knows a good thatcher."

"I'm sure she does. The question is, does she also know someone in the market for a good kidney?"

Both of the girls look at me with expressions of pure adolescent naïveté. I realize my mistake at once. Naturally, neither one of these girls knows anything about financial hardship; the one because she's twelve, the other because the uncle who dotes on her is a millionaire.

"I'm sure Uncle Nicholas will give you the money to fix it, Ellie," Rachel says, proving my point to a nicety.

"Yes, I know."

"Do you want me to ask him for you?"

"No, I don't."

Something of the tight reserve in my voice must carry over to the older girl, because she only gives me a queer look before allowing the subject to drop. I'm grateful enough not to have to fall into lengthy explanations as to why a young woman living in a mistress's keep might be reluctant to accept monetary gifts from the lord of the land that I willingly turn the talk back to werewolves.

Oh, the lengths to which a desperate woman will go.

"You might as well keep going. What else do you have on that list of yours?"

"Let's see . . ." Rachel once again peruses her list of common werewolf myths, squinting around the blurred edges of the watermark. "Ah! Here we were. Fact number three: The only way to protect yourself from werewolves is to put a sprig of monkshood under your pillow at night. Kind of like with garlic and vampires."

I snap to attention. "Wait a minute—"

"I don't see anything in the book about monkshood." Lenora wrinkles her nose and peers closer at the tome, which I assume has been borrowed from the village museum on an extended lease. "Eleanor? Is that one true? Does that monk stuff repel werewolves?"

I snatch the list from Rachel and scan it. Everything appears to be written in her own hand. "Where did you get this?" I ask.

"We made it." She blinks up at me, a furrow in her brow. "As everyone was leaving the fête meeting yesterday, we asked them what, if anything, they knew about werewolves."

"You did *what*?"

"You were outside pretending not to wait for Rich King," Rachel says, the picture of innocence. "And we thought it might help with the research. You know, to interview locals to discover what they've heard about werewolf legends. Or if they've ever seen anything that might have been one."

By all rights, I should be outraged. Not only have these girls picked up the reins of their werewolf investigation and gone way off course with it, but they're doing it under the guise of my leadership.

I need to put my foot down. I need to control my charges. I need to—

"What did they say?" I ask, my heart beating faster. "Has anyone seen one?"

"Unfortunately, no," Rachel sighs. "The general said there was a pack of stray dogs that came through here about five years ago, but they mostly hung around outside the butcher shop hoping for scraps."

"Is he the one who told you about the monkshood?"

Rachel looks at Lenora, her lips pursed in thoughtfulness. "No, it wasn't him. Or the vicar or Mrs. Cherrycove, because they only knew about the silver bullets. And your dad was the one who told us about the full moon theory, Lenora."

"It was Mrs. Brennigan," Lenora supplies.

I swivel to stare at her. "Really?" *Sweet Mrs. Brennigan? Friendly Mrs. Brennigan? Enjoying-her-second-honeymoon-thanks-to-yours-truly Mrs. Brennigan?*

"Oh, yeah," Rachel says with a snap of her fingers. "It *was* her. She stayed and talked with us the longest, and she didn't act like we were being annoying the way some of the other ladies did. I like her, Ellie, don't you?"

"I do like her," I admit. "But what I don't like is the idea of either of you going anywhere near monkshood. That stuff is toxic, you guys—*really* toxic."

The two girls share a knowing look.

"I'm not kidding. One touch, and it can kill you."

Their knowing look doesn't dissipate in the slightest.

"*How* does it kill you?" Rachel asks.

"Yeah," Lenora adds. "What are the exact symptoms?"

The fact that Sarah Blackthorne died of wolfsbane poisoning isn't common knowledge yet. Like the pig's missing heart, the news will probably get around the village eventually, because, well, that's what news does in places like this. For now, however, the word is that she was poisoned, end of story.

I'm debating the wisdom of being the one to impart the news to these two young, impressionable women when a knock sounds at my door. Never one to give credit to unseen forces, I nevertheless cast up a silent prayer in thanks. The monkshood-wolfsbane-violent-death conversation wasn't one I was looking forward to having with these two.

"Ooh, is that someone coming to order a spell from you?" Lenora asks as she springs to her feet. "Quick—what should I say?"

"Not a single word," I reply. "And if you absolutely can't help yourself, a simple *hello* will do the trick."

Lenora giggles. My powers of clairvoyance tell me she's going to once again delight over what a comedienne I'm turning out to be, so I block her out and rise to answer the door.

I don't share Lenora's belief that it's a potential customer. Not only would the back door be a more likely entry point, but I haven't seen *any* clients since Sarah Blackthorne died—not even anyone passing through and hoping I sell cannabis, which is an unfortunately common occurrence. If I thought I could get away with becoming a pot dispensary on top of everything else, I'd do it. Alas, even I'm not willing to push Inspector Piper that far.

"Lewis!" I cry upon seeing the less glorious of the two King brothers on the other side of the door. He looks much as he always does, which is to say his clothes could use a good ironing and his facial hair has once again reached the overgrown shrubbery stage. He also looks, unless I'm very much mistaken, even more exhausted than he did the last time we met. "Come in, please. I was just, uh, holding a lecture for my two apprentices."

I will the two girls to put all evidence of werewolf-related research materials out of sight of my guest, but my powers fall flat.

"L-lecture? Apprentices?" Lewis peers around me to examine the scene for himself. He makes as if to back away, but I'm not about to lose this opportunity to continue our chat. "I should c-come back. . . ."

"No, no. We were just finishing up in here. It's a school night, so they should be getting home."

"But, Ellie, it's only—"

"Four o'clock already, I know." I feign a heavy sigh. "There's just not enough time in the day, is there? We'll try to get the rest of this done tomorrow."

My powers fail here, too. Neither Rachel nor Lenora budges from the spot, both of them showing an alarming tendency to become permanent residents.

"Maybe you can help us, Mr. King," Rachel says in a sweet voice I instantly mistrust. "We're researching werewolf folklore for Lenora's school project and are hoping to get firsthand witness accounts. Have you ever encountered one? In real life, I mean?"

I groan inwardly. It's hardly the ideal question to put to a man whose aunt recently died from wolfsbane poisoning, but there's no taking it back now.

"M-me?" he asks, eyes wide. "N-no, of course not. Why would I?"

"Well, I don't know. That's why we're doing research." She flutters her long lashes in a way that's alarmingly beguiling. If the boys at the art gallery aren't lining up with offers to take her out, my elixir must be seriously defective. "What about werewolf legends? Do you know any?"

"L-legends?"

Lenora, no longer pleased to play second fiddle to her idol, pipes up with a clipped, academic air, "Werewolf mythology dates back to the ancient Greeks, and almost all Western cultures have their own variation. Even the Babylonians had a few."

"Y-yes, w-well." Lewis's stammering grows more pronounced, and his gaze shifts uneasily to mine. "I don't know anything about the B-Babylonians. I only wanted to . . ."

Whatever he wanted is lost to the beads of perspiration gathering on his brow. He pulls out a handkerchief and mops his forehead, looking at me with such desperation I immediately take pity on him.

"Can I get you something to drink, Lewis?"

His relief is so profound it's almost comical. "Yes, p-please. Do you have more of that c-cordial?"

I have several bottles of it, in fact, all of them waiting for just such a demand on my hospitality. I also have several bottles of stronger spirits that might help soothe him, but if he intends to keep sweating like that, he's going to need to hold on to as many of his fluids as he can.

"Yes, of course. I'll grab an extra bottle for you to take with you. Would your brother like one, too, do you think?"

His limbs jerk, and he bumps his hip on a side table. All of the contents—a book on poisons I've been reading, a stack of

Horse & Hound magazines I can't convince the publisher to stop sending me, and the box of elephant tranquilizers brought by the postman earlier today—fall in a heap to the ground.

Lewis barely seems to notice the disarray. "M-my brother?"

"I met him yesterday at the vicarage. A nice man. He seemed quite popular with the ladies."

"Richard is here?" He casts a wild look around. "N-now?"

The girls are starting to show signs of uneasiness, almost as though Lewis's nerves are contagious. I can hardly blame them for it; this whole jump-and-sweat routine is starting to make *me* twitchy.

"Why don't you sit down?" I find myself saying. "Have a drink, relax, maybe even stay for a bite to eat. Have you been finding it any easier to sleep now that you've settled in?"

"S-sleep?" he echoes, his voice incredulous. "*S-sleep?*"

Never, in all my life, have I come across a man who needs it more. "Yes," I say firmly. "Sleep. I can give you something to help with it, if you'd like."

My offer is soundly rejected. With another of those strange jerks, he shakes his head and begins backing toward the door. "I'm sorry. I have to g-go." He sees the girls sitting open mouthed and watching him and adds, "It was a m-mistake to come here."

The only mistake, as far as I can see, was mentioning his brother, but I don't regret making it. Not when it resulted in such a violent reaction. I might be the person with the most access to poison around here, but I had no motive to murder Sarah, no grudge to hold against her.

Lewis King, however? Spasmodically nervous Lewis? Cordial-guzzling Lewis? Not-getting-any-inheritance-because-it's-all-going-to-the-Tennis-Foundation Lewis?

He wastes no more time on pleasantries. After a few fumbling attempts to rearrange the spilled contents from the table, he turns on his heel and flees out the front door.

Almost immediately, I wish I'd thought to flee with him.

"Lenora, did you see the color of his eyes—?"

"I saw. And did you notice all that wild hair everywhere—?"

"I noticed. Plus, how pale and sweaty he was, even though it's cold outside—?"

"That too. And his excessive thirst. That was in one of the articles—"

"And that big old book. You know what this means—?"

"Oh, yeah. I know."

I turn on the girls, an expression of firm resolve on my face. "Don't you dare say it, you two. I know what you're thinking, but there's no way Lewis King is a—"

"*Werewolf!*" They speak, or rather scream, the word in unison.

I pinch the bridge of my nose, feeling the weight of my years crashing down on my shoulders. If this is a punishment for all those decades I spent making people believe their homes were haunted, I can only assume the worst is yet to come.

Granted, the girls aren't completely off base. There *is* something seriously strange about Lewis King, if only the fact that he's been in a downward spiral since he arrived here. The man I met at the pub hadn't been a sparkling conversationalist, by any means, but he was genial enough in an ordinary, my-aunt-just-died sort of way.

Yes, his facial hair does seem to grow awfully fast for a normal human male. And, sure, that musky smell of his leaves a little to be desired. But the man isn't a *werewolf*. It's probably just poor personal hygiene.

"It's a great theory, you guys, really it is, but you have to remember that Lewis wasn't even here when Mr. Worthington's pig was killed. I found Regina late on Thursday evening, and he didn't arrive until Friday morning. He took the early train from London."

At this sound piece of logic, Lenora's lower lip protrudes in a pout. Rachel, however, shows none of that youthful tendency toward moping. Her look is much more cunning, her eyes pulled upward as though she's working through a series of particularly difficult sums.

"One-oh-three," she mutters. "Two-sixteen. No, that's the fifteen-ninety. Ha! I knew it."

"You knew what?" I ask, not liking the self-satisfied smile moving across her face.

"There is no early train on Fridays."

I blink. "There isn't?"

"Nope." Her self-satisfied smile deepens into one of pure delight. "With all the commuting I have to do for my internship, I've got just about every route that goes back and forth between here and London memorized—and Friday morning's train is an outbound one, not an incoming one. Either he lied about when he got in, or he didn't travel by train at all. What did he tell you?"

I think back on that first meeting with Lewis, of Nicholas's obvious dislike of the man and the rumpled state that led me to sympathize with his hurried train travel. Lewis never actually confirmed that he took the train—he only cast me that bewildered look when I hazarded a guess.

Now that I think about it, that look could have meant anything. Especially since I've come to know Lewis a little better, and it's obvious that hirsute disarray is his natural state of being.

"He didn't tell me the exact time he arrived," I admit, somewhat sheepish. "I just assumed—"

"Aha!" Lenora jumps to her feet, her hands clasped in front of her. "So he *is* a werewolf."

I hold up my hands to slow her down. Yes, I make mistakes from time to time, but there's a difference between misreading a travel-rumpled shirt and accusing a man of shapeshifting into a beast of the night.

"You know what this means, Lenny," Rachel says.

Oh, sure. *Now* Rachel gets to her feet. *Now* she makes a motion to depart.

"Since when are we calling her Lenny?" I ask.

"I like it. Lenora makes me sound like an old woman. Lenny is a sleuth. A bloodhound. A gumshoe." She flashes her signature toothy grin at Rachel. "And, yes, I do know what it means."

That makes two of us. I've spent enough time in the company of these two girls to realize that werewolves have nothing on their bloodthirsty determination. They won't rest until they've torn this case apart with their bare hands.

"We're heading to the train station," Lenora says with a pump of her fist in the air. "Field trip!"

I hold back my sigh. Short of calling up *Lenny*'s stepmother and having her come collect her wayward burden, there's not much I can do to stop this pair. I can only accompany them and hope that my attempts at responsible adult supervision will keep me from being permanently banned from all future school activities.

"Don't forget to add the bus station, taxi stand, and private airfield into the mix," I say as I reach for my shawl. At their look of sudden inquiry, I add, "Anything worth doing is worth doing all the way. Even if he didn't arrive by train, he still had to get here somehow. Maybe we'll get lucky and someone will remember when they saw him come in."

"You mean . . . ?" Rachel's eyes widen.

What I mean is that if Lewis King didn't arrive by train on Friday morning, as I originally thought, then there's no accounting for his whereabouts the day of the pig's death . . . or the evening of Sarah Blackthorne's. For the first time since I started this whole investigation, it seems I officially have a suspect.

But "I mean you did great work" is what I tell her. "You have a good memory, Rachel. I'm not sure I would have known about the train schedules on my own."

She shows every sign of falling into enthusiastic glee at this, but I stop her before she manages to fling her arms around me. "But a word of warning—and I mean this with every fiber of my being. You two will not do any investigating without me, understand?" I lower my voice so Lenora can't overhear. The younger girl is busy shoving papers and books into her backpack. I have no idea how she'll make them all fit, but at least it keeps her busy. "Lenora looks up to you. She trusts you. I don't mind if you keep researching werewolves together, but you'll stick to books and museums while I'm not around, or I'm ending this entire project."

To her credit, Rachel accepts my authority with a solemnity worthy of a Hartford. "Of course, Ellie. I'd never do anything dangerous." She pauses, choosing her next words carefully. "Does this mean you think Lewis might really be a werewolf? As in, for reals?"

"The world is a strange and mysterious place," I say, unwilling to commit myself one way or another. "In my lifetime, I've seen—and heard—many things that defy explanation."

My dead sister, for example. There's no denying that her voice falls under the strange and mysterious category.

I stop and start, recalling all too clearly my visit to Sarah Blackthorne's kitchen, when Winnie mocked my theory about the rat poison with her usual laughing air. I hadn't paid much attention at the time, but I remember now that Lewis asked if I'd spoken aloud. It was almost as though he, too, had heard her voice speaking from afar.

But that's ridiculous. No one hears Winnie but me. No one except Beast, anyway. And maybe that mouse at the crossroads. And . . . *Oh, dear.*

"What is it, Ellie?" Rachel asks. "What's wrong?"

"A werewolf is technically an animal," I say.

"I know, right? That's what makes them so cool."

True. It's also what makes them not real. They're fake.

Make-believe. An unreliable myth in a world full of rigid rules and natural laws.

Just like the possibility of a woman speaking to me from beyond the grave.

A man is hovering outside my back door when I return home.

The survey that Rachel, Lenora, and I made of the numerous transportation outfits in this part of Sussex took much longer than I anticipated. What remains of the sun—a watery, feeble vessel that's close to giving up altogether—is now crossing over the horizon, leaving me standing in the dawning twilight with nary a soul to be seen for miles.

Except, of course, for the strange man.

"Hello?" I call, careful not to startle him into fight or flight. Neither one of those things is an ideal outcome when standing alone in the dark. Fight, because I'm a small woman and I don't carry weapons on my person; flight, because if it's Lewis again, I don't want to scare him away before we have a chance to talk.

Especially after our findings. No one at the bus station, train station, taxi stand, or airfield could remember seeing Lewis come in, even under the deep persuasion of Rachel's batting eyelashes. We also visited a few of the nearby gas stations in hopes that he might have rented a car and filled up along the way, but the man seems to have appeared from out of nowhere.

Or, according to my sidekicks, he transformed into his wolf form and ran through the hillsides under the light of the waxing moon.

Giddy adolescent girls, as it turns out, don't make the best sidekicks.

"Can I help you with something?" I add, drawing closer. There's a rain gutter to my right that I might be able to pull down and wield like a club, should the need arise, but there's something about that slight form that looks familiar. A spot of orange light extinguishing in the growing darkness and a waft of smoke washing over me confirm it.

"Hello, Inspector," I say. "I see the lollipops aren't working out as well as you'd hoped. Case getting to you?"

Inspector Piper steps out from the shadows. He looks much as he always does, sharp and suspicious, and he's wearing a grimace I assume is the result of being caught cigarette handed.

"They always do," he says. And then, with a slight tilt of his head, "I came to inspect your garden."

"In the dark?"

He glances up at the black-tinted sky. "It was daylight when I got here."

Considering I left with the girls a little after four o'clock, that gives him several hours in which he could have been sitting here waiting for me. If he's smart—and he is—he already took a good, hard look at the garden and all its contents.

Not that he'd have found anything. The previous owner of this cottage did an incredible job with the grounds, transforming a small, walled-off plot of land into an herbal and floral retreat from the world. I've added a few plants of my own, but with the exception of those duplicitous daffodils, there's nothing growing in it that could be used to harm another human being.

"And?" I ask. "What did you find?"

I unlock the back door and push it open, gesturing for the inspector to follow me in. He makes a show of wiping his feet on the mat, leaving a heavy smattering of mud behind.

Oh, yeah. He definitely took a good, hard look at my garden.

"You said you have a cat," he replies.

"I do have a cat."

He makes a show of looking around him. "Where?"

I follow the path of his gaze, skimming over all of Beast's favorite spots—curled in front of the AGA stove, perched on the windowsill, staring ominously from the doorway. "Huh. She wasn't outside?"

The inspector shakes his head and reaches for his interior coat pocket. He stops halfway with an inward curse.

"Here." I slump my bag on the table in a gesture that would do Lenora proud and dig around until I extract several packages of gum. We had to buy *something* in all those gas stations we stopped at, and it was the only thing I could afford. "Try these."

He takes one of the cellophane-lined packages and stares at it.

"It's sugar free. Same great distraction, none of the calories." When he still hesitates, I laugh and start gathering the tea things. "I could make you some artisanal water, if you'd prefer, but something tells me you'd just end up sending it in to be tested."

With a shrug, he opens the gum and pops a piece in his mouth. Although he drops the wrapper to the floor in a move I swear is designed to irritate me, my plan works. Almost immediately, he relaxes, his shoulders coming down and another of those appraising looks cast around my kitchen. "What's its name?"

It takes me a moment to register his question. "The cat? Beast. She should be around here somewhere—I leave the window above the sink open so she can come and go as she pleases. Take this and waft it around the house, will you?"

He accepts the half-opened can of tuna with a grimace.

"It'll draw her out. It's like luring spirits, except she'll bite you instead of haunt you. Did you find any poison in the garden, by the way? Am I the murderer?"

He hesitates. "You should talk to my Aunt Margaret."

"Why? Is *she* the murderer?"

He releases a chuffing sound that might be a laugh. He also wanders into the living room, holding the can of tuna out in front of him. A light switches on, and there's a long pause that I assume is a thorough—if not very secretive—search of the room's contents.

"You're wasting space out there," he eventually says. "Rosemary should always be planted next to sage. Fennel should be far away from everything. A ring of marigold will keep most pests away."

I poke my head into the living room. That sounds an awful lot like helpful advice. "You seem to know quite a bit about gardens."

"My Aunt Margaret knows quite a bit about gardens," he corrects me. "Is there a reason your living room looks like you're plotting a werewolf takeover in the middle of a rainstorm?"

I laugh and finish putting the tea things on the tray. There's not much food left since the advent of Lenora and Rachel into my domain, but I find a sleeve of mildly stale biscuits and place them in the middle.

"I assume you've heard that Lenora MacDougal is my apprentice?" I ask. Without waiting for an answer, I add, "Behold the evidence. She and Rachel have decided that we have a werewolf on the loose."

When I walk into the living room, it's to find that Inspector Piper has given up on the can of tuna and is crouched among the haphazard pile of books and papers that Lenora hadn't been able to squeeze into her backpack. There's quite a few of them, so she must be running out of space in there.

Inspector Piper pokes through the slog with the tail end of his pen, taking a moment to shake off the water that's been collecting through the roof in my absence.

He twists his head to peer up at me. "You told them about the wolfsbane?"

"Of course not." I place the tea tray on the middle of the coffee table and pour out two cups, ignoring the drip of ceiling water that lands in one. "But between the dead pig and the fact that teenage girls love a good underdog story—see what I did there?—this is what happens. If you know of some way to quash their youthful fervor without sending them off on an attempt to trap werewolves by the light of the full moon, I'd love to hear it."

His answer is a grunt and a return to his paper poking. He bypasses the scattered copies of *Horse & Hound* and raises an eyebrow at the tranquilizers before lifting the cover of the leather-bound werewolf book. Reading it only long enough to ascertain that it's museum property, he moves on to the smaller, pamphlet-style notebook next to it.

"What's this one?" he asks.

I can't recall seeing it before, but that doesn't mean much considering how many books Lenora lugs around in the general way of things. Picking up the smaller tome, I notice that it appears to be a hand-bound collection of beautifully pressed pages, all tied at the binding with a strong, reedy twine.

"Turns out Lenora is really good at finding useful old books," I say as I open the cover. "To be honest, she's kind of a wizard at it."

"A wizard?" he echoes doubtfully.

"A dab. A prodigy. A genius. Not everything has mystical ramifications, you know."

He leans closer. "It doesn't have the museum's sticker on the inside. They're usually good at cataloging their collections."

"Maybe she picked it up from a bookstore. I wouldn't put anything past her."

"And everything in it is handwritten," he points out.

"Does that matter?"

"It does when the first page looks like this."

He takes the book and shows me the page in question. There's nothing on it but a sketch of a pentagram—and a terrible one at that. The line segments are all of unequal length, as though the artist couldn't be bothered.

"Well, that's just silly," I say. "Why draw a pentagram if you aren't going to take your time with it? It's supposed to be the golden ratio, beloved of mathematicians and Satanists alike."

"So you recognize it?"

Soft laughter escapes my lips. "Yes, Inspector Piper. I'm familiar with what a pentagram looks like. As is almost everyone who's ever watched a horror movie."

Interested now, I take the book back and begin flipping through the pages. The tome looks, at first sight, to be exactly what the pentagram and worn cover promise: a handmade notebook filled with various witchy scrawls. Pentagrams, pentacles, and ominous markings of all shapes and sizes—it's basically the same type of thing I carved into the outside of the box that once contained Mr. Worthington's pig-binding elixir.

In other words, complete malarkey.

"What does this have to do with werewolves?" Inspector Piper asks. His breath is warm on my shoulder, his head mere inches from my own as he examines each page with me. The scent of stale cigarettes and strawberry gum makes for an interesting mix.

"It doesn't," I say. "In fact, if I had to take a guess, I'd say it's a Book of Shadows."

"A Book of Shadows?"

"It's not as sinister as it sounds, I promise." When the only response I get is a kind of wary disbelief, I add, "It's basically a journal for witches. I have one, too. It's where I take notes on the potions I make, track the cycles of the moon, that sort of thing. See this marking right here, the one that looks like two line snakes facing off for a showdown?"

Inspector Piper has to tilt his head a few times before he sees it. "Sure. Why not?"

"Well, it's a pretty common symbol for unity between lovers. It signifies a strong relationship or the perfect couple. I might use it if I was working on a love spell."

"So it's a spell book?" the inspector asks.

I glance down again, a worry snagging at the back of my mind. "Well, yes and no. Take this page, for example. It's written in all the traditional magic symbols, the way you might write a spell, but it's not like any I've ever seen. There are no ingredients or instructions, not even a chant or two. There's just this curved symbol here and a series of numbers. I have no idea what it means."

"And you say this notebook belongs to Lenora MacDougal?"

Given how interested the girl is in witchcraft, it wouldn't surprise me to find that she's been playing around with a Book of Shadows on the side. I had one at her age, too, though it contained fewer pentagrams and more doodly hearts around different boys' names.

I'm no snitch, however. I shrug. "Probably. I asked her to look into all instances of the occult in this area, so there's no saying who it belongs to. I wouldn't be surprised if she borrowed it from Aunt Margaret."

"I would," the inspector says. At my questioning look, he adds, "She's an herbalist, not a witch."

I laugh. "That's what we all say."

My laughter, though honest, is short-lived. For one, all these visits from Inspector Piper are starting to make me nervous. It would be one thing if he was asking my advice or filling me in on the details so I can provide a helping hand with his case. But he's examining me—he's questioning me. That means he's no closer to finding the real culprit than I am.

For another, the can of tuna is still sitting untouched on the coffee table. Solving Sarah Blackthorne's murder is important, yes, but so is finding my cat. Now that I think about it, I can't remember the last time I saw her. She wasn't around when I got home from the fête planning committee yesterday, and she wasn't in the room while the girls were going over their werewolf list, which is strange for her. There's nothing that cat loves more than to preside over a coven at work.

"It's not like her to stay away for so long," I say as I pick up the can and give it a tentative sniff. It's fishy enough to tempt the most feline of palates. "I wonder where she could be."

A huge drop of water falls onto the inspector's forehead, beading down the line of his nose. With slow, methodic carefulness, he reaches into his pocket and extracts a handkerchief.

"Maybe," he says as he wipes the drip away, "she found somewhere dry to take shelter for the night."

"Here, Beastie, Beastie." I stand crouched at the entrance to the garden, the tuna in my hand and a crooning note in my voice. "Come out, Beastie, Beastie. I promise not to watch you eat this time. Word of a witch."

The only sound that greets my ears is the whisper of wind rustling through the gate behind me. As soon as Inspector Piper left, I came out here with the full expectation of finding Beast playing a trick on me.

She loves this garden. During the daytime I can often find her sunning herself by a leafy frond or two. At night, she'll sometimes perch on the top of the wall so she can keep a vigilant watch over the cottage and all its contents. It's part of the reason I'm so sure there's a piece of Winnie in her somewhere. Not because I'm being sentimental, but because that cat sees things. She *knows* things.

"The temperature is going to get close to freezing tonight, you silly creature," I call, trying not to let the panic creep into my voice. "And I'm not getting up at three o'clock to let you inside once you finally realize it. I mean it this time."

Still nothing. Just wind and rain and a moon creeping toward its full luminous height. Three days, I told the girls, until the werewolf power is at its peak. Three nights, and that glowing orb will contain all the power of the universe.

"It's just a myth," I say, my voice wavering. "Werewolves aren't real. Regina's death was just a fluke."

The comforting words don't help, especially once I recall one of my first conversations with Lenora, when she told me all about how her brother traps mice from the field out back of their house because their own cat went missing about a month ago.

During the last full moon.

A chill that has nothing to do with the night air moves through me. I wrap my arms tight around my midsection and try not to think of missing cats and slaughtered pigs and women poisoned in church basements.

Beast can survive anything. That cat doesn't have nine lives—she has ninety.

As if to prove it, I catch sight of something moving in the distance, near the peak of a hill that slopes gently out of sight of the road. At first, I think it's nothing more than my worry and imagination working in tandem to play tricks on me. It wouldn't be the first time—you'd be surprised how much influence a spooky setting and a feeling of hysteria can have over the mind. It's a thing I've relied on more times than I care to admit, trading on atmosphere to make people believe in the impossible.

But the blur of movement passes over my peripheral vision once again, and I turn sharply toward it. "You silly cat," I mutter as I start moving that direction. "You scared the bejesus out of me, disappearing for so long."

It's just like that animal to put me in a pucker, frolicking about without a care in the world. Like Winnie, she's off in a world of her own making, where murders and werewolves are nothing more than an evening's entertainment.

Before I make it halfway up the hill, the wind picks up in a sudden cool burst, carrying with it a familiar tang. A few weeks ago, I might not have thought anything of it, but a few weeks ago, I hadn't spent quite so much time steeped in that scent.

Sharp. Metallic. *Bloody.* And underneath it all, an undeniable animal musk.

I pick up the pace. Instinct warns me to take cover and approach from the side, taking care to hide myself from whatever creature is carrying that scent, but I force myself to ignore it. It's probably just a mouse caught in Beast's fangs, a gift in exchange for all the care and food I lavish on her. Cats are weirdly generous that way.

But as I approach the site where I first saw the movement, I realize I'm not stumbling upon a mouse. Nor is the kill this time the least bit fresh.

I gag, my hand over my mouth, as I reach yet another body left decomposing for all to see.

No, not all, I think. *Just me.*

I'm not sure whether to be proud of myself or not as I immediately identify the animal as a cat at least two days gone, deposited at the hill's crest in its current postmortem state.

"Beast?" I ask, my voice wavering. My heart thuds heavily in my chest, a wrenching feeling not unlike the one I experienced at the loss of my sister threatening to take over. "Beast, are you—?"

My answer comes—not from Winnie and not from beyond the grave—but in a blue collar that I know, in an instant, doesn't belong to my cat. The initial wave of relief this realization brings is quickly brought to rest when I realize that another dead animal, this one almost on my back porch, is hardly *good* news. Especially since that blur of movement I saw couldn't have been caused by this animal moving on its own four feet.

Something—or someone—is on the prowl. And something—or someone—is determined that I be aware of it.

I whirl, my eyes narrowed as I try to make out the huddled lumps and dark blotches in the distance, but I don't see sight of anything moving. At least, not unless you count the tree branches swaying heavily to and fro and the gentle shimmer of a cloud moving over the moon.

"I'm not scared of you!" I call, even though the prickle at the nape of my neck feels an awful lot like fear. "I've seen worse than this before. This one isn't even ripped open. I bet it still has its heart and everything."

Though true, I'm not all too keen on having decaying carcasses thrown onto my property, especially considering how recently Inspector Piper stopped by unannounced. He'd take one look at this poor animal and assume I'm adding sacrifice to my regular rituals. Since I have nothing but love for creatures of the four-legged variety, I say a quick chant over the body and make a mental note to bury it first thing in the morning. I also take one last lingering look over the darkened landscape, hoping against all reason and likelihood that Beast will appear to put my alarm to rest.

She doesn't.

The best I can do is take a deep breath and say, "Watch over her for me, will you, Winnie? That cat will probably be back tomorrow without a lick of fur out of place, but it's always better to be careful. Even with an animal as indomitable as that one."

I'm not sure whether the words are meant for me or my sister, but it doesn't matter. As a howl sounds in the distance, mournful and so unnerving it sends a shiver down my spine, neither one of us seems to have anything to say.

Chapter 10

There's only one person in the village I trust to tell me the truth, the whole truth, and nothing but the truth when it comes to neighborhood gossip.

"Eleanor!" Vivian is alone in the castle, sequestered in her bedroom against both the cold and any outside invaders. Her room has always been the warmest place in the castle, as it contains one of the only working fireplaces. Today is no exception. She's celebrating the warmth with a tropical muumuu-style dress and a bottle of my elderberry cordial that I assume she had Rachel pinch from the cottage during one of her frequent visits. "What are you doing here? I thought you were busy investigating Sarah's murder."

I allow a note of apology to creep into my voice. "I am. In fact, that's why I'm here. I hate to be a bother, but I'm in something of a bind."

"And you want my help with it? Oh, dear." She reaches for the bottle, her hands fluttering with the cork. She's perfectly capable of opening it on her own—her actions are meant to convey both an air of fragility and an inability to follow through with any gestures of hospitality.

"None for me, thanks," I say. I'm familiar with the script. "I just had a huge lunch. I couldn't possibly eat or drink anything else."

My confession has its intended effect, which is to quell any fears Vivian has that she'll be expected to play the role of hostess. She's still wary about that whole being-in-a-bind situation, though, so she continues to act like a bird released from its cage for the first time.

"It's always nice to see you, dear, but I don't know how I can help." She sighs. "Everyone seems to want something from me lately. Vicar Brown has been badgering me to help fund the new bell tower, and I've received I don't know how many visits from life insurance salesmen who seem to think I have one foot in the grave. Those would be bad enough on their own, but then Penny came by with one of her cakes this morning."

"You got a cake?" My mouth waters at the prospect of one of those chocolate towers sequestered somewhere in the castle. I haven't lost a loved one recently, but I've been around enough death that I think I've earned a slice. Burying that cat this morning was no small feat. "What on earth for?"

"I can't imagine. I've been nothing but nice to her lately. She should know better than to saddle me with that much responsibility."

I find nothing odd in this statement. The only thing Vivian likes less than visitors is having food in the pantry that will increase the likelihood of them stopping by. "I'm sure you can count on Rachel to do away with it before anyone finds out," I say. "She's been eating me out of house and home."

Vivian's eyes take on a shrewd look. "Don't mention that girl's name to me. Do you know how many hours I spent discussing werewolves with her last night?"

I feel nothing but sympathy for her plight. I'm starting to loathe the very mention of that creature. "I can guess."

"I assume this is your doing. Whatever you're up to this

time, I don't want any part of it. Regular men are bad enough. If you start encouraging her to drag home ones covered with fur, I won't be held responsible for my actions."

I can't help but laugh. "I solemnly promise not to saddle Rachel—or you—with any wolf men I find lying about." Since I know I'm not going to get an invitation to sit, I lower myself into the nearest chair. "But that does put me in mind of what I wanted to talk to you about."

"As I told my granddaughter already, no, I haven't encountered any werewolves in my lifetime and, no, you may not set up a shapeshifter hunting party on these grounds. Honestly, Eleanor, can't you control them with your mind or something?"

"Teenagers or werewolves?"

She picks up the bottle of cordial and uncorks it with all the flourish her earlier attempts had been lacking. "At this point, I'll take either one."

That makes two of us. Unfortunately, my mystical influences work best on the desperate and downtrodden—two adjectives that neither Rachel nor Lenora can be accused of falling prey to. And I can't control werewolves because *they're not real.*

It's a phrase I've been telling myself over and over again all morning. It wasn't a werewolf depositing a cat on my hill last night. It was someone sending me a message—warning me against getting too close to this investigation. I'm a hundred percent sure of it.

Or at least ninety percent, anyway.

"I'm doing my best," I promise. "But first, I need you to tell me everything you know about Lewis King. Especially why everyone in the village seems to dislike him so much."

She pauses in the middle of filling her glass. "What makes you think I know anything?"

I remember what the general said that day in the pub, about how there's room in a village this size for only one strong-willed and influential matriarch, and know exactly what to say. "Because you hated his aunt, and you're not one to begrudge a grudge. Come on, Viv. Even Nicholas doesn't seem to care much for him, and he doesn't have strong feelings toward *anyone*."

Except, of course, for me, but even that sentiment is suspect these days. Here I am, embroiled in the middle of a murder investigation, finding dead cats in my backyard and being hounded by the local police into closing my business, and he's off reaping his millions.

I guess that's what happens when one ship is profoundly more successful than the other. He has oceans to traverse, high seas to sail. I'm mostly just paddling around in a sludge-filled pond of my own making.

"I don't know what you're talking about," Vivian says primly, but there's a cackle of delight lingering at the back of her throat. "If Sarah Blackthorne's nephew wants to spend her entire life savings investing in schemes that any idiot with two eyes can see are a sham, it's no concern of mine."

I scoot my chair closer.

"I honestly don't know what he was thinking, Eleanor. A dating service for dogs?"

"No way. That was an actual thing he did?"

Her cackle becomes more pronounced. "Not for long. The company went under after a prize Pekingese got knocked up by a mongrel masquerading as a spaniel. Which, incidentally, wasn't nearly as disastrous as the key-carrying delivery service that would go inside your house to drop off packages. They say over three hundred thousand dollars' worth of jewelry and electronics were stolen by the employees in the first week."

"Poor Lewis," I can't help saying. Granted, he's rapidly jumping up my list of murder suspects, but it's impossible not to feel a *little* sorry for him. The village pariah is a tough role to play.

Trust me. I know.

"He does seem rather . . . underwhelming a man," I add. "Especially when compared to his brother."

Vivian snorts and leans back in her chair. Now that her glass is full and I've promised not to put her out in any way, she's relaxing into our chat. "Richard King—now *he's* the one you should feel sorry for. He's had to pull his brother out of his financial messes enough times to buy Buckingham Palace five times over. Not that you heard it from me. I don't gossip."

"Of course not," I say.

On the surface, I'm all bland agreement, but my insides are roiling with possibilities. In cases of murder—poison or otherwise—there are three motives worth looking out for. Love is one. Power is another. And money usually undergirds them both.

"Did you know that Sarah signed over her life insurance policy to a tennis charity?" I ask. "Her nephews aren't getting a single penny."

"I'm not surprised." Vivian shakes her head. "Sarah Blackthorne was a miser and a cheat. She probably cut Lewis and Richard out for spite. She was that type, the kind who would kick a Girl Guide in the knee and take her lunch money."

In other words, she was a bully. Cruel to both humans and animals. A killjoy.

Lonely.

That last one catches me off guard. It doesn't come from Winnie, but I don't need my sister's otherworldly wisdom to realize the truth. Sarah Blackthorne might have been one heck of an unpleasant woman to be around, but she deserved our pity more than poison. I've been living in the village for months, and I'd never even heard of her nephews, let alone seen them stop by for a visit. Those are hardly the actions of a loving family.

As if in agreement, Vivian softens. "I will say one thing for her, though—she was good to those boys of her sister's. More than they ever deserved, if you ask me. Richard almost never came to visit her, and it's common knowledge that Lewis would have been bankrupted without her. He was the reason she moved from that nice stone house on the hill to her tiny row home."

"So that's why Nicholas and Annis don't care for him," I say without need for further explanation. Nicholas might be an ironic, impenetrable fortress and Annis a fiercely loyal servant of God, but the one thing they've always had in common is a strong sense of right and wrong. A young man reducing his aunt to penury is an unforgivable offense no matter which way you look at it.

"Medical treatment is what he says he needed the money for, but what condition he's suffering from is beyond me. *And* Dr. MacDougal, I might add. She sees to him whenever he stays here in the village, and she's never found anything wrong with him that a firm talking-to won't fix."

"Porphyria is believed to cause werewolf-like symptoms," I muse, mostly to myself. "That would be expensive to treat."

"That's it. Out."

I glance up, half startled and half laughing, to find Vivian glaring at me with all the ferocity a rich, seventy-something noblewoman in a muumuu can muster. "Vivian, I was *kidding*."

"You're as bad as Rachel, coming in here and scaring a poor elderly woman with apocryphal tales."

"As if I could!" I protest, still laughing. Vivian is neither poor nor elderly, nor, if her reaction to her castle haunting last year is any indication, the least bit frightened of anything apocryphal. "And you have to admit he looks the part. Those wide, hunched shoulders, all that hair that keeps growing back . . ."

"His brother was the same way until those television executives got hold of him. Laser surgery, every centimeter of him. I saw him in his swim trunks once. His chest looks like it belongs on a wet seal."

I rise up from my seat and press a kiss on her cheek. She smells of elderberries and the expensive amber-scented Baccarat Rouge perfume Nicholas buys for her in bulk.

"Thanks for your help, Viv," I say. "And for the company. I'll send a whole crate of that wine over with Rachel the next time I see her."

"Will you, dear? How lovely." An appropriately beatific expression settles on the lines of her face, which hint at the beauty she once was—and, in many ways, still is. "Be a dear and take that chocolate cake with you when you go, won't you? I don't want Rachel finding it and inviting the whole village over for a party. It should be down in the kitchen. I asked Penny to carry it down there."

"I suppose, if you really want me to . . ." I say with a good show of reluctance. Inside, I have to force myself to slow down and go through the normal human motions of departing. I don't want to give her a chance to change her mind.

The hallway is freezing after the sauna-like conditions of Vivian's room, but I don't mind the long, cold walk down to the kitchen. In fact, I rather enjoy it. With one of Penny's chocolate cakes on the line, I'd willingly walk my way down to the South Pole—and back again.

They're that good.

Of all the crimes wrought on the village over the past few weeks, none are quite as disheartening as the theft of Penny Dautry's prize chocolate cake.

As I slog through the muddy lane back to my cottage *without* a delicious cake in my possession, I curse all those involved.

Vivian, for promising sugary delights and not delivering.

Penny, for hoarding her secret recipe and parceling the cake out only upon literal pain of death.

Lewis, for taking his aunt's money and thereby rendering himself odious to the cake maker.

And Nicholas, for luring me to this village in the first place.

"Before I came here, I'd never heard of Beast or Nicholas Hartford the Third or Penny Dautry's chocolate cake," I mutter as I turn up my walkway. I'm soaked almost all the way through, but it doesn't matter, since it looks as though one side of my roof is about to cave in. Apparently, aquatic living is something I'm going to have to get used to. "My life was rich. Full. Now I've been ruined for anything else but those three."

"Oh, dear. Did I come at a bad time?"

I halt midstep, more startled than I care to admit at the sight of a thin, nervous-looking woman sitting hunched on my doorstep. Given how popular my cottage has been lately, I shouldn't be surprised to find yet another visitor stopping by.

But I can't help it. It's too fantastic, even for me.

"Did I conjure you?" I ask, blinking at the vision before me. Not at the woman, whom I recognize on sight as Penny Dautry, but at the towering confection on the step next to her. Three layers, each one a perfect circle, folds of glistening chocolate ganache smoothed over every edge . . . My mouth waters almost instantly.

It's the cake.

"Conjure me?" she echoes. "Why would you do that?"

She grabs the porch handrail and struggles to her feet, propelling me into action. I wish I could say that my instincts are pure chivalry, a young woman helping an older one in the act of standing, but I'm mostly worried she's going to topple onto the dessert.

"I was just up at the castle talking to Vivian about you," I reply with a smile meant to allay any fears of malicious gossip. "I find that a simple conversation will sometimes draw a person toward me."

"Will it?" Penny says. "Oh, dear."

I keep my hand on her elbow as she straightens her knee-length tweed skirt and serviceable khaki mackintosh. She also has on one of those plastic floral rain bonnets I always eye when I'm at the grocer's. They look ridiculous on anyone under the age of fifty, but Penny seems awfully dry under there. Her cake has been subjected to the same treatment, a kind of plastic wrap tent around it to protect it from the drizzle.

"I hope I haven't kept you waiting long," I say with a sidelong look at the dessert. I have no idea how well ganache stands up to the elements, but I can't imagine all this rain is helping. "Please, come in. My home is always open."

Like most people, she hesitates on the threshold, wary lest that footfall into my abode will cast a curse upon her head. The cauldron catching drips in the middle of the living room doesn't help matters, but she notices the wainscoting and white-painted fireplace and decides to risk it.

I'm not too far behind, the chocolate cake secure in my loving embrace.

"Is it too much to hope this is for me?" I ask as I kick the door to a close behind me. Jostled by the movement, a large piece of ceiling falls away and plops in the cauldron. I peek inside and grimace. The plaster seems to be breaking down into some kind of paste-like substance in there. "And, uh, don't mind the mess. The rain sprites are a little angry at me right now, but we're working through it."

"Rain sprites?" Penny echoes doubtfully.

"A joke," I say. "The thatch needs to be replaced."

"Oh, of course. How silly of me." She laughs nervously, her breath caught on a pause. "Were you really discussing me up at the castle?"

I nod down at the cake in my hands. "Technically, we were discussing this masterpiece right here."

"You were? But Vivian didn't—I was supposed to take it—"

"Vivian didn't want it? You were supposed to take it to the kitchen?" I smile warmly in an effort to soothe her. "You did much better to bring it here, believe me. She might have eaten a bite or two, but she'd have let it sit on a shelf and get stale before she told anyone it was there. I, on the other hand, promise to love, honor, and cherish this cake until death us do part."

My words, don't, as I hope, lessen her anxiety. In fact, as my tongue trips over the long-term implications of the traditional marriage vow—*death*—she gives a visible start.

For the first time, I find myself wondering about the cake's contents. It would have been very easy for her to slip some wolfsbane into the glistening chocolate ganache, murdering people left and right. No one would be the wiser. How could they? Anywhere this cake is served, there's never a crumb left to examine for clues.

"It was only good things, I promise," I say as I begin to pull out a couple of plates. Strange though it may seem, I'm willing to risk imminent and painful death for a slice. "Your cake is famous, you know."

"Yes," she says, looking profoundly sad. "I know."

Like the lives of most of the people in the village, the basics of Penny's life are fairly well known. She's in her late fifties to early sixties, unmarried and uninterested in changing that state of affairs. Rumors have it that she once trothed her love to the passionate French pastry chef who taught her everything she knows, but I assume that story has more rumor than truth to it, if only because no rational woman would let a passionate French pastry chef slip through her fingers that easily.

"It's difficult, isn't it, being recognized for one sole skill in this world?" I slide a generous wedge of cake onto her plate and an even more generous wedge onto mine. "It doesn't matter what you can do or how many ways you can do it—when a person becomes whittled down to just one thing, it's almost impossible to get people to see you any other way. Especially in a small village like this one."

Her expression lightens almost immediately. "Yes. Yes, it *is*, isn't it?"

"Vivian Hartford is the eccentric, which means she's expected to bar herself in her room and refuse all social overtures. Dr. MacDougal is the calm, cool medical practitioner, so she has to rise to every occasion with grace. And me, well, I'm the witch. I can't have a leaky roof and glutton myself on dessert. I'm supposed to be mysterious and all seeing at every turn."

To show how resistant I am to such pressures, I kick off my shoes and take a hefty bite. The cake is rich and moist and so perfectly decadent, I actually emit a low moan.

"And you," I say around a thick mouthful. "You're expected to bake. When the world is falling down around you and the only thing you want is to pack up and move to France, everyone expects you to roll up your sleeves and churn out cakes like you're working on an assembly line."

She leans across the table, her fork dangling from her fingertips. I focus on the earnest entreaty in her pale blue eyes and thin, chapped lips rather than the fact that she hasn't touched her own cake yet. I really hope she hasn't poisoned it.

"It's true!" she says. "When I walk down the street, all anyone sees is my cake. Not Penny Dautry, the human being. Not Penny Dautry, the *woman*."

I nod, feeling only slightly guilty about my gentle manipulations. Nothing I've said is a lie, even if my motives are only to reduce Penny's nerves enough to manipulate her further. For whatever reason, she visited Vivian today with a bribe in hand. What she wanted—an overture of friendship, information about the family—I can't say. But when it didn't work, she brought the bribe to *me*.

It doesn't take a psychic to realize there's meaning in that.

"I'm an artist—did you know that?" she demands. "A poet."

"I can tell," I say. "Your eyes carry a certain wisdom."

Color rushes to her cheeks. "Well, I don't know about that. . . ."

"I do. There's more to you than meets the eye, Ms. Penny Dautry, I'm sure of it. But you aren't touching your cake."

She stabs her fork in the sponge and shovels a large piece into her mouth. Watching her chew and swallow causes my stress levels to drop a ridiculous degree. I wasn't looking forward to joining Winnie in the afterworld just yet.

"As much as I appreciate you sharing this cake with me, it's not why you stopped by," I say. "You want something."

She hesitates.

"It's okay, Penny. You can tell me. People often entrust their deepest, darkest desires to a woman in my situation. I've seen much of the world—both this one and the next. Nothing you have to divulge will surprise me."

"Why do you say that?" The nerves are back in place again, her skin ashen. "What do you want me to tell you?"

"I don't want you to tell me anything you're not comfortable with," I soothe. "But I'm guessing you're here because of your relationship with Sarah Blackthorne. I saw you the night she died—you were the first to rush to her aid. It shows what a nice person you are, especially since the two of you didn't always get along."

Her fork halts in midair. It shakes once, shivers twice, and drops to the table. Any color that remained in her face is wiped away. Any lingering doubts I have are wiped away, too. It seems the general was right when he said that Sarah made enemies of everyone at the committee meeting. It had to take a real piece of work to get on the wrong side of a sweet woman like Penny.

Then again, maybe it's not so difficult to do. . . .

"What do you know about me and Sarah?" Penny asks, her voice becoming shrill. She pushes back from the table, her actions surprisingly agile for a woman who had such a difficult time rising from my stoop not more than fifteen minutes ago.

Partially to calm her and partially because I have more questions I'd like to ask, I wear my most serene expression. I'm grateful that I took the time to dress before I visited Vivian, my vintage floral wrap dress a little optimistic for the weather, but perfect for giving the impression that I'm one with the elements.

"I know enough," I say. "But don't worry. Your secrets are safe with me."

"I won't do it, you hear me?" She casts a look so frantic around the kitchen, I'm suddenly grateful my knives are tucked away in a drawer. "Not today. Not tomorrow. Not ever. I've had enough, and I don't care what you plan to do about it."

"Penny, it's okay. I only want to be your friend."

Penny's whole body jerks. "When Sarah died, I thought that would be the end of it. I thought it was over. I thought I would finally be fr—"

Free.

She doesn't have to finish the sentence. Aware that she's said too much, Penny clamps her jaw tight. She makes a fumbling attempt to put her rain cap on, but all she does is tear the plastic along one side.

"How dare you, Madame Eleanor." She holds the rain cap up as if to blame me for its rough handling. "They said you were different, that you actually cared. But you don't. You're just as bad as she was."

I open my mouth to defend myself, but I have no idea what I'm supposed to defend myself *against.* As far as I can tell, I've done nothing more than offer support and guidance and, yes, friendship. Above all else, it seems as though Penny could use a friend.

"Here." She reaches into her purse and extracts a long pink billfold. With a shaking hand, she extracts two fifty-pound notes and throws them onto the table. They flutter like the wings of a butterfly, not stopping until they land and stick in the chocolate ganache.

"There's no charge—" I begin, but she's no longer listening. Pausing just long enough to kick angrily and ineffectively at the cauldron, she whisks herself out the front door.

I stand, my fork still in hand, and watch her go. Part of me wants to chase after her and demand an explanation, but there's no need. My psychic senses have already determined what it is she's hiding.

Penny Dautry, like so many other people in this village, wanted Sarah Blackthorne dead.

Of course, what I don't know is why. Or how. Or what on earth I'm going to do next. I might be a hundred pounds richer and the sole possessor of a chocolate cake designed by the gods, but that doesn't mean anything if people are going to run screaming from my house at the first sign of kindness.

"I'm *not* like Sarah," I say as I shut the door and appraise my house—cold and empty, without even a sign of my cat to make it feel like home. "I have apprentices. I have friends. I'm not miserable and alone."

I hold my breath and wait, willing Winnie to jump in and reassure me, but she's just as silent as before. She and Beast both.

Which makes me a little miserable, to be honest. And, considering that the steady drip-drip in the cauldron is the only sound I hear, also makes me alone.

Chapter 11

"Wait—I don't understand. You ate the *entire* cake? By yourself?"

"Don't judge, Liam. If you tasted this masterpiece, you'd understand what drove me to it. It's almost animalistic, the things this cake makes you do."

A sigh sounds through my phone. "You mean, like forcing otherwise reasonable women to consume fifteen thousand calories in one sitting?"

"Actually, I was thinking more along the lines of slaughtering pigs and cats for no discernible reason."

The sigh becomes a heavy pause. At least, I assume it's heavy. I'm currently slogging through yet another muddy lane on my way to the village. Part of it is for exercise, since those fifteen thousand calories of cake are no laughing matter, but I also have to meet up with my apprentices for yet another afternoon of questionable supervision.

The wind whistles around me as I walk, the afternoon gloom filled with the sounds of Mother Nature wreaking her vengeance. I envy her that.

"Do you feel a sudden compulsion to murder animals, Ellie?" Liam eventually asks. "Because if that's the case, I think you should double-check that whole poison thing. Don't bath salts make people get weirdly violent?"

"Why do you think I ate the whole thing?" I ignore the bulk of his commentary, since its sole purpose is to frighten me into giving up England and going back to New York to roost on his couch. "If I left any lying around, Rachel and Lenora would have sniffed it out. I was saving them from an untimely death."

"A true hero."

"You're missing the point. It's a *good* cake. Penny knows it, which is why she only bakes one when someone is dead or she wants something. She's like a postapocalyptic kingpin hoarding all the water reserves."

"England is making you weird."

"I hate to break it to you, brother dear, but I was weird long before I jumped across the pond."

He uses my confession of oddity to segue into what's *really* bothering him. "Have you, uh, heard from Winnie lately?"

Unlike my brother, I don't need an excuse to draw our sister into the conversation. She's a topic I would happily discuss to the ends of the earth and back again—which, to be honest, is what this walk is starting to feel like. "No, and I'm freaking out about it. She hasn't said anything since Beast went missing."

"Your cat is missing?"

"Yes. I've searched everywhere, but she's disappeared—run away, or been kidnapped, or . . ." I trail off, my voice wavering as I try to quash the image of last night's carnage. Beast couldn't have been killed the same way. I'd feel it if she were. I'd *know* it. "I didn't make the connection right away, but I can't avoid it now. I think Winnie's either gone to watch over the cat, or, and I know this sounds strange, she *is* the cat."

Another weighty pause greets me from the other end of the phone. For about twenty seconds, I'm afraid I've lost my cell phone connection—a thing that happens in these parts much more often than I'd like—but Liam eventually speaks up. "Has anyone else seen this animal? Like, touched it and can confirm its physical existence?"

I can't help but laugh. "Yes, Liam. She's a flesh-and-blood animal. I have her rabies vaccination papers to prove it."

His sigh of relief is lost in the wind. This time, our connection really does start to crackle, so I sign off.

"Don't worry so much," I say, though I'm not sure how much of it he can hear—or how much he believes. "I'm getting oodles of fresh air these days thanks to the holes in my roof, and I'm a hundred pounds richer than I was yesterday. Things are looking positively optimistic around here."

It's a bald-faced lie, but I don't know what else to say. Besides, even though I don't have a roof or a murderer or even much of a career, I do have suspects. Lewis's erratic behavior and money troubles with his aunt place him at the top of my list. Penny's up there, too, what with her obvious relief at Sarah's death and the fact that she's acting strange, throwing money and chocolate cake at me.

As for the werewolf, well . . . It's only Wednesday. There are still two more days before the full moon hits. I'm sure it will all be explained away before then.

I'm so preoccupied with my thoughts that I don't notice the car right away. I *should* notice it, since it's bright teal and whizzes down the unpaved lane in a manner that can only be described as erratic. Although quite a few families around here have vehicles, it's much more common to see the villagers on foot or traveling via bus. The roads are so terrible, it tends to be both faster and safer that way.

The car proves it by thumping its front wheel against a particularly large stone working loose from the mud-soaked lane. The sound it makes, the wrenching of metal being ripped from the undercarriage, causes me to jump.

"You really should slow down along these lanes," I call, my voice sharper than I intend thanks to the adrenaline coursing through my veins. The car was never close enough to hit me, but with so much moisture rendering the road barely navigable, it came a lot nearer than it should have.

The door pushes open and a man staggers out, his hand clutched to his head. It takes me a second to recognize the blood coursing from his temple; two to realize I'm looking at none other than Lewis King.

It might seem strange that it takes me longer to recognize the man than the injury, but he's reached such a state of disarray that he barely even looks human. His beard hasn't been trimmed since I saw him yesterday, and his yellow eyes are sunken and bright. The rain and blood make it difficult to tell for certain, but it looks as though he's perspiring heavily. A quick peek at his wrinkled shirt confirms it—the sweat stains are undeniable, as is that musky scent I'm coming to recognize as his natural body odor.

"Lewis, are you all right?" I ask. Unwinding one of the scarves from around my person, I devise a makeshift pad and hold it out. "You don't look so well."

"I'm f-fine," he says, jumping away from my proffered first aid with a nervous start. "It's this blasted c-car."

I'm no expert, but the *blasted car* is some kind of vintage sports model that looked, until it ran over that rock, to be in pristine condition.

"It's a nice car. Too nice for this weather. They keep a Land Rover up at the castle to make it over some of these roads." Never one to let an opportunity go to waste, I add, "Did you drive her down from London? I thought you said before that you took the train."

A nervous, sweating wreck Lewis might be, but he's no fool. His glance is sallow but sharp. "I did t-take the train. I *always* t-take the train. The train is all I can afford. This"—he breaks off to kick one of the tires—"is my b-brother's car. You seem to know things. How much d-do you think it c-cost?"

I've managed to get my wrapped shawl near enough to Lewis's head to staunch the flow of blood, so I'm able to hide my surprise under the guise of industriousness. For him to bring up the topic of money—unprompted—is a stroke of luck I wasn't expecting.

"Cars aren't really my forte, but if I had to guess . . . Twenty thousand?"

His short laugh is meant to put me in my place. "Maybe *n-now*," he says with a meaningful look at the torn metal.

"He makes a good living working in television, doesn't he?"

An expression that can only be described as a glower descends upon his brow. "Y-yes."

"And you don't, do you?" I fall into my Madame Eleanor voice—that soothing, soothsaying tone I've perfected over the years. It comes so naturally by now, it's almost like falling into a trance. "You struggle for each penny, make each one stretch as far as you can, but it doesn't matter. They never make it all the way. It must be difficult, watching your brother buy all the luxuries you can't, knowing that even with your struggles, your aunt still preferred him to you."

A heavy resignation settles on his shoulders, making him look even more exhausted than before. I'm not proud of adding to his troubles, but that slump confirms the suspicion I just voiced aloud.

"Were you coming to see me again?" I ask. "Is that why you were on this road? To finish our conversation?"

He glances up and holds my gaze long enough for me to notice that his pupils are enlarged. Fear, I think. And a lot of it.

"I'd like to help if I can," I add.

He hesitates for a long moment, balancing as if on the precarious edge of a fence. I wait, unwilling to push while he's in such a state.

"You're an expert in w-witchcraft stuff, right?" he asks. "Like spells and c-curses?"

He spits out that last word, as if merely by saying the word *curse*, he's opening himself up to the possibility of one taking possession of him.

"I don't curse people, if that's what you're asking," I reply. Especially not if he's going to pick up his aunt's thread about all that evil eye stuff. "But, yes, I'm familiar with the general practice thereof."

"What are the s-symptoms?"

"The symptoms of being cursed?" I'm thrown for a momentary loop. Of all the strange questions I've been asked throughout the course of my career, this one has never crossed my path before. How *to* curse someone, sure. How to lift one that's already there, of course. But in my experience, the only thing needed to diagnose one in the first place is a healthy imagination and a tendency toward hypochondria. "Well, it depends on the curse, I suppose. They're all designed to do different things. For example, do you want someone to feel pain? Have a run of bad luck? Fall under your control?"

"You c-can control someone?"

"Theoretically, yes." Sensing another opportunity to mine for information, I add, "But there's a limit to what you can force another human being to do. Mystical powers can influence a person, but they can't make you do anything you wouldn't normally do. For example, I can't make you put poison in your aunt's coffee, and I can't make you steal your brother's car and run it off the road—at least, not unless those were things you were already contemplating doing."

Each accusation I level at Lewis's head has the effect of turning him even paler and sweatier than he was before. Nerves can account for excessive perspiration, but it's so cold out here I'm starting to lose feeling in my toes. This man must be carrying a monstrous burden of guilt to be heating up like that.

"Aunt S-Sarah never drank c-coffee," he says.

"Perhaps not," I allow, "but this is your brother's car, and it's currently standing in a watery ditch. That makes you one for two."

He gives a spasmodic twitch. "Are you g-going to tell him?" he asks. Of the two accusations, he seems the most preoccupied with the latter, which I find strange. Automotive theft carries a much shorter prison sentence than premeditated murder.

"I don't know your brother very well, but I imagine he'll be able to see the damage and come to a fairly accurate conclusion." Both pity and a strong desire to get out of this rain prompt me to add, "Would you like me to drive you back to the village? I can take the long way, and we can have that talk you wanted. Better yet, you could relax and take a nap. . . ."

"A *n-nap*?" A spasm overtakes him, causing him to jerk away and toss my shawl back at me. "Now? Are you k-kidding? There's too much to d-do and not enough t-time until—"

"Until?" I prompt. There are several ways I can think to conclude that sentence, each one more interesting than the last.

Until the police come to the natural and inevitable conclusion that I murdered my aunt.

Until I manage to flee the country with my brother's car and life savings.

Until the full moon and my transformation is complete.

But it's too late. Apparently deciding he's said too much, Lewis turns around and squelches back to the car. I'd feel sorry for him, what with the weight of his aunt's death on his shoulders and the disfavor of the entire village at his back, but he doesn't even think to offer me a lift.

Then again, maybe it's best *not* to get in a car with that man right now. Not only has he confirmed that his financial struggles are a very solid, very real source of agony in his life, but his agitation only grows as he starts up the car and revs the engine in an attempt to pull out of the slog. The poor guy. I can't help but feel it'll be a wonder if he makes it back to the village without accidentally running that car off a cliff.

But then his wheels finally grip the road, casting showers of mud into the air before splattering them upon my head, and I almost wish he will.

"Don't ask." I sit delicately on the end of the library chair, careful lest the mud covering nine-tenths of my body transfer itself to the upholstery. The only way the librarian at the front desk would even let me in was by my solemn promise that I wouldn't touch anything. "It's been that kind of day."

Rachel makes a cluck of sympathy from the other side of the research table. I scheduled today's meeting at the library to avoid having to buy another one of those extravagant high teas, but that was before my hundred-pound windfall. I shouldn't spend the money Penny gave me, I know, but I've soothed my conscience by promising I'll only use the funds to help solve Sarah's murder. Whatever is agitating Penny is clearly tied up in it.

Besides, she still might end up being the killer. In that case, it would be a crime *not* to accept the payment and bring her to justice. Right?

Despite the lack of tea service, Lenora came prepared. She extracts several candy bars from her backpack and lines them up in the middle of the table. Since there's also an enormous stack of books on wolves, British wildlife, and railway timetables, I let the candy slide.

"What's on the agenda today, my pretties?" I ask. "Besides Maltesers, that is."

I mentally prepare myself for another lengthy discussion of werewolf characteristics and how Lewis King fits the bill, which is why I'm so surprised when Lenora jumps right in with, "So, I called the Animal Control Service this morning, right?"

"You did?" I blink at her. "How did you know?"

"Know what?" Lenora asks, blinking at me.

I open my mouth to tell her about the warning I received last night—and then immediately shut it again. I might not be a good influence over this child, but even I know better than to add a dead cat to her already fertile imagination.

"Nothing," I say. "It's just that I don't remember asking you to call Animal Control."

Rachel grabs one of the candy bars and rips it open. "You didn't. But I had dinner at Lenora's house last night, and her brother, George, came in holding this huge dead field mouse he caught out back."

Lenora pulls a face. "It was so gross, Madame Eleanor, you don't even know."

On the contrary, I have a rather good idea of just how foul something like that can be, but I keep my mouth shut. Regarding that topic, anyway.

"You ate at Lenora's?" I ask, looking back and forth between them. "Without an invitation?"

"Dr. MacDougal didn't care at all," Rachel promises. "She said I'm welcome to join them anytime I want, and she even helped us with some of our research."

"Oh, she did, did she? I wonder why?"

My question is a rhetorical one, since I already have my answer. A hint—it rhymes with pillionaire.

"Calling Animal Control Services was her idea," Rachel says. "She said you can tell a lot about predators in an area based on what sort of animals they have to clean up off the side of the road. Only there aren't any in England."

"Dead animals?" I ask. On the contrary, my life seems to be teeming with them lately.

"Predators," Lenora says. "Except for foxes and badgers, but they'll only kill small things the same way cats and George do."

"Don't forget birds," I offer.

"Birds?" Rachel echoes.

"Yeah. Ones like hawks and owls." Which, according to Dr. MacDougal, will pick up entire pig hearts. For a woman who wanted me *not* to feed her stepdaughter tales of werewolves scavenging for parts, she seems to be taking an awfully keen interest in this whole predator/prey theory. "But I imagine they fall under the 'small things' category, too. I don't see a hawk picking up something the size of a cat."

Or, to be fair, leaving it on a hill for me to find in the dead of night.

Rachel leans across the table, an air of excitement hanging around her head. "But that's the thing, Ellie. According to the woman Lenora talked to this morning, they've had a larger than usual number of cats go missing this past week."

"A larger than usual number?" I echo.

"And you know who else has been here for a week," Lenora supplies with a knowing look at Rachel. Rachel's response is a convincing wolf howl that draws a deep shushing sound from the front desk of the library.

"We don't know that for sure, you guys," I protest, more for form's sake than anything else. I can't help remembering that musky scent underlying the tang of blood—or the way Lewis looked this afternoon. "I didn't see Lewis until Friday, remember? That's the earliest we can place him here for sure."

Lenora pushes the railway timetable at me. For the first time, I note that there's a bright red circle around one of the times. "Nope. We can place him last Wednesday."

"What?" I grab the paper and examine it, though there's not much to see. You can pick these up at almost every train station. I think we grabbed this one on our tour yesterday. "How do you know? We asked, but no one remembered seeing Lewis."

"I know, but that's because we didn't ask the right way." Rachel reaches into her own backpack, which is starting to rival Lenora's in terms of size. She extracts two images that I recognize at a glance as her own work.

Her sketch artistry skills have come a long way since the last time I used them. I take both images in my hands, examining first one and then the other. The image on my left is Lewis as we almost always see him—unkempt, bedraggled, in desperate need of rest. The image on my right is Lewis as he appeared after he shaved and showered that day at his aunt's home. The hair has been removed from his jawline and some of the exhaustion wiped from his expression, but that cherubic face is unmistakable.

"No one remembered seeing the hairy Lewis," Rachel explains as she taps the first picture. "But *this* one—the normal guy? I went out while Lenora was at school today and got two separate confirmations. He definitely came down on Wednesday. *Before* Mr. Worthington's pig was killed."

"Yes, but—" I begin, but I should have known better than to have an opinion around these two. Or any semblance of authority.

"He's getting worse," Lenora says. "We saw him in the village center yesterday, and he looked terrible. Even my dad said something about it, and he wouldn't notice if I dyed my hair black and pierced my nose. It's because we're getting closer to the full moon. He's transforming."

Rachel nods as if this makes perfect sense. "And he's hungry. You'd better lock up Beast, Ellie. There's no telling where he'll feed next."

I take a deep breath, more out of an effort to give the impression that I'm frustrated with the pair of them rather than because I *am*. In truth, this revelation is far more helpful than either of these girls realize. Arriving on Wednesday wouldn't only give Lewis enough time to slaughter that pig. It also places him well within the timeline to have killed his aunt.

"I'm going to keep these, okay?" I ask and, without waiting for an answer, fold the pictures in half and pull them close. "And I'm officially pulling you two off werewolf duty from here on out. No—don't argue. I know it's unfair and stupid and the same boring adult treatment you'd expect from your parents, but I mean it. You can't keep going around asking questions and not expect Lewis to hear about it. If you get any closer, your lives could be in danger."

Lenora stares at me with wide eyes, but she doesn't speak. It takes Rachel to put into words what she's thinking.

"You mean he really *is* a werewolf?" She reaches for Lenora's hand, the pair of them taking comfort from one another in a gesture that clenches my heart. Once upon a time, Winnie and I were like that, too. "You think he might attack us if we know the truth?"

"I think it's best that you two stick to a tight curfew from now until the full moon," I reply, neatly sidestepping the question. "And I think you should start researching something else."

"Like what?" Lenora asks. "Werewolves were the only thing I could find, remember?"

I have to think fast. Under normal circumstances, I'd be all too happy to train Lenora in my myriad other mystical skills. She could help me grind herbs and boil flowers, maybe even dry sage for my smudging bundles. But I need to focus my attentions on this murder investigation—and I'd like to do it with her as far away as possible.

She needs something safe. Something academic. Something that has nothing to do with Sarah Blackthorne's murder or her nephew's strange condition . . .

"I know," I say with a snap of my fingers. This time, it's my turn to reach into my bag. Unlike the backpack twins over there, I carry a vintage medical valise that looks as though it's been used to remove a limb or two. It's just as covered in mud as I am, but the layer of dirt only adds to its appeal.

The inside is as dry and safe as ever, so the pentagram notebook is none the worse for my little adventure with Lewis.

"Why don't you focus on this?" I toss the notebook on the

center of the table, watching as it spins in a perfect 360-degree rotation before coming to a stop in front of Lenora.

Rachel eyes the book with suspicion, but Lenora greedily snatches it up and starts flipping through the pages. "Smashing!" she cries as she lands on the lopsided pentagram. "Did you make this yourself?"

"Well, no." I glance back and forth between the two girls. "You brought it to my house with all the werewolf materials, remember?"

Rachel keeps her hands firmly under the table, a wary expression settling in her violet eyes. Lenora is equally suspicious, but her emotion takes the form of a questioning tilt to her head. "I don't know what you're talking about. I've never seen this book before in my life."

"But it was in the pile with everything else," I say, my own suspicions mounting. "That's where I found it."

Rather, that's where Inspector Piper found it. *Or so he said.*

"Ellie, we would have mentioned something like this straightaway," Rachel says. "It gives me the creeps, to be honest. Why is everything written all scratchy?"

I lift the notebook from Lenora's hands and study it anew. Once again, I'm struck by how homemade it looks—both the book itself and the notations. "You're sure this didn't travel with your stuff? It's pretty small. It might have gotten mixed in with the werewolf materials."

Lenora makes the motion of an *X* over her chest. "Cross my heart, Madame Eleanor. I'd have noticed something this cool. Is it written in code or something?"

"Yes," I say, somewhat hesitant. Now that I'm unsure about the notebook's origins, it feels almost ominous in my hands. "It's a kind of witch code, actually. Most of what you're looking at are traditional magic symbols. They're pretty universal, so I was thinking you might be able to look them up online and try to decipher them—see if they make a meaning of some sort."

Lenora breathes out a long and excited exhalation. "I love cryptography and word puzzles. Can we start working on it now?"

I don't hand it over right away. For some reason, I can't seem to shake the idea of Inspector Piper planting this in my house. But what I don't know is *why* he'd have done it. Is it a clue he wants me to solve? Evidence he plans to use to arrest me? The man lives to thwart me, certainly, but I don't see him going that far to frame me for a murder I didn't commit.

"Rachel, do you think you could make an accurate copy of this?" I tap the front cover with my forefinger. "That way, I can keep the original while you two try to figure out what it means."

"I *could*," she says, reluctance in every line of her bearing. "But are you sure I should? What if writing this stuff down gives it power?"

It's on the tip of my tongue to tell her that the only power a book like this has is whatever nonsense you infuse it with, but I don't. It's *good* that she's wary of the unknown, that she believes in the power of something greater than herself. It means she'll be that much more careful as she ventures out into this wide, scary world of ours.

Then again, I *do* still want her to copy it, so . . .

"Ad hominem," I chant. "Mea culpa. In loco parentis. Casus belli."

Lenora's starting to give me the side-eye as I recite a list of common Latin phrases, so I finish by making a motion of the cross over the top cover of the notebook.

"There. That should do it. The safety charm will last until sunset. Will that give you enough time to get it copied?"

Rachel takes the book in careful hands. "Yes, as long as I get right to it. Lenora, you'll help?"

"You know it. I have an empty notebook somewhere in my backpack."

Thanks to the vast clutter of Lenora's backpack, the search for her notebook occupies a good five minutes, during which time Rachel delicately leafs through the pages, her brow growing more and more wrinkled as she goes along.

"Rachel, if you don't want to, it's perfectly fine," I say. "I can just as easily go through it myself. It seemed like something Lenora might like to do, that's all."

"That's not it," she says, and in a voice low enough that Lenora can't overhear. That's when I know she's serious—these two have been joined at the hip ever since this whole investigation started, their excitement and their appetites feeding off one another. For her to show concern for the younger girl speaks strongly of her current state of mind. "I think I recognize this book."

My glance is sharp. "You do? Whose is it?"

"Not the writing or any of the stuff in it," she amends. "But the literal book. I'm pretty sure you can buy them at the Saturday market from that nice old lady who makes the soap out of sheep's milk."

My heart stutters. "*Aunt Margaret?*"

Now Rachel's the one with the sharp look. "You have an aunt named Margaret?"

I flutter my hand in an attempt to wave her off. "She's not my aunt. She's Inspector Piper's. Rachel, are you sure you've seen her selling these?"

Her brow furrows even more as she turns the notebook over in her hand once more. "Not this one specifically, but I remember she had something similar last summer. A whole stack of them, actually. I thought one would make a nice sketchbook, but the next time she had her stall set up, she was all sold out."

"And he said she was just an herbalist," I mutter. "That

scrounging toad. If you can't trust law enforcement to tell you the truth, who can you trust?"

"Who's just an herbalist?" Lenora asks, her attention caught.

Me, if I don't start piecing some of these clues together. It might be the only option I have left. If I want to get back to selling my potions—and I do—I need a lot more than the eerie suspicion that Lewis King is a werewolf and that Inspector Piper knows more about this murder investigation than he's sharing with me.

"No one, sweetie. Did you find what you were looking for? Good. I need you two to finish that up as soon as possible."

"Why?" Lenora asks.

Because even though I hate to do anything at Inspector Piper's instigation, it seems I have one last visit to pay in my mud-spattered glory.

"Why, it's a Book of Shadows, love. Surely *you*, of all people, must know that."

I accept a cup of tea from Aunt Margaret but don't drink. I also don't bite into the gorgeous piece of pound cake she's placed in front of me. I'm not saying I've been poisoned, but that cake of Penny's is weighing pretty heavily in my gut by now. Perhaps I needn't have eaten the *whole* thing.

"I do know it," I reply. "What I don't know is where it came from. It's not yours, is it?"

She releases a trill of laughter that sounds like puppies and rainbows. If I'm the Wicked Witch of the West in this strange thing that is my life, then Aunt Margaret is Glinda in a pink apron instead of a ball gown.

A woman less like Inspector Piper I have yet to meet. Oh, there's the slight physical resemblance, yes, but she shows no sign of habitual tics as she moves easily around her living room to arrange her chair across from my own.

Liam, Winnie, and I never met our grandmother, but I like to think that if we'd put our collective heads together and conjured one up, she'd look exactly like Margaret. Puffs of silvery hair dance around her ears, where giant pearl earrings dangle like fishing tackle. She has a matching pearl necklace, which is layered over a sprigged cotton dress that looks like springtime. High heels complete the ensemble, even though she is, from all appearances, home alone. I imagine she goes to bed every night in a frilled nightie with feathered slippers on her feet.

"My dear child, I haven't kept a Book of Shadows since I was in my twenties, and even then it was more of a little black book than a spell book. It's how I kept track of all my lovers—I had quite a few in my day."

"I bet you did," I reply. There are dozens of pictures of a smiling woman in that same strand of pearls on the mantel above the fireplace. In each one, the dishy young Margaret has her arms around a different—and equally dishy—young man.

If I didn't like this woman before, I'd adore her now.

But I still have to ask. "You do sell these notebooks, though, right? My—uh—friend recognized it from your market stall."

"Oh, yes." Margaret finally completes her arrangements with the chair and takes a seat. She sits daintily, her bottom perched on the edge and her legs crossed at the ankle. In my mud-spattered attire, I feel downright slovenly. "I press all the pages myself using flowers from my garden."

"Do you know who you sold this one to?"

She blinks at me over her cup. "Of course not. I sell at least twenty dozen of these a year. They're quite popular with the tourists. You wouldn't believe how much I get away with charging them."

Hmm. I turn the book over in my hand, wondering just how much work goes into making something like this. Surely it can't be much more difficult than vodka-based perfumes? Perhaps it's time for Madame Eleanor to branch out.

"That one was sold sometime in September, if it helps," Margaret offers.

"How do you know?"

"Those are my hybrid tea roses." She taps the page with one perfectly sculpted pink fingernail. "They never bloom until summer is almost over. Most of the tourists have long since packed up by then, so it probably went to one of the local ladies. They're my second-best customers. Mrs. Brennigan has been after me to make a dozen for the spring fête."

Mrs. Brennigan again? "When did she make this request?"

"Oh, a few days ago. Who can tell anymore? Time stops being absolute once you reach my age." She sets her cup down and examines me, those kindly eyes a little sharper and shrewder than they were a moment ago. "Peter said you'd be stopping by to ask me about my garden. Did you want to see it?"

It takes me a moment to register Peter as Inspector Piper, since I'm not in the habit of referring to him by his given name. However, I'm more than happy to light on him as a topic of conversation, since he's the reason I'm here in the first place.

"Yes, please. He didn't seem to think much of mine." I wait until she gets to her feet before rising and following her to the back door. "He doesn't seem to think much of *me*, period."

"Really?" Her hand closes on the doorknob, surprise showing in the elegant arch of her brows. "I understood you were instrumental in closing that murder investigation up at the castle last year."

"I wasn't instrument*al*. I was the literal instrument. He couldn't have done it without me."

She laughs, showcasing a line of even white teeth that shine as brightly as the pearls around her neck. "He also told me you're helping him stop smoking. I've been after him to do that for years."

We've stepped out onto the garden, which is everything I wish my own could be. Margaret lives not too far from the evergreen crossroads, her home a quaint stone structure with a roof that's perfectly sound and a neatly trimmed yard that extends for several acres. She doesn't have a walled garden, the way I do, but rows of neat boxes lined up like graves.

That's where any analogy to death ends. Her garden boxes are literally teeming with life, plants and flowers spilling over in an abundance of horticultural glory. I have no idea how she's managed to grow so much this early in the year, but the results are spectacular.

"Are you sure we're talking about the same man?" I ask.

"Peter doesn't have many friends," Margaret says by way of answer. "He never has—part of it's the job, but most of it is that abrupt way of his. It puts people off."

"Including his ex-wife?" I suggest.

She just laughs. "That's why it's so nice that you're willing to overlook his manner and extend a helping hand. Well, there it is. Third box from the back. From what I can tell, the cage was cut sometime last week, but I can't say for sure which day. It's been raining so much that I haven't had to come out here to water."

There is so much about what she's just said that I need to unpack—the first, of course, this accusation people keep leveling at my head about Inspector Piper and I being friends. A friend is, objectively, someone who doesn't try to pin a murder on you. I refuse to accept any other definition.

However, that bit about the cage has me mightily interested. . . .

"Your garden box has a cage around it?" I ask as I glance toward the third box from the back.

My question is answered the moment my gaze alights on it. There are a total of twelve garden boxes in all, but only one with restricted access. Although most of the contents seem innocent enough, there are five padlocked iron cages spread out among the growth. At first glance, they look almost like birdcages with heavy-duty black bars, but their purpose becomes clear as I draw closer. A sign affixed to the bars of the first cage bears the image of a skull and crossbones as well as a warning that the cage contains hemlock.

"Hemlock?" I ask, more excited than I should be to find myself facing not one, not three, but five different types of deadly poison growing in front of me. I turn to the next cage, which bears a similar sign. "Belladonna? Strychnine? Foxglove? You grow all that right here in your backyard?"

By the time I make it to the fifth and final cage, I'm starting to gain an understanding of why Inspector Piper was so eager for me to pay Aunt Margaret a visit. It looks as though a pair of bolt cutters have been taken to this one, leaving a gaping hole big enough to pull out one of the familiar purple plants by the roots.

"Wolfsbane," I say and emit a long whistle. "So, that's it. Sarah's poison came from your garden."

Margaret sighs as she joins me at the edge of the box. "So it would seem. I've always known it's a risk, keeping these plants out here in the open, but I'm careful to warn the homeowners in this area not to let their kids or pets play near the boxes."

"Who knew about this?" I ask.

"Oh, lots of people. The neighbors, my friends, Peter . . . I've never kept it a secret. And you'll note that each plant is carefully marked and protected. My insurance company insisted."

I do note it. Not only does each caged plant's sign bear the skull and crossbones warning, but it includes the common name, the scientific name, and the exact nature of the grisly death you can expect to experience at its hands. It's a serial killer's dream come true.

In fact, if I were a police detective investigating a recent poisoning, it's the very first place I'd look—*not*, as some people did, at the local friendly witch just trying to get by making a few harmless elixirs.

"You mean he knew it was here all along?"

"Who?" Margaret blinks at me. "Peter? Of course. There have been police crawling all over this place trying to discover who cut the cage. I hope they find out soon—I'd hate to have to dig up and discard the rest of these plants. Most of them are perfectly benign in the right dosage. The hemlock is the only thing that makes my joints stop aching in this weather."

As much as I sympathize with an herbal-minded woman doing what she can to get by in this world, I cast my attention away from Margaret and scan the darkening horizon instead. Access to this garden would be easy enough to gain, since there are only a few low rock walls between her yard and the pasture that lies beyond it. The lights of the farmhouse next door catch my eye.

"Who lives over there?" I ask.

"The Gilfords," she says. "Nice people. They raise the sheep whose milk I use to make my soap. Peter's already talked to them, but they didn't see anything, unfortunately. And their poor dog, the one who's usually so good at barking whenever there are strangers about, has gone missing."

That last bit causes my head to swivel her direction. "Their dog is missing? Since when?"

A sympathetic clucking sound issues from the back of her throat. "I couldn't say. He never was the sort to go running off. They're absolutely heartbroken over it."

"Does Inspect—" I clear my throat. "Does *Peter* know about the dog?"

"Of course. He's quite good at his job, though I expect he's hit a bit of a wall, which is why he's brought you on." She turns her back on the garden box and addresses me directly. "Well? Is there anything else you'd like to see? I wish I could help you more with deciphering the notebook, but I'm not nearly as well educated in the occult as I used to be. I believe that rounded bit at the bottom of each page has to do with wealth, but that's as far as I ever got. Wealth, beauty, and sex—that was the only real use I had for any of those spells. Nowadays, it's all joint relief and cursing Mr. Worthington when his pig gets out and eats my prize begonias again."

For the second time in as many minutes, I find myself at a loss. Villages as small as this one are likely to be paved with paths that wind and cross and overlap, but this is becoming downright eerie. No matter how many times I try to focus on the murder of Sarah Blackthorne, Mr. Worthington's pig keeps wandering back into the picture.

Its escape. Its death. Its missing heart.

And at the center of it all—the lingering question of a werewolf in our midst.

"You heard about Regina, didn't you?" I ask. "That she was, um, attacked by some kind of animal the night after Sarah's death?"

"Was she?" Margaret makes a tsking sound. "I'm not surprised. That animal has been a menace since the day Old Worth brought her home. Did you know she could eat right through those fence posts?"

I hold back a groan. "Yes, thanks. I've since been made aware of that fact."

That pig was nothing short of miraculous, apparently—and everyone in the village knew it except me. What she couldn't do, however, no matter how determined she might have been, was bite through an iron cage over the top of a wolfsbane plant. That was done by human hands.

I swallow. At least, I assume those hands were human.

"One more thing before I go," I say, hesitant to leave just yet. Margaret's company is soothing in the same way Vivian's is—free of expectation or judgment—and the only place I have to get back to is my own damp cottage. "You said that your nephew *brought me on* to help solve the case, as if it were a thing he did on purpose, like we're working side by side. But he's never asked me for my help. In fact, I was under the impression he considered me a candidate for murder."

"Well, of course he didn't ask for help. A police inspector

turning to a suspected witch for help solving a case involving wolfsbane poisoning? What would the authorities say?"

"Forty to life is my guess."

She laughs and winds her arm through my own. "Now that our business is done, it's time for pleasure. Have I ever told you about the time I sailed across the Atlantic in the company of an American yacht-racing crew? No? Well, it was a dark and stormy night. . . ."

Chapter 12

"Nicholas Hartford the Third, you have some serious explaining to do."

"Hello, my dearest, my darling, my delight. How did you know I was back?"

I push past both the man and the front door leading to the castle. Both are heavy; both are stalwart. Only one of them, however, is made of wood.

"Do you have any idea what you've done?" I ask. I don't wait for a reply. "There are currently no fewer than three—count them, three—men prancing about on my roof. There were four, but one of them fell through the thatch above my bed. I awoke to a pair of hairy ankles dangling through the plaster."

It's difficult for me to make out all the details of my beloved through my righteous indignation, but I suspect that Nicholas's lips twitch in his familiar attempt not to laugh. He reaches out a hand and plucks a piece of powdery white ceiling tile from my hair.

"Evidence of your wake-up call?"

"It's not funny!" My righteous indignation abates enough for me to notice that Nicholas isn't looking his impeccable best. He's still attractive, of course, his white button-down crisp and clean, his craggy features finding the right balance between charming and jaded, but there are dark shadows under his eyes and a scruff of hair along his jawline.

"Oh," I say. "You just got in."

He checks his watch. "Technically, I got in thirteen minutes and twenty-two seconds ago, but, yes, my arrival is of recent origin."

I peer closer at his eyeballs for signs of any redness. "Have you slept?"

"That depends on your definition of the word. I napped a little while the plane was on autopilot over the Pyrenees."

"You did not."

"They practically fly themselves these days," he replies mildly. "I find the whole process quite soporific. And ravening. I'd ask you to breakfast with me, but I haven't yet had a chance to lay in supplies. Have the roofers fallen through your kitchen ceiling yet, or can we go there?"

Reminding me of the roofers isn't Nicholas's smoothest move. I lift a finger and point it at his chest, stopping just shy of making physical contact. "How dare you bring them in behind my back. And without so much as a by-your-leave."

"I've always wondered about the origins of that expression," Nicholas muses, taking in my finger with no more than a blink. "Shakespeare, I think. *Merchant of Venice*. It's fascinating how many of our sayings originate from the Great Bard."

"I told you I was fine." If he's going to ignore the real crux of the matter, then I'm going to ignore the bulk of his elitist commentary. "I said I had the roof situation handled, and I do. I don't need you to send in your fleet of incompetent thatchers, and I don't need you to risk life and limb flying all night over mountain ranges to check up on me."

He blinks. "Is that what you think I did?"

"Well, *I* didn't hire them, and I doubt they're up there out of the goodness of their hearts."

Once again, he sidesteps the actual argument I'm trying to make. "I'm not here to check up on you, Eleanor. I came home early because I missed you."

The ability to manipulate time is one of those tricks I used to practice on the regular, winding back clocks and changing cell phone settings in an effort to make circumstances seem as spooky as possible for my clients. However, it's not something I've done since I moved here, since a witch has much less call for that kind of mysticism than a psychic.

Which is why it's so strange for time to stop all on its own. As I stand in the castle foyer looking at Nicholas—the weary lines of his face, the dark scruff of his stubble, those gray eyes that see so much—the entire world falls away. Nothing seems to matter. Not the recent deaths or the poison, not my missing cat or the werewolf who took her. There are only the two of us: a con woman with an investigative streak and the rich, powerful, gorgeous man who seems, for some incomprehensible reason, to like her.

Well, what are you waiting for?

It's not Winnie's voice this time. It's mine—and I don't have a good answer. Pride and independence are all well and good, but the more time I spend peering into Sarah Blackthorne's life, the more I realize what it means to be alone. *Really* alone. The kind of alone that turns into misery and joylessness, that makes an entire village happy to see you gone.

Which is why I throw myself into his arms and show my appreciation the best way I know how.

"That's more like it," he says after an interval that feels like minutes but might be hours. We're still standing in the doorway to the castle, and some of the plaster from my hair has made its way onto Nicholas's now-rumpled suit, but I find it difficult to care.

He missed me.

People don't miss me very often. Oh, Liam feels a pang or two for my absence, I know, and I occasionally get a sweet note from Peggy, Winnie's primary caretaker in the years before her death, but as for the rest . . . Why would they? You don't hire a psychic or a witch when things are going well in your life.

"A welcome like this one makes up for almost crashing into the summit of Aneto," Nicholas murmurs as his arms wrap more firmly around my waist.

"Still not funny," I reply. There are several romantically appropriate ways in which I could continue this conversation, but none of the sensations I'm feeling are more pressing than the one bubbling on the end of my tongue. I pull back and peer up at him. "But I don't understand. If *you* didn't hire the roofers to come out and replace the thatch, who did?"

Nicholas shakes his head, his lips—now reddened by my dark lipstick—quirked in a lopsided smile. "Absence might have the traditional effect on my heart, but I see yours is as it ever was."

"You have to admit the timing is rather suspect. Hairy ankles *and* your return on the same morning?"

He sighs and releases me. After taking a quick moment to wipe his lips with the handkerchief he invariably keeps in his breast pocket, he offers me the crook of his arm. "I suppose there's nothing else for it, is there? Come along."

I eye that arm suspiciously. "Why? Where are we going?"

"To the mistress's keep, naturally. It'll be breakfast *and* a show. I've never seen a man fall through a roof before."

"Careful, son, careful. You'll want to raise it a little bit higher there. . . . Yes, right there."

The sound of the general's voice reaches my ears long before

Nicholas and I make it all the way up the drive. The walk was a muddy one, as the hem of my ankle-length peasant skirt can attest, but Nicholas has managed to make it through unscathed. I'm not sure how he does it, unless he just naturally walks on a cloud of air.

"Oh, there you are," the general says as we come into view. He seems unsurprised to see the pair of us. "Paying a morning visit to the castle? I've always loved the sunrise there. Well? What do you think?"

He turns and surveys the cottage with a self-satisfied air. Like Nicholas, he doesn't seem the least bit damp or dirty despite the fact that the only vehicle parked in the drive is the roofer's work van. It must be the tweeds everyone around here wears—there's a reason they all look the same color as the English countryside. You can tramp for miles and never show a speck of dirt.

"What do I think about the castle sunrises?" Nicholas asks. "Personally, I've always found them to be best in winter after fresh snowfall. Summer sunsets are worth a look, too, especially near the rise out back. Eleanor hasn't seen one of those yet."

I nudge Nicholas with my hip to quiet him. He knows very well what the general was asking, but he's always faultlessly literal when he's trying to be smart.

"Are you responsible for this?" I ask. "The roofers, I mean?"

Self-satisfaction takes over the general's expression, the ends of his mustache twitching like a puppy's tail. "I've been meaning to talk to you about it for weeks, but with one thing and another, it slipped my mind. Spring can get a bit nasty around these parts. You need a watertight roof or you'll get drowned out."

"Um, yes. I discovered that."

"That's what I was afraid of." He points a finger up toward the roof. "The one with the beard is my sister's nephew on her husband's side. Family discount, you know."

A sinking feeling weights me to the ground. Family discounts are all well and good, but I doubt a connection as branching as that one is going to be of much use. "That's so kind of you, but I'm afraid you're going to have to ask them to stop."

The general plants his feet and fixes me with a hard stare. "Stop? *Now?*"

I can also feel Nicholas's interested gaze on me, but I'm careful not to look at him as I reply. "Yes. Unfortunately, domestic upheavals should only be conducted under the waning moon cycle. If you'd asked me first, I could have warned you." Since the general shows every sign of opening his mouth to argue, I add, "That's probably why your sister's nephew landed on my head. The timing is inauspicious."

"Inauspicious?"

"Ominous."

"Ominous?"

I allow my voice to drop. "Doomed."

"Now, see here." The general turns on me with a tightly furrowed brow. "I was only trying to be neighborly. There's no need to start dropping curses on my head. A young woman all on her own in these parts in a cottage everyone knows is leakier than a sieve—and with only the Hartfords to turn to. It's not right, that's all I'm saying."

Nicholas gently clears his throat. It's an obvious warning to anyone who knows him, but the general isn't easily put off.

"Well? That castle roof has been leaking for the past seventy years, at the very least. A little rain obviously doesn't bother your lot."

I smother a laugh. Nicholas would happily and gratefully overhaul that castle from its dungeons to its rafters, but the only thing Vivian hates more than houseguests is domestic upheaval, waning moon or not.

I reach for the general's hand and give it a squeeze. "Thank you for your offer, General. It's sweet of you to look out for me, it really is, but there's no way I can allow them to finish under these conditions. When the moon stops waxing, I'll give your sister's nephew a call and have them return."

He laughs. "That's what you think. The roof's half off now—if you kick them to the curb, you'll be floating along like Noah in his great ark by nightfall. And they're all paid up, so nothing's going to stop them until they're done. A stickler for duty, Harry is. He was a soldier just like me."

I cast a bewildered glance at Nicholas, but he's watching General von Cleve with an intent look. "Was he? Just like you?"

The general's mustache droops, but he turns to me with a smile and a clip of his heels. "I hope you don't mind, but I helped myself and the boys to some tea while you were out for your walk. You're out of the green sort."

"Oh, of course." I can't think of a polite way to protest either the intrusion or the roofers currently making my home a habitable one. Not only was it an incredibly generous gesture for the general to arrange and pay for this, but he wasn't kidding about Noah's ark. If those dark clouds hanging overhead decide they'd like to drop their burden anytime soon, I'm going to have to transform myself into a mermaid. "I'll pick some up the next time I'm in the village. I didn't realize it was your favorite."

"Picked up the habit in Korea," the general says by way of explanation. "Some things are impossible to shake."

"And about the roof," I add, somewhat uneasily. "I can't let you pay for it. When they're done, please send me the total, and I'll—"

I'm not sure how to finish that sentence in a way that doesn't involve a life of crime or the wholesale bargaining of my organs, so it's for the best that the general draws himself up to his full stature and glares at me.

"I'll do no such thing, young lady, and I resent the implication that I'd order a job done and pass the bill off to you. This roof is a gift, and I'll thank you to remember it as such."

There's so much dignity in him, he's almost impossible to refuse. Still, I have to do it. If I won't accept a roof from the man I'm dating, I can hardly accept one from a kindly old military man I barely know. Before I can figure out how, he opens his mouth again.

"I never had a daughter, you see," he says, his voice firm. "My best years were given over to Her Majesty's Service. I don't regret my sacrifice—not by a long shot—but by the time I found myself ready to settle down, my ways were too set to change. And from what I can tell, you don't have much in the way of family yourself. Seems like taking care of each other is the least we can do."

That comment is the final nail in my coffin—or in the thatch, as the case may be. *Taking care of each other* is the one thing village life is supposed to be about, the one thing that continues to elude me no matter how hard I try to grab hold. But here it is, being offered to me with no strings attached.

At least, not any strings that I can see yet.

"Thank you, General von Cleve." I lean in and press a kiss on his cheek, the brush of his mustache prickly against my skin. "I appreciate this more than you know. You're a sweetheart to be thinking of me."

His face flushes with color, and he coughs heavily before pulling away. "Yes, well. You're one of us now, aren't you? Nicholas, always a pleasure. Send your mother my love."

"Aye, aye, sir," he says in his usual urbane tone. "But what am I saying? That's navy, isn't it?"

The general's mustache gives another one of those strange twitches before he turns away. He calls out a few more instructions to the roofers—including the need to watch their step or risk breaking through to the bathroom—before taking himself off down the drive.

We watch him go, Nicholas and I, waiting only until his bulldog-like tread takes him out of our line of sight before speaking.

"You were a little rude to the general, don't you think?" I ask.

Nicholas's brows raise. "Was I?"

"I know he's a bit of a wartime relic, but his heart is in the right place."

"I'm sure his heart is as pure as the driven snow, but Reginald von Cleve has not now, nor has he ever, seen anything of war."

I turn to glance up at Nicholas, sure that in this, as in most things, he's being ironic. But there's a firm set to his jaw that indicates he's one hundred percent in earnest. "What are you talking about?" I ask. "He's a general—or, rather, he *was*. He was a POW in Korea. He told me so himself."

"And you always believe what someone tells you? For shame, Madame Eleanor. I thought you were more cynical than that."

I was. I am. At least . . . I *used* to be.

"No," I breathe. "Really?"

He inclines his head in an assent. "It's not common knowledge in the village, but it's my understanding that he spent most of his youth in a Swiss sanatorium. Oh, not for his own health—that man has the constitution of a horse. But his mother was sickly, or so she believed. She dragged him all over Europe seeking cures for her various nervous conditions. By the time she finally succumbed to one of them, it was too late. He couldn't go to university, couldn't join the armed forces, was unable to pursue any real kind of career. A shame, really."

"So he manufactured an illustrious military past instead?"

Nicholas hunches his shoulders in an elegant half shrug. "Why not? All it takes is a few jackets and medals picked up from the nearest surplus store."

"Well, really," I say. Even though the general has long since walked out of our range of sight, I find my gaze drawn to the empty lane. "He must have known that the only way to make a lie like that stick is to make it believable. A generalship is flying awfully high. He should have stopped at captain. Or major, if he absolutely couldn't help himself."

A slight snort escapes my beloved. "Is that a Madame Eleanor trade secret? Only sell the lie if it's a believable one?"

"Laugh all you want, but I wouldn't be surprised if it comes around to bite him one of these days. How many people know?"

"Other than you and I? None, I imagine. Reginald predates almost everyone who lives in the village. My mother knows, naturally, since the pair of them were schoolchildren together, but I doubt she knows she knows it. He could have claimed a pioneering trip to Mars and she'd have accepted it as truth, just as long as she wasn't required to participate in any way."

"Your mother is too pure for this world."

"My mother is a plague and a menace." Nicholas places a hand on the small of my back and propels me toward the house. "All the women in my life are. I wouldn't know what to do with myself otherwise."

I fill Nicholas in on the current state of my investigation over breakfast.

One of his greatest skills in this world is manufacturing culinary delights out of the barest of ingredients. He claims it's the inevitable result of growing up in a house where food is considered a luxury rather than a right, but I suspect he enjoys the task more than he lets on. No one puts sprigs of parsley on a plate unless they're showing off.

"You could have saved me a lot of trouble if you'd just told me that Lewis King is a financial tapeworm," I say around a mouthful of scrambled eggs. I have no idea what he's done to them, but after two minutes of poking around in the garden, he managed to find something to transform them into magic. "I wasted at least two days snooping around his past."

He pauses long enough to chew and swallow. "I didn't know that Lewis King is a financial tapeworm."

I put my fork down and stare at him. "What are you talking about? Both you and Annis acted as though you'd fallen into a tar pit the moment he entered the conversation, and your mother told me all about the financial schemes he's invested in using his aunt's money. I thought that was why you disliked him so much."

The sounds of footsteps and men shouting overhead force Nicholas to pause longer than he normally would, which is why it's so disappointing when the cacophony stops and all he says is, "I don't dislike Lewis King."

I pick up my fork again, but this time, it's to point it at him. "You do too. I saw it in your face that day in the pub."

"You saw it in my face?"

"Yes."

"Any particular part of it? My nose, perhaps? Or my chin?"

"Don't be ridiculous. It was everywhere, like reading a newspaper headline. Nicholas Hartford the Third, unruffled by ghosts and witches and men falling through roofs, seriously dislikes Lewis King."

He leans across the kitchen table, thrusting his face toward mine. His lids come down halfway over his steely eyes in the way common among kids when they're preparing for a staring contest. "I had no idea you were so talented. What's my face saying right now?"

"That you're a stubborn jerk who won't admit when he's wrong." I lean forward to meet him halfway, dropping a quick kiss on his lips so he won't take offense at that jerk bit. "And like I said, it wasn't just you. Annis had a negative reaction to him, too, but she wouldn't tell me why. Only that he was unpleasant as a kid."

"He was."

"You do realize that I can place him in the village on the

night of Sarah's murder, right?" I start ticking off on my fingers. "He had the timeline. He had motive, since he needed money, even if he didn't know his aunt was going to give it all to the tennis people. He had access to the poison, or easily could have by cutting through Margaret's garden cage."

"And?" Nicholas asks.

I pause. "How do you know there's more?"

"Because, Eleanor." He's given up on all pretense of eating by this time, still leaning close enough to hear me over the sound of the roofers. Clasping my hands in his, he gives them a squeeze. "Unlike you, I really can read your face. There's something you're not saying."

He's right. There is. But telling a man as determinedly realistic as this one that there's a werewolf on the loose isn't as easy as one might hope. Especially since the only real proof I have is a dead cat on a hill, a mauled pig in the woods, and a man who's a little hairier and sweatier than the norm.

I'm also unwilling to admit how uneasy I am about my own cat's disappearance. Not because Nicholas won't be sympathetic, of course, but because he *will*. He'll whisk me into his arms and tell me not to worry and stand watch outside to ensure my sleep is safely guarded. All of which sounds delightful at first, but will seriously impede my progress on this case.

And I *need* to solve this case. If not for my missing Beast, then for the people of this village. They deserve better than to live in fear. They shouldn't have to lock their pets up at night and their children during the day.

"So you admit that Lewis King was unpleasant as a child?" I ask, determined to focus on the few facts I have. "What do you mean? What did he do?"

Nicholas pulls himself away and returns his attention to his meal. "One of these days, my dear, there's *not* going to be a murder to solve, and you and I are going to have a long chat about your priorities."

"Does this mean you're not going to tell me about Lewis?"

He sighs. "There's not much to tell, to be honest. He wasn't the sort of boy who made it easy to like him, that's all. He didn't participate in sports, he made it a point to go telling tales to his aunt every time there was a disagreement, and his behavior could be erratic at times."

"At what times?" I ask sharply.

"When things didn't go his way, usually."

"There wasn't a pattern to it?" I persist. "A cyclical pattern, perhaps? Every few weeks? Or . . . monthly?"

There's a dawning look of recognition in Nicholas's eye, but he holds it at bay while he contemplates my question. "Not that I can recall, no. But I wasn't a burgeoning mystic who tracked the moon's cycle, so there's no way to know for sure."

"I never said anything about the moon."

"You didn't have to. I heard about the wolfsbane."

Well, there it is. It's out in the open now. Nicholas knows that I'm pursuing a werewolf, that I've thrown all common sense out the window and am committing to the supernatural. I shift my gaze to a more comfortable spot above his shoulder. "Your mother seems to think he has health issues of some sort. She said he needed his aunt's money for his medical condition."

"Is this where you ask me if I ever saw him foaming at the mouth?"

"That depends. Did you?"

He laughs and relaxes against his chair back. "I'll say this for you, Eleanor Wilde. There's never a dull moment when you're around."

"I'm taking that as a no."

"Alas, he never transformed into his werewolf form around me. I never saw him sprout hair or catch mice in his teeth. I never saw him loping around the playground on all fours. He *did* always have a strange body odor, but so did his brother, Richard. And it doesn't seem to have prevented the latter's success in this world."

I blow out a long breath. As pleasant as it's been to spend time with Nicholas, this conversation hasn't been as productive as I'd hoped. All signs still point to Lewis King as the culprit, but I can't shake the feeling that he's no guiltier than I am. The murderer is capable of causing terrible agony—of slaughtering animals and leaving them behind for poor, defenseless women like me to find. Lewis's behavior is odd, yes, but it's less like that of a killer and more like that of a man on the edge—maybe even a man in pain. In fact, of everyone in the village, he's the only one who actually seems to care that Sarah Blackthorne is gone.

"Well, Madame Eleanor?" Nicholas asks, an inquisitive lift to his brow. "Short of catching Lewis in the act of transformation, how are we going to prove or disprove your theory?"

It's on the tip of my tongue to tell him that there's no *we* about it—that Lenora and Rachel would be all too happy to set a late-night trap that would lure Lewis out into the open—but even I have to balk at such a plan. For one, Lenora still has to go to school in the morning.

For another, I just realized there's a much easier way to get the answers I seek.

"Finish your breakfast," I say, ignoring the thump of the roofers overhead. "You and I have an errand to run in the village."

Chapter 13

"Oh, I'll wait out here, thanks." I cross my legs demurely at the ankle and fold my hands in my lap, looking the picture of innocence in the waiting room of the small clinic where Dr. MacDougal plies her trade. "I don't want to intrude."

The pained martyrdom on Nicholas's face practically begs me to intrude, but that would defeat the entire purpose of my plan. From the moment we walked into the clinic, dripping apologies for showing up without an appointment, Oona has been eating out of the palm of Nicholas's hand. It might distress me, the adulation showered upon this man by a well-educated, respectable woman who should know better, but she's behaving exactly as I expected her to.

Besides—poor Nicholas is going to need all the pandering he can get after this. You'd think I'd asked him to fake leprosy for all the dust he kicked up.

"I'm only here in a supportive capacity," I add with a wave of my hand. "Pretend I'm invisible."

More than happy to be rid of me, Oona gestures toward the swinging door behind her. "Come along, Mr. Hartford," she says with all the respect and geniality one would expect of a professional in her position. "I'm sure we'll have you feeling as good as new in no time. Tell me, how did you find your mother this morning?"

I'm guessing he did his best not to find her at all, but he makes good on his promise and lays on his most charming smile as he follows Dr. MacDougal to the examination room. He has explicit instructions to keep her back there for at least ten minutes. The medical exam should only take about half that, seeing as how he's never been in better health, but I'm counting on Oona's social ambitions to take care of the rest.

I might not be willing to use the Hartfords to give me a financial leg up in this world, but I'm not above leveraging petty snobbery to solve a murder.

I sit back and assess the waiting room, which is empty save for me and the receptionist behind the desk. I'd hoped that, in arriving unannounced, Nicholas's presence would have thrown the office off kilter enough to allow me access to the medical files I can see lining the wall behind the front desk. However, the receptionist looks to be firmly installed, a pair of cat-eye glasses perched on the end of her nose and a stack of paperwork by her side that should keep her busy from now until the end of days.

Or until a witch intervenes.

"Hello," I say as I saunter up to the desk, my smile bright and innocuous. "It's Zahra, right?"

"Uh, yes?"

"I thought you'd be here today. It was foretold in the stars."

A wary look descends upon the woman, her dark brown eyes wide behind their plastic rims. I recognize both the woman and the expression from the many times I've seen her around the village. She's youngish—in her early thirties, is my guess—and pretty in a retro, brainiac sort of way, as evidenced by her choice of eyewear. However, no glasses are able to hide the wrinkled lines of exhaustion that make me think she doesn't get nearly enough sleep at night.

Which makes sense, since I've often seen her at the grocer's accompanied by a tall, good-looking Scotsman with a pack of young children in tow. *Lots* of young children.

"Have we met before?" she asks.

"Not officially, no." Since her fingers are currently holding her place in the middle of the form she'd been filling out, I forgo the handshake. "But I've always wanted to introduce myself. You have six kids, don't you?"

She blinks again, this time to reveal a look that's a combination of recognition and wariness. In other words, she's realized who I am, and she's not happy about being accosted by a witch at work. To be fair, it's a common reaction.

"A lucky number, six," I say, losing none of my smile. "It belongs to Venus, to lovers, to all things of the heart and home. Which makes sense, if you think about it. You wouldn't have that many children unless you and your husband were doing something right."

Her wariness turns to a deep flush of color, but not in a way that signals she's uncomfortable with the topic under discussion. If anything, that dusky pink is full of delight—and with a husband who looks like hers, it's no wonder.

"Gordon, Gary . . . I'm sorry. I don't quite remember his name, but I believe it starts with a *G*."

"It's Gavin," she supplies. "But how do you—?"

"Oh, I know many things," I say. "Including that the two of you haven't had a night alone together in ages. I know, I know—it's almost impossible while the kids are so young, but a tree is only as strong as its roots. You can tend to the branches all you want, but unless there's a solid base to hold them up, what's the point?"

"I'm sorry, but what—"

"Does this have to do with me? Not much. But I do have one

or two potions here in my bag that might be of use." I make a show of rummaging around in my satchel for a theoretical supply of tonics. Unfortunately, all I have is the empty eye of newt bottle and the last of my lavender attraction elixirs. The eye of newt comes out first, causing Zahra's eyebrows to raise, which is just as well because I need a second to knock the cork loose on the attraction elixir before I place it on the counter next to it.

"I'm really not interested in any kind of hocus-pocus—" she begins again, this time with a distracted look at her paperwork.

"No?" I'm careful to appear unoffended. "No worries. I understand. It's not for everyone. But I *am* pretty close to Rachel Hartford and Lenora MacDougal—you know Dr. MacDougal's stepdaughter, right?—and they were just telling me the other day that they're planning on starting a babysitting service. I wonder if . . . No, never mind. I've taken up enough of your time already."

I make a motion for my bottles and am stopped short—predictably—by Zahra's outstretched hand.

"No, wait!" she cries. "Do you really mean what you said, about Rachel and Lenora? Dr. MacDougal never said anything about her daughter wanting to mind babies."

Given what I know of Lenora's intellectual precocity, I imagine that minding babies is literally the last thing on earth she wants to do, but this is an emergency. Besides, she still owes me twenty pounds for bribing Benji at the museum. In a way, this is payback.

"Well, Lenora is still so young," I say. "I believe they thought doing it as a pair would be best, at least to start out, since Rachel just turned eighteen. They'll take a tag team approach, as it were. Ideal for a pack as large as yours."

Zahra nods, her lips pursed thoughtfully. I can practically see all those possibilities of nights out on the town taking shape inside her head, an elusive taste of freedom on her tongue.

"I could pass on your information, if you're interested," I

offer. "They're just building up their client roster, and I'm sure they'd love to add you."

The bait proves too tempting to ignore. "Would you?" Her hands flutter over her paperwork as she searches for a scrap piece of paper. "We—Gavin and I, I mean—would really appreciate it."

"Of course," I promise and, when her attention is distracted with the piece of paper she's finally located, I knock the lavender elixir over with my hand.

I feel a pang of guilt for whatever medical records I've just destroyed with that floral scent, but only for a fleeting moment. Zahra is on top of things, whisking the important files out of the way as she jumps to her feet.

"Oh, I'm so sorry!" I cry, making a convincing show of regret. "I can't think how I came to be so clumsy."

"It happens to the best of us," she reassures me.

Since I highly doubt she'd call me the *best* of anything if she knew my true motivations, I let that comment slide. I also stand back and watch as she shakes the pages off and mutters something about grabbing some towels. The less I intrude on her attempts to clean the spill, the better.

"I'll be right back, yeah?" she says. "Don't go anywhere—I still want to get you my telephone number."

I solemnly swear to stay in the immediate vicinity of her desk. It's a promise I keep, too, even after her long ponytail swishes out of sight. The filed medical records are technically within the immediate vicinity.

Pausing only long enough to make sure the coast is clear, I duck behind the desk and hightail it straight for the middle portion of the alphabet. It takes me a few false starts before I locate the *K*s, my fingers flying over the files as I locate the one I'm most interested in: King, Lewis.

There isn't time to make a copy before Zahra returns, so I'm forced to resort to good old-fashioned theft. With a solemn and silent vow that I'll put the files back at the first opportunity that affords itself, I tuck them into my valise and scoot back to the other side of the desk.

"There!" Zahra returns to clean up the spilled elixir and to press not just one, but two copies of her phone number into my hand. "No real harm was done. And I'm giving you two in case they each want one."

"I'll make sure these get where they need to go," I promise before apologizing once again for my clumsiness. I know it behooves me to sit quietly in the waiting room until Nicholas finishes his examination, but the files are burning a figurative hole in my pocket, so I escape on the pretense of needing to use the ladies' room.

"Okay, Lewis," I mutter as I lock the restroom door behind me. It's not the most secure location to peruse my stolen wares, since there's one of those two-sided windows that you open to pass laboratory samples through, but I flip the file open and scan it anyway. "What medical condition do you have that would give you cause to bleed your poor old auntie dry?"

I know, in my heart of hearts, that it would be too much of a stretch to hope for a diagnosis of lycanthropy or porphyria, both of which have been historically associated with werewolves. Lycanthropy is technically a mental disorder, yes, and the best that porphyria would explain is some of his excessively hairy patches, but there's something about the idea of them that feels so fitting for this investigation.

Imagine my disappointment, then, when all I find is a tendency to fall prey to the occasional bout of strep throat and an ongoing prescription for the treatment of hyperhidrosis.

"He sweats a lot?" I mutter as I turn the pages this way and that. "*That's* the mysterious medical condition that's supposed to account for everything?"

It's as good of proof as any that Lewis King's claims of medical necessity are invalid. Whatever else he might say, any and all money he got from his aunt went to line his own pockets and his somewhat shady schemes.

Put a check in the guilty box.

Unfortunately, that diagnosis also explains why he always looks so nervous. Excessive sweating is just his natural state—at least unless he's been regularly taking his atropine, as the prescription form in his file tells him to.

And a check in the not-guilty one, I guess.

Fortune might not have been on my side for this part of my mission, but Zahra is nowhere to be seen when I return to the waiting room, so I'm able to slip the file back in place without anyone being the wiser. There's nothing left for me to do but sit and wait until Nicholas has finished working his magic with Oona MacDougal.

And to be grateful that one of us, at least, has magic that gets the job done.

There's just enough time to send Nicholas home to get some well-deserved rest before I have to meet my two protégées at the library. I'm finding it difficult to believe that all the other kids are this diligent in logging their apprenticeship hours, but Lenora is insistent that we meet every day.

"Sorry I'm late, Madame Eleanor, but you won't believe the day I've had."

Considering I coerced my law-abiding boyfriend to break several laws with me, I'm fairly certain I will. "Nothing bad, I hope?" I ask as Lenora settles into her chair.

"Terrible." She sighs and pushes a cloud of hair out of her face. "I don't have the notebook anymore."

"You lost it? That's okay. Mine's in my bag. I'm sure Rachel can make another copy."

"What can Rachel do?" Rachel plops onto the chair next to Lenora. This morning was one of her internship days—her *real* internship, not this mystical sham—so it looks as though she's arrived straight from the train station. "Whatever it is, I hope it involves snacks."

Lenora shakes her head. "I don't have any chocolates today. Oona confiscated my stash. She confiscated *everything*."

"Even the Flakes?" Rachel asks.

"Even the Flakes. After you left last night, she went through my room like a banshee." Lenora casts her doleful eyes up at me. "A banshee is a spirit that—"

"I'm familiar with their kind," I interrupt dryly. "And I don't think it's a very nice thing to call your stepmother."

"But she sounded exactly like one!" Lenora protests. "We didn't mean to let her see the notebook—really, we didn't—but Rachel was over to work on it last night. My dad came into my room and asked us all these questions. *He* thought it was a great project, but then he told Oona about it. He tells Oona everything. He's worse than George."

"Rachel was at your house again?"

Lenora nods. "We wanted to start decoding it straightaway. But the second my stepmother saw it, she threw a fit."

"That wasn't a fit," Rachel informs her friend with a sad sigh. "My mum used to throw *real* fits. Potted plants tossed at people's heads, teacups smashed on the ground, the whole show."

"That was a fit for Oona—believe me," Lenora says. "She never gets mad in front of company. But you can tell when she gets all pale and quiet that the storm is coming later."

"Hang on a second," I command the pair. The librarian is making her regular rounds through the stacks, so I lower my voice. "Your stepmother has a problem with the notebook? That's strange. When I saw—"

I cut myself off before I make the mistake of finishing that sentence. Odd though it is that Oona didn't mention anything about the project while I was at the clinic today, I don't want this pair asking me questions about my activities. The fewer people I rope into fraud with me, the better.

"When I saw her in town today, she didn't mention it," I amend.

"Well, I tried telling her it was for a code-breaking class, but she knows our school doesn't have anything fun like that. She pretended not to care while Rachel was there, but she took it away the moment she left. And she took all my candy. *And* what was left of my allowance."

"Maybe you could earn some more money babysitting," I offer by way of consolation. I'm about to inform her that I might have accidentally pledged her services already, but I'm distracted by the contents in my bag. Or, rather, I'm distracted by the lack of contents in my bag. "Huh. That's weird. I could have sworn I had it in here last night."

I start pulling the items out one by one and placing them on the table in front of me. The two elixir bottles—both empty now—my wallet, several lipsticks in varying shades of red, hairpins, and a scarf are all part of my usual baggage. Lately, the Book of Shadows notebook has been in there, too, but it's nowhere to be seen among the rest of the paraphernalia.

"I must have taken it out without realizing it," I say, mostly to myself. I can't recall seeing it at the medical clinic, which means it must still be at home. "I guess that cuts our plans today rather short, doesn't it?"

"I bet she took yours, too," Lenora says with a jut of her lower lip.

I laugh. "She'd have to be a magician to have pulled that off." Either that, or a witch. I don't know how else she'd have managed to sneak inside my house and taken it without my knowledge. This bag rarely leaves my side. "Maybe it's for the best that we take a few days off. You've been working too hard anyway."

"But we almost had it figured out," Lenora objects. "There were only one or two villagers we couldn't place. The ale one, remember, Rachel? That could have been anybody, though I still think it's that Mr. Markham who makes the cider for the pub."

Rachel snaps her fingers. "And the one with all the poisons, remember? Unless that was your mum, since she's a doctor."

I glance back and forth between them. "Villagers? Ale? What are you guys talking about?"

Both heads turn to me as one, but it's Lenora who speaks up. "The book, Madame Eleanor. Before Oona got her hands on it, we were almost there."

"Almost where?"

"To knowing who each page was. Yours was easy, obviously, since you were assigned an upside-down pentagram. That's black magic, because you're a witch."

"Uncle Nicholas and Grandmother were easy, too," Rachel supplies unhelpfully. "A rich man and a noble lady. Technically, we're not noble, but most people assume we are."

"Inspector Piper was the scales of justice."

"And the general, of course. For war."

"Oh, of course. He had the most numbers." Lenora turns to me with an expectant blink. "We never did understand the numbers."

I find it prudent to call a halt to their chatter. And to hand Rachel a pen from my bag. "Whoa, girls. Slow down. Tell me all that again, but with actual explanations this time. And a diagram, if at all possible."

Rachel seems wary. "I didn't memorize the book or anything, Ellie."

I gesture at her hand. "Then paraphrase. It sounds as though you remember quite a bit."

She bites on the end of the pen and thinks for a moment, reminding me so much of her uncle that I have to laugh. I made a request, which means she'll carefully and deliberately ponder it until she's ready.

"All right, so every page had one or two symbols on the top, right?" she eventually asks. "And then some of them had those huge lists of numbers at the bottom."

I nod. That much I recall. The numbers had been accompanied by Aunt Margaret's symbol for wealth. Like dollar signs, in a way.

Rachel makes an offhand sketch of an upside-down pentagram and taps the page with the end of the pen. "This symbol is how we figured out it was a book of villagers. It was the last entry in the whole thing, and the writing was darker, like whoever wrote it had gotten a new pen. So they added you when you moved here."

"Yeah, because the page before it was a cross and staff," Lenora says. To me, and as one speaking to a particularly uninformed infant, she adds, "That's Nigel, Vicar Brown's curate. He moved here right before you did. He didn't have any numbers, either."

"Not everyone did," Rachel says. She draws the cross and staff for me. "Anyway, once we figured out that those two meant you and Nigel, we were able to start working on the rest. Whoever wrote all that stuff must have been living here for a while, because they knew just about everyone in the village. Each person was assigned their own symbol and page."

A spark of something is beginning to take shape in the back of my mind, but it's an intangible thing, difficult to pin down.

"Each page represented a villager?" I echo. "Some with a list of numbers and some without?"

Rachel nods.

"Who had numbers?"

"General von Cleve, like I said already," Lenora supplies. "And the lovers, which was another one we didn't figure out."

I nod. That was the two snakes facing off for a showdown. It was the one I used to point out the book's magical properties to Inspector Piper.

"And the ale guy," Rachel adds. "He had almost as many as the general."

"That's it?" I ask. "Just those three?"

"Oh, no. They were everywhere—those ones just had the most. There was another one that filled the whole page, but it had been crossed out. We thought it might have been a farmer of some sort."

"It *was* a farmer," Rachel agrees. "I didn't tell you, Lenny, but I was thinking about it later, and I decided it was Old Man Petersham. He died of a heart attack a few years ago, so that would explain why it was crossed out."

The dark, cloudy shapes in the back of my brain seem to be gathering speed. Are we talking about a Book of Shadows or something darker, more sinister? *Like a hit list?*

"What about the one you thought might be your stepmom?" I ask. "With the medicines?"

"Poisons," Rachel corrects me. "One was arsenic, for sure, and I think another one was cyanide. That one didn't have numbers, though. It was a clean page."

"That wasn't Oona MacDougal," I say, picking up the threads of their theory. None of this should be making sense, but it does. This village has always been at the center of this case—its people, its fêtes, its quarrels. This notebook and its strange catalog of residents is somehow a part of it. "My guess is that it's Aunt Margaret. Rachel, do you think you can draw the ale one for me?"

"Most of it, yes."

The pink tip of her tongue shows between her lips as she works. The image is more elaborate than many of the others, a triangle holding a half circle up like a chalice, with two smaller semicircles off to the side.

"The middle part is a drinking cup, see?" Lenora points out. "That's the only thing we could find that was close. I don't know what the rest means."

I can tell the exact moment the image registers, because the unmistakable taste of chocolate fills my mouth. "I do," I say. "It's Penny Dautry."

"But Penny Dautry doesn't drink," Rachel protests. "Or only a sip or two at holidays, I'm sure. She doesn't even like to take communion."

"It's not ale," I say and point out the additional details she's drawn. "It's the traditional things that accompany it. The cup means drink, yes, but the things around it are refreshments. Like bread. Like *cake*."

As neither girl was present when Penny's chocolate cake was unloaded on me—along with that angrily flung hundred pounds—they don't feel the prescience of this statement. All they show is excitement at having another one of their riddles solved.

"Cake! Of course."

"I haven't had a piece of Penny's cake in ages."

"You're lucky. I only had a bite one time, and that was because I stole it from my dad's plate. Oona thinks too much sugar is bad for kids."

As much as I'd love to debate the merits of Penny's secret recipe, I stop the girls before they fall too deep into their rabbit hole. Knowing what I do about the general's *real* wartime associations—and about Penny flinging money at me in fear and anger—I don't have time for rabbit holes.

On a hunch, I ask, "Which of the pages belonged to Sarah Blackthorne?"

Lenora stops and blinks at me. Rachel tilts her head and ponders the question. Neither girl has an answer forthcoming, which resolves me on one thing: I need to figure out where I left the notebook. Unless I'm very much mistaken, it has a very important bearing on the murder case. And not because it's a hit list. If my suspicions are correct, it's even worse than that.

"Mrs. Blackthorne didn't have a page," Lenora eventually says.

"Yeah. We didn't see anything that might have been her."

Of course they didn't. Why would they have, when she was the one who wrote it?

"Okay, you two. That's everything I need." I push myself up to a standing position, taking a moment to clear away all the sketches Rachel has made. No way am I leaving evidence like this lying around in a library where anyone can find it. "You've done excellent work figuring that notebook out. I can't thank you enough."

"But what do we do now?" Lenora asks.

"Yeah. Oona took our copy away, so we can't finish."

"You don't need to." It's a point I'm very firm on. "The information you've provided is more than enough. You two are going to take the weekend off and behave like normal human girls instead."

They seem unimpressed by my decree. "How do normal human girls behave?" Rachel asks.

"Yeah, and what about the full moon coming up?"

"Go to the cinema," I order and scour my admittedly dusty repertoire for other activities that might appeal to two intelligent and lively young women. "Take selfies in front of national monuments. Shoplift. I don't know. You must have had lives before all this werewolf stuff happened. Can't you just go back to it?"

The two girls share a look that spells trouble with the caps lock on. "I mean it, Rachel," I warn. "Remember what we talked about before."

Rachel nods with a solemnity that does her credit, but there's a spark in Lenora that makes me uneasy. "And call Zahra from your stepmom's office," I say, fishing the pair of phone numbers out of my bag. I slide them across the table. "She has a proposition for the pair of you."

That, at least, distracts Lenora enough not to press the issue. Assuming that proposition is a euphemism for important record-keeping work rather than the care of six squealing children, she slips the number in her pocket.

"What are you going to do, Madame Eleanor?" Lenora asks.

"I'm not entirely sure yet," I admit. But paying a visit to Penny Dautry tops the list.

I'm only about a kilometer outside the village before the scent hits me. At first, I blame it on hunger. I haven't eaten since Nicholas's eggs this morning, and we already know I have a weakness for all things sugar- and chocolate-related.

"Is someone making s'mores?" I ask aloud.

It's a rhetorical question, since there's no one around to answer me. It's also an unnecessary one, since I've arrived at my destination. I follow the trail of that smell around the side of a cute whitewashed clapboard house to find not just a campfire, but a full bonfire taking place. A heap of scrap metal appears to be ablaze on a pyramid of firewood, and next to it, Penny Dautry is emptying an industrial-sized bag of flour on top.

The flour does a pretty good job of quenching the bulk of the flames, which means they die down enough for me to identify those pieces of scrap metal as baking pans. *Lots* of baking pans, all of varying shapes and sizes.

"Hello?" I call, afraid to startle Penny into throwing herself onto that fire. She's covered from head to toe in white powder, the checkered apron she's wearing over her dress doing little to protect that garment. "Penny, are you all right?"

She turns to find me standing a few feet from the fire, dressed in my usual dark layers, the flames flickering on my face. The image must be a startling one, because she starts laughing in a way that seems wholly inhuman.

"You're too late, Madame Eleanor," she says as she throws another large bag onto the fire. This one must contain sugar, because the scent of toasted marshmallows magnifies tenfold. "I'm not giving you any more money. I found a way out."

One of the pans buckles under the weight of all that burning sugar, sliding off the heap and sending ashes flying in every direction. I don't dare pick it up, since I have no idea how long it's been burning and I don't have a pot holder handy, but the grass is damp enough that I don't fear an immediate brush fire.

"Maybe you should take a few steps back," I warn. "That pyre doesn't look very stable."

She doesn't heed my advice, opting instead to draw closer to the flames. Whipping the apron off, she adds it to the top like a floury garnish. "There," she says, watching the fabric burn. "That's the last of it. I'm never baking anything ever again."

I'm happy to report that my first feeling on hearing this isn't, as one might suspect, a pang of hunger for all the lost chocolate cakes. Relief is my prevailing emotion. Penny sounds less like a woman who's about to immolate herself on the altar of baked goods and more like a woman who's reached a decision.

The former is tricky. The latter I can work with.

"Good for you," I say as I draw a few tentative steps closer to her. "Now you can concentrate on your poetry."

She doesn't pull away, but she doesn't appear very conciliatory, either. She mostly just looks hot. The combination of the exertions of the bonfire and the heat of it have beads of sweat breaking out on her brow.

"Why don't we go inside and see if we can't find you something to drink?" I suggest.

She raises a finger at me. "I mean it, you know. I don't care who you tell or what you try to get the others to believe. My baking days are over. Now I really am free."

I nod. There's that word again, *free*, the release from bonds that are somehow associated with Sarah Blackthorne. *And you*, the remaining money in my bag says.

"I can't wait to hear all about it," I say. "But I really think you should go inside and sit down. You look exhausted."

I'm not kidding—she does look rather worn down, her hands

covered in flour and ash, her hair blown loose from its knot—but it's not until I say the words aloud that she seems to feel it. Penny sags as though I've just cast a spell, her shoulders drooping as her knees bend. I hurry to her side and prop her up, urging her away from the fire and into the house.

Her kitchen is a testament to the decision to cast her baking supplies into the netherworld. Cupboards are thrown open and the contents spilled all over the counters and floor. A trail of flour leads from the pantry through the mudroom to the back door. Even the refrigerator hangs open, an empty pink box with chocolate residue sitting alone on one of the empty racks.

"The living room, I think," I say in a voice of firm decision. I pause to fill a glass with water from the tap before leading Penny into her main room, where a pair of comfortable chairs are arranged in front of her fireplace. That, too, bears the signs of a recent plundering, the wood bin emptied and a box of matches spilled on the mantel.

I push the water glass in her hand and wait until she drinks every drop before settling into the seat opposite her.

"Now," I say. "I want you to tell me everything. Starting with how long Sarah Blackthorne had been blackmailing you before she died."

Her glance at me is sharp but unsurprised. That lack of surprise, that dull acceptance of my appearance here, tells me everything I need to know: Penny has been expecting me. Penny has been expecting me because she believes that I have every intention of picking up where Sarah left off.

"A few years—three, maybe." Penny sags in her chair, her head resting against the floral needlepoint cushion. From where I sit, the flowers look eerily like wolfsbane. "It's hard to say because it didn't *feel* like blackmail at first."

I nod. "She presumed upon your good nature the first few times, begged help under the guise of friendship."

Penny's voice wavers. "She told you that?"

"No, Penny. She didn't tell me anything. She didn't have to."

She accepts this with a wary look, unsure if I'm referring to my mystical abilities or my role as Blackmailer 2.0.

"It wasn't much money at first," Penny says somewhat vaguely, as one recounting a long-ago tale. "Just a few pounds here and there. I didn't mind helping her, not really, not when I know what it's like to be a woman living alone without any independent source of income."

I nod, all too aware of the parallels to my own situation.

"I would have kept helping her, too, if she'd only asked. But she didn't ask. She demanded. She—" Penny's voice breaks off in a sob. I take a risk and lean over to clasp her hand in mine. There's burnt flour caked into the creases of her palm, but I rub my thumb over the lines of it anyway.

"How much did you give her?"

"Over the years? Thousands, most likely. I had to. She said she was going to tell everyone—" She breaks off and turns her head away. "It sounds so silly when I say it out loud, but you don't understand, Madame Eleanor."

I clasp her hand tighter. "I *do* understand. More than most. Where does the cake really come from?"

She heaves a sigh. "It's a shop about halfway between here and London—you probably haven't heard of it. No one has. That's how I was able to get away with it for so long."

I subdue the selfish urge to pry the name of the bakery out of her. As much as I'd like a long-term pipeline to those chocolate cakes, the mere idea that they still exist somewhere in this world will have to be enough.

"How did Sarah find out?" I ask.

"She followed me one day. It was after Old Man Petersham died. I slipped out early on the morning of his funeral—I always take my little Mini—and she was waiting for me when I got home. She acted like it was a great joke, a secret between the two of us, and left it at that. But then she showed up a few weeks later, and . . ."

And began a long-term assault on Penny's good nature, threatening the exposure of her chocolate cake ruse for the sake of a few extra pounds.

"The funny thing is, I'm really very good." Her eyes meet mine. "At baking, I mean. I used to make a chocolate cake—my own chocolate cake—that was quite scrummy. Nothing compared to the other one, but I never got any complaints. Unfortunately, I was terribly behind for the school bake sale one day and thought it wouldn't matter if I donated something store bought. Just the one time, you understand."

I understand that part, too. Once you start lying—once the deception takes hold and delivers in a big way—there's no turning back. It doesn't matter if you're talking about a chocolate cake and the admiration of an entire village or fake mediumship and being able to pay your sister's medical bills. Our paths are essentially the same.

The only difference is, I never got caught.

I reach into my bag and extract all the money of hers I have left. "This isn't everything you gave me the other day, but I ran into a few expenses I wasn't anticipating."

Penny opens her mouth, but I prevent her from speaking by pressing the bills into her hand. "I'll give you the rest back as soon as I have it. It was never my intention to make you feel threatened, Penny. I promise on my honor as a witch and your friend."

"My friend?" she echoes.

"Well, I *hope* we're friends, but I understand if you aren't feeling too kindly toward me right now." I attempt a smile. "And I want you to know that I support whatever decision you make. I meant it when I said your secrets are safe with me. I like you—and that chocolate cake—far too much to just throw them away."

"Well," she says, the single word carrying a wealth of meaning. "Well."

"Although we should probably head out back and extinguish the flames either way, because I'm afraid you're going to set your neighbor's shed on fire."

She laughs, so startled by the sound that she immediately claps her hands over her mouth.

"It's not the cake that brings them comfort, Penny. I mean, it *is*, obviously, since I don't know a man, woman, or child alive who doesn't dream of it on their plate, but it's more than that." I get to my feet and extend a hand her way, holding it there until she slips her palm against mine and rises alongside me. "It's the ritual of it that really matters. Death comes for us all, eventually. Even though we can't see it coming, we know there will be some things—family, friends, neighbors, Penny and her chocolate cake—that will always be there when we need them."

It's one of my better speeches, if I do say so myself, full of mysticism and hope and the dark promise of the great beyond, but I forgot one small thing: death. As in, *literal* death, Sarah Blackthorne lying cold in a morgue until her murder is solved, a killer somewhere on the loose in the village.

Five minutes in Penny Dautry's company would convince even the hardest of police detectives that she's no guiltier of killing Sarah than she would be a fly, but she can't see that. Not when she so clearly has a motive *and* was present at the committee meeting.

"Madame Eleanor, it wasn't me. I didn't—I couldn't—If you could just—"

"I know," I say. "And don't worry. I will."

"But how do you know what I'm going to ask?"

Because it's the same thing everyone has been saying to me since this whole business started. Unless I'm very much mistaken, it's also why Penny took the cake first to Castle Hartford and then to me.

Bribery, plain and simple.

Bribery for the one person in the village who's friends with Inspector Piper. Bribery for the one person in the village who can force him to turn the tides of his investigation elsewhere. Of all the reputations I've been saddled with in this lifetime, this one remains the most inexplicable to me.

"I'll take care of Inspector Piper," I promise as I lead her to the backyard. I have no idea how we're going to extinguish that blaze, but I have high hopes that the rain will kick in and lend a helping hand. "But tell me one thing first—do you know anything about a notebook Sarah might have carried? In her purse or on her person, full of strange markings?"

Confusion puckers her brow. "No, I never saw anything like that. Sarah didn't care much for reading—or for writing."

I'm not surprised by that. The notebook isn't a journal or a memoir, and it's definitely not some light reading before bed. In fact, I'm pretty sure it's a list of all the people in the village Sarah Blackthorne was blackmailing before she died. Old Man Petersham. Penny Dautry. General von Cleve. The mysterious lovers.

All those people, all those potential murderers.

And a single book that holds the key to it all.

Chapter 14

"You're wearing an awful lot of clothes for dancing naked in the moonlight."

I jump as the low sound of Nicholas's voice accosts me from the back door. Years of sneaking through rambling old houses in search of ghosts means that few things can scare me anymore, but a warm, living man speaking inches from my neck is one of them.

I whirl to find him standing even closer than I at first suspected, leaning so close I could easily kiss him. "Where the devil did you come from?" I demand.

"I walked down in hopes of convincing you to spend the evening together, but I see you've anticipated me." He casts an appraising look over me, his omnipresent smile lingering on the edge of his lips. "I don't suppose you're not wearing anything under that trench coat, are you?"

I cinch my belt tighter. "Are you mad? It's pelting down rain out there. I have on like eight layers to protect my nether limbs."

"There go all my plans." He sighs. "All right. Lay it on me.

What are we doing, and what's the likelihood that one of us will end up dead by morning?"

The irony in his voice doesn't escape me. "I don't recall inviting you to share my adventure. In fact, I don't recall inviting you at all."

"I know, but if I sit around waiting for you to come to me, I'll die an old maid. I was hoping to take you dancing—and no, not the moonlight kind. The real kind."

The real kind? As in, two people enjoying a night out on the town? As in, arms and legs entangled as two bodies move as one?

"What's wrong?" He tsks and feigns a worried look. "Uh-oh. Can't you dance? Did I finally discover the one thing Madame Eleanor doesn't excel at?"

"Of course I can dance," I say, my voice sharp. I can't help it—he's caught me so far off guard that it's a wonder my mouth works at all. Here I am, up to my knees in blackmail and murder, and this man can only think about whisking me away for a night of carefree entertainment?

I spent *hours* this evening searching my cottage for that blasted notebook, but it wasn't in any of my usual hiding places. I can hardly go running to Inspector Piper without that proof in hand, and even if I did have it, I don't know what it would be proof *of*.

That Sarah Blackthorne was a terrible person, yes, but everyone already knew that. That one of the villagers on that list is responsible for the murder, sure, but which one?

Nicholas's arm is around my waist before I have a chance to voice any of this aloud. By the time I've managed a single bat of my eyelashes, he's swooped me down into an expert dip, my body held aloft only by the grace of his strength. I'm completely at his mercy, a fact he uses to his unabashed advantage by determinedly *not* kissing me.

"I'm not such a bad dancer, either," he murmurs, his gray eyes flashing down into mine. "Well, my dear? Are you going to tell me why you're skulking out under the cover of night, or will I have to tail you and find out the hard way?"

"You don't have to make it sound so suspicious. I just didn't want to bother you after that stint at Oona's office, that's all."

"You're *not* a bother to me, Eleanor." His reply is vehement—almost overwhelmingly so—but it's softened by the kiss I've been waiting for.

There's something about being so wholly trapped by this man's embrace that makes the touch of our lips that much more electric. He's deceptively strong, my Nicholas. And deceptively passionate. If he truly let himself go, the havoc he'd wreak on me—mind, body, and soul—would be devastating.

But the kiss doesn't last, and neither does the moment. Which is just as well, I suppose, seeing as how the sun has almost finished its own suave dip below the horizon. Nicholas sets me back on my feet.

"There," he says, triumphant at having thus unsettled me. "*Now* can I come with you? I promise to feign as many illnesses as you need to get the job done, but I feel I should warn you that Oona MacDougal is no fool. She knows you were up to something."

There's nothing for it but to give in. I'd hoped to discharge this particular errand alone, but there's no denying it will help to have an extra pair of eyes.

"Did you happen to bring a flashlight?" I ask.

"Alas, I left it in my other trousers. If you'd told me we were going werewolf hunting, however, I'd have brought a whole arsenal."

I glance sharply at him. "I never said we were werewolf hunting." Then, because he's not too far off the mark, I add, "To be honest, what we're actually hunting is a cat."

"A cat?" he echoes.

I nod, my chest grown suddenly tight. "It's Beast. She's gone—has been gone for several days now. I thought at first it might be a fluke and that she'd come home on her own, but animals have been going missing around here since before this whole investigation began."

I don't mention the part about my sister also being gone, but I don't need to. "One of them showed up dead on my hillside a few nights ago, but I was afraid to mention it. I think . . . I know it sounds paranoid, but I think the werewolf left it there on purpose. To warn me, maybe? To let me know that Beast is next?"

It says a lot about Nicholas that my confession doesn't elicit the bat of a single eyelash. "Oh, Ellie," he says. His arms are around me and holding me close before I know what's happening. It's one of the things he's best at, moving from inertia to action faster than it takes most people to breathe, his languid indolence a mask for how alert he is to everything going on around him.

He's also quite good at hugging, though you wouldn't think it to look at him. When a man is as stiff and starched as this one, it's easy to assume that his embrace would be wooden, that he'd always hold a piece of himself back. Neither of these things is true. His hands are warm and strong, holding me fast and tangling in the intricate coils of my hair. If anything, *I'm* the one who shows reserve, still unsure of myself after all this time.

"She can't have gone far," he murmurs, the words spoken into the side of my neck. His breath is a warm whisper across my skin. "I'm sure she's just enjoying a bit of freedom, that's all."

When I don't respond except to sniffle into the pristine front of his shirt, he drops a soft kiss on my hairline. "And even if it were the werewolf, I'd lay odds for that cat against any supernatural being in existence. She's terrifying."

I release a reluctant—and watery—laugh. "You're just saying that to be nice."

"I can count the number of things that scare me on two fingers. One of them is that cat." His hand lifts to my chin, his forefinger propped underneath and forcing my gaze up. His eyes are serious but warm, and they don't shift as he drops a soft kiss on my lips. "The other, my dear, is you."

Scaring fully grown, extravagantly wealthy men isn't new to me. The ability to terrify all mortals is a necessary tool for psychics, mediums, witches, and anyone else who thrives on the mysterious. A scared man will believe a lot. A scared man will pay even more.

Somehow, however, I doubt that's what Nicholas means.

"Nicholas, I—" I begin, but a low howl sounds from somewhere in the distance.

Confirmation of a werewolf on the loose is the last thing I want right now, but I am grateful for the interruption, if only because I don't know what I want to say next. That I'm grateful for his support, yes, but also that I'm just as scared of him—of the things he represents, of the things he makes me *feel*.

"Maybe I should head back to the castle and grab those flashlights after all," he says, more amused than alarmed at that sound. Probably because I haven't told him about the blackmail yet.

"There's no need. I have lots of candles."

"I'm sure you do, but I doubt they'll be much use if we're creeping over rocks and through forests in the dead of night. My cell phone has plenty of battery left. We'll use that."

I agree without further dissent. Considering what a difficult time Penny and I had quelling her bonfire, I'm more than happy to avoid open flames for the rest of the day.

"It was my plan to stick to the main road for a spell and then turn off toward the evergreen crossroads," I say as we head out. Nicholas doesn't have nearly as many layers on as I do, but living in the castle has made him impervious to the cold. "Those crossroads have more to do with this whole thing than they should. I think it's because they tie Mr. Worthington's farm to the rest of the village."

"And *I* think we should head in the direction of the old stables," he says as he takes me by the hand. His other hand is held out in front of him, a wide arc of light emitting from his phone as he leads us out into the twilight. "It's not in use for equine residents anymore, but it does tend to fill up with newborn mice and birds this time of year. If I were a cat, that's the first place I'd go."

I dig in my heels. "Wait—you think Beast abandoned me for no reason other than to fatten up on poor, defenseless babies?"

"Undoubtedly," he replies.

"That's terrible."

"That's a cat."

"It's no excuse," I maintain. "She could at least hunt the creatures that have a chance to fight back."

"The females who live in this cottage have a tendency to prey on the weak, I'm afraid," he says with a gentle tsk. "If you think the cat is bad, you should see what the woman who owns her can do. Fully grown men, scampering across the countryside at her bidding. It's scary."

"I wanted to go on the road," I point out.

Despite the lighthearted conversation, we move quickly past the grounds outside my cottage toward the relative direction of Castle Hartford. I think I know the stables Nicholas is talking about, since I've passed them a few times on my ramblings over the land. I'd always assumed they were a barn of some kind, but it makes more sense that they'd have been used to house the vast number of horses required to keep Hartfords of centuries past at the top of the social food chain.

"Here, kitty, kitty!" I call. "Come out, kitty, kitty. Beast of my heart, where are you?"

"Beast of your heart?" Nicholas asks in a slightly strangled voice. "I thought she hated you."

"She does," I say. "But we're kindred spirits. She just refuses to admit it."

"And what, if you don't mind my asking, makes one's spirit kindred with another?"

As is almost always the case with this man, I'm not sure if he's genuinely interested in the answer or if he's mocking me. When we first met, I'd assumed it was the latter—always the latter. He's a cynic and a skeptic, like me, but my willingness to believe in the extraordinary for the sake of a buck gave him a slight edge in that department.

But he's here, and he's holding my hand, and for reasons I haven't yet worked out, he seems to want to stick around doing just that.

"Do you want the *Anne of Green Gables* definition or the *Wuthering Heights* one?" I ask.

"I was hoping for yours."

"I don't have one. All of my ideas are stolen from the literary greats."

He takes his eyes from our surroundings long enough to cast me a sideways glance. "Which definition do you prefer?"

"The *Wuthering Heights* one, naturally. Whatever souls are made of, hers and mine are the same."

"Yours and a cat's?"

I nod. It's a strange thing to admit, I know, but we're tied, Beast and I. We have been since the moment we met. Some relationships—deep and inborn, burned into the flesh—defy explanation.

"What about yours and mine?" he asks.

I trip on a rock. I've been so focused on scanning the horizon, searching for signs of a sleek black animal laughing from afar, that I haven't been paying attention to where I step.

Fortunately, Nicholas has. He's there to catch me before I even realize I'm falling. As his phone falls to the ground and plunges us both into darkness, his arms are around my waist, his entire weight bracing mine. I'm not sure if my sudden breathlessness is the result of my stumble or because of the fierceness of his grip, but I'm glad to have Nicholas there cither way.

That overwhelming gladness is why I immediately right myself and step away. For almost twelve years, I've done everything on my own, carried the weight of the world on my shoulders and my shoulders alone. It would be so easy to start shifting that burden to this tall, rich, handsome god of a man.

Easy and dangerous. Once you manage to unload a burden like that, it's almost impossible to start carrying it again.

"Yours and mine?" I echo.

He doesn't respond, content to stand there and stare at me, his eyes boring holes into mine. My mouth goes dry, my confession caught in the dry landscape of my tongue. But it's there all the same.

Whatever our souls are made of, his and mine are the same.

Grabbing him by the shirt collar, I yank him down to the ground, the pair of us falling flat on the earth in a tangle of limbs. Because of our respective positions, he lands on top of me, but not uncomfortably.

"Well, well," he says in a low rumble, his lips hovering over mine. "I suppose that's one way of answering."

I slap my hand over his mouth before he says anything more. His lips feel soft against my palm, but I don't have time to appreciate the sensation. With a gentle nudge, I turn his head in the opposite direction. "Shh. There's something over there. Look."

A heavy sigh escapes his lips. "Of course there is," he says, but he obliges me by looking.

Sure enough, a dark, shadowy figure moves furtively over a hill to our right. The figure is slightly hunched and moving at a careful pace, almost as though he's more animal than man.

"The werewolf is back," I say on a gasp.

"You know, I'm starting to believe my mother was right when she forbade us from mentioning that creature in her presence."

"Be quiet," I hiss. "You'll scare him away."

Without his phone illuminating our path, it's difficult to see the details of the creature ambling over the rocks, but the clouds part just enough to allow a ray of moonlight to slip through. It's a well-timed—if eerie—burst of light, and even Nicholas is intrigued enough to stop talking long enough to watch where he goes.

"He's heading toward the crossroads," I whisper, thinking of Regina. . . . And of Beast. "We have to follow him."

"You want to follow a werewolf into the darkness in order to save your cat from being ripped open and devoured?" Nicholas asks. The question must be a rhetorical one because he sits up and begins brushing off his sleeves. "You're probably right. Let's go."

I barely manage to subdue my shout of appreciation in time. Nicholas might be stiff and starchy, but he's always game for an adventure.

"Wait." I still him with a hand on his arm. "Did you bring any kind of weapon with you?"

"My gun is in the trousers with the flashlight. Will my fists do instead?"

"It's no laughing matter," I warn, thinking of the last time I saw Lewis King, his erratic driving and even more erratic behavior. "Some*one* killed Mrs. Blackthorne and some*thing* is out killing animals. I'd rather not run into either one without some kind of protection in place."

"You do have protection," he says and pulls me to my feet. At my look of inquiry, he adds, "You have me."

There's nothing for it after a declaration like that but to follow him into the darkness. The figure is moving in such an ambling, awkward way that we're able to catch up within seconds; in fact, we have to slow our pace to a near crawl to avoid drawing too close. Wherever he's headed, the creature isn't in a hurry to get there. He pauses and looks around, occasionally raising his head as if sniffing the air.

"He's hunting," I say on a breath.

"No," Nicholas says grimly and points to the ground. "He's already hunted."

A glint of red winks up from the rock below. I crouch and lay my hand there, even though I already know what I'll find. My palm comes away slick with blood. Upon closer examination, I find that the pool at our feet is just one of several that follow the same trail the creature has been taking.

I have no way of determining what kind of blood it is, but a deep sense of foreboding tells me it's feline. *Beast.*

"We have to stop him," I say, my throat raw. "I don't care if we have a weapon or not. He's not getting away with this."

"Eleanor, you can't—" Nicholas begins, but it's too late. I'm already off and running, determined to close the gap between me and that monster.

The creature recognizes the signs of chase almost immediately. As soon as I draw close enough to make out that the build is a masculine one, a howl escapes his lips, breaking the silence and the panting sound of my mad flight over the rocks. Nicholas is right behind me, but I'm smaller and faster than him. I'm also more determined, since I have such a personal stake in his capture.

The werewolf moves with a determination that feels almost impossible, coming as it does on the heels of that stumbling, exploratory gait. However, it takes me only a few seconds to realize that it's not speed propelling him so much as an intense familiarity with the landscape. While I stagger over the uneven ground and pick my way through the occasional scrubby bush, my prey seems to know exactly where to step to avoid stumbling.

Even Nicholas, who spent the bulk of his childhood rambling over these lands, is unable to match him step for step. By the time the clouds close like a curtain, drawing darkness back over the night, we're well on our way to having lost the trail.

Never one to give up easily, I continue my pursuit despite my deep, labored breaths and the growing hitch in my side.

"Eleanor, stop," Nicholas calls from somewhere behind me.

I don't heed him. I can still hear the snuffing, shuffling sounds of the creature's escape. There's still time to catch him.

"Eleanor," he calls again. "For God's sake, *stop*."

I do, but only because I'm hit with a flying weight tackling me from behind. It hits my legs and sends me to the ground in a thump. My knees bang painfully onto the hard earth, my palms hitting the ground in a whirl of loose rocks and debris. Neither of those pains register, however, once my head slams into the ground. With a dizzying whir, the world slides and tilts around me, causing my stomach to slide and tilt with it.

Even with the slipping and sliding of the world around me, however, Nicholas's familiar voice assails my ear. "I'm so sorry," he says. His hands move gently over my head and neck, checking me as if to ensure himself that I'm still fully intact. "I didn't mean to hurt you, but it was the only way."

"The only way to what?" I ask, my voice thick.

I get my answer a few seconds later as my vision clears and I'm able to take stock of my surroundings. In the direction the creature ran, a mere foot to my left, there's nothing but the hard edge of a ravine—a ravine that drops several hundred feet to a rocky outcropping below. An overpowering sensation of vertigo takes over at the sight of it.

One more step in that direction, and I would have learned all the mysteries of the universe at once. One more step in that direction, and I would have died.

And the werewolf knew it. He was leading me there with just that end in mind.

Chapter 15

"You'll have a nasty headache for a few days, and I'll need to give you a tetanus shot before I leave, but you'll live." Dr. MacDougal whips her stethoscope back around her neck and stares hard at me. "I also strongly suggest you keep the nocturnal wanderings to a minimum until you're more familiar with this area. There are hundreds of places to slip and fall around here—many of them dangerous, as you almost discovered for yourself."

"Thanks," I say weakly. "I'll remember that."

"In fact, you might want to stick to city living from here on out," she says. "Not everyone is cut out for life in a village like this one."

"Noted."

She sighs and shakes her head, the sharp edge of her bluntly cut hair swinging like a curtain. "You have no intention of following my advice, do you?"

"Not really, no." I smile and then immediately wince. The stitches render every movement of my face an agony. There are five stitches in all, extending from the edge of my eyebrow toward my temple. The one thing my witchy reputation has been without all these years is a gnarly facial scar, so I'm not *too* upset at having them. "Thank you for coming on such short notice."

"Yes, well." She clears away the tools of her trade, which have been laid out on my kitchen table. "It's the least I could do for a friend."

I highly doubt it's *my* friendship that brought her out for a house call as late as this one. She smiles up at Nicholas, thus confirming that belief. The people around here can't seem to get enough of the man, exalting him like a hero. Considering he saved me from an untimely death tonight, I can understand why.

"I don't see any signs of concussion, but I'd feel more comfortable if she didn't sleep alone tonight."

He nods once. "I'll take her up to the castle with me."

"No thanks," I promptly reply. "I need to be here in case Beast returns."

Nicholas looks as though he'd like to argue, but, like Dr. MacDougal, he's too dignified to do it in front of an audience. He closes his mouth in a tight line.

"Beast—that's the missing cat you were out searching for?" Oona asks.

The nonchalance in her voice is impossible to miss. It's careful, calculated—which, in my experience, means it's not nonchalant at all. "Yes. She's been gone for five days, and I'm starting to get really worried. Lenora told me that your cat disappeared recently, too."

She frowns at the mention of her stepdaughter's name. "Yes, unfortunately."

"That makes your cat, my cat, the cat on the hill, the Gilfords' dog, and Mr. Worthington's pig," I say. "That's an awful lot of animals in peril."

"Please don't tell me this is part of the werewolf legends you've been having Lenora research."

"There was something out there. I saw it. *We* saw it."

Dr. MacDougal casts a disbelieving look at Nicholas, making me fear that I'm about to be cast in the role of wayward hysteric, but he heaves a deep breath and hunches his shoulders in a shrug. "I'm not saying it was a werewolf we chased over the cliff's edge, but there was something out there."

"Some*thing*?" she asks.

"Someone," he corrects himself. "Bipedal."

She sighs and starts prepping the tetanus shot. "Well, the next time you see bipedals scampering about at night, I highly recommend you call the police instead of chasing them through the darkness. A few more steps, and that could have been a nasty accident."

It's on the tip of my tongue to tell her that there was nothing *accidental* about what happened to me out there. That person—that creature—had been trying to propel me over the cliff's edge on purpose. Near-death experiences have a way of bringing wisdom, however, so I hold my tongue.

On that topic, at least.

"By the way, Lenora told me that you confiscated the notebook she and Rachel had been working on," I say.

"Yes, I did." Oona stabs the needle in my arm.

My only reply is a wince. She doesn't have to be *quite* so enthusiastic about this whole thing.

"While I understand that the nature of your work is steeped in the occult, I'd thank you not to introduce my child to Satanism just yet." She smiles, but it's a wan thing that doesn't reach her eyes. "Let's at least wait until she's a teenager for that, shall we?"

The shot complete, Oona makes quick work of cleaning and packing up her supplies. "That arm will probably feel tender tomorrow, but not nearly as tender as your head, so I doubt you'll notice."

I'm not ready to let the subject of the notebook drop. "I absolutely agree with you about Lenora, and I'm sorry to have let them run away with the project," I say.

Oona looks only mildly suspicious at my meek acceptance at having my livelihood thus disparaged, but Nicholas is watching me with a curious lift of his brow. I'm careful not to look at him as I add, "I don't suppose I could come get the notebook from you, could I? If I promise to keep it out of their reach? It was kind of important."

"Oh, dear," Oona says with a sympathetic cluck of her tongue. "I wish I could, but it's long gone by now. I tossed it out with the medical waste at the clinic today."

I get to my feet, ably assisted by Nicholas's waiting hand. "You did?"

"I never would have presumed, but the girls told me it was only a copy they made. They said you had the original safe and sound."

"I did, but—" I cut myself off, unwilling to divulge more while I'm still so unsure of my ground. I think of a quick lie. "But Rachel did the drawings in that one. I like to hold on to her work whenever I can. That girl is going to be famous someday."

"But a copy would never be worth as much as an original, would it, Madame Eleanor?" she asks, emphasizing my name with careful deliberation. "It carries none of the value, none of the importance. Take care of that wound, and don't hesitate to call if you have any more questions."

I do have more questions—dozens of them, in fact—but I don't dare voice them aloud. Something about the way she phrased that last bit, almost as though she was leveling me with a threat, gives me serious pause.

Moving as one, Nicholas and I walk Oona to the door and bid her a grateful good night. Pressing my back against the door as it comes to a close, I shut my eyes and try to hold on to the moment for as long as I can. Something the doctor said is niggling at the back of my mind, an unsettled feeling taking shape.

"My poor dear," Nicholas says with a low, soothing tsk. "Let's get you to bed. Does it hurt very badly?"

My eyes fly open again, and it takes me a second to register that he's showing genuine concern for my well-being. "No, I'm fine," I say, giving my head a small shake. "It's not that. I mean, it does hurt, but that's not what's bothering me."

He makes another comforting noise and begins propelling me toward the stairs. I let myself be led, but only because I'm busy thinking.

Or, rather, I'm busy *trying* to think. That blow to my head must have taken more out of me than I thought, because although the threads of an idea are still there, I can't seem to make them take shape. Especially not when Nicholas gives up on my slow tread up the stairs and whisks me into his arms.

"What are you doing?" I ask as I find myself weightless and encapsulated against his chest. It's warm there, and reassuring, and I find myself burrowing sleepily closer. "You don't have to carry me. I can walk. In fact, you can probably go back to the castle despite Dr. MacDougal's dire warnings. I promise to call if I start seeing unearthly spirits moving through my vision or anything like that."

Nicholas continues his easy trot up the stairs and to my bedroom, then deposits me tenderly on my bed. At some point during the day, the roofers must have come in here and cleared away the debris, because there's nary a piece of plaster to be seen. Or rainwater. They must have made some good headway up there.

"You heard the woman," he chides. "Doctor's orders. It's either spend the night in your old room up at the castle, or deal with me sleeping on your couch."

The thought of sleeping in the castle's yellow bedchamber sends a shiver running through me. That room might only be haunted by unpleasant memories now, but that's enough paranormal activity to keep me away—especially since I'm starting to feel battered and bruised from my fall. Dr. MacDougal had warned that it would take a few hours for the full aches and pains to settle in, but that it would hit with a vengeance when it did. She wasn't wrong. My body feels as though it's been tossed into a dryer set on high.

I suppose that's what happens when a man throws himself at you and knocks you to the ground in a frantic effort to save your life.

"My hero," I say and pat the space on the bed next to me. "Are you sure you wouldn't rather stay nice and close tonight? You can keep a much better watch on me that way. And I guarantee you'll like what you see."

His eyes flare with interest, but he's immovable from where he stands. "You're only saying that because you haven't looked in a mirror yet."

My hand flies to my temple. "Oh, no. Is it awful?"

"Like you fought a werewolf and lived to tell the tale," he says and traces the line of my stitches with his finger. "I rather like it. Very medieval."

I laugh, but it's only a token effort. "I don't trust Oona," I say. "That notebook we were talking about—it's not just a notebook, Nicholas. And I think she knows it."

"Probably. We'll talk about it tomorrow."

"I haven't had a chance to tell you about it yet, but I think it's tied to the murder."

"You'll figure it out. You always do."

"And we'll need to make a survey of the evergreen crossroads in the morning," I add. "The werewolf may have left some clues behind. I want to get out there before they're washed away."

"We will," Nicholas promises. He also presses a soft kiss on my forehead. With it comes a bone-deep exhaustion I'm finding more and more difficult to suppress. "But first you need to get some rest. Sweet dreams, Eleanor. After a night like this, you've earned them."

Chapter 16

"You villainous traitor."

"Good morning to you, too, sunshine."

"You overbearing sludge-demon."

"I took the liberty of preparing a tea tray downstairs. It's ready whenever you are."

"You primeval juggernaut."

"That one sounds rather nice, actually. Thank you."

I throw back my covers and launch myself out of bed. Well, to be strictly accurate, I *start* by launching myself out of bed, but I make it only a few steps before every part of my body screams its protest. There's enough stiffness in my joints and in all the places where I hit the ground last night to turn me into a zombie, but even that pales in comparison to the dull, steady throb in my temple.

And to the throb of anger I feel at the sight greeting me outside my bedroom window.

"It's well past noon," I accuse as I point at the dim bulb of the sun peeking out from behind a cloud. One of my many strange skills in this world is my ability to tell time by the movement of the sun. In this case, I'm not pleased by what it's telling me. Half the day is gone already. Not only will all signs of the attack last night be washed away, but there's a full moon in less than twelve hours.

I whirl on the man sitting calmly next to my bed, a stack of newspapers at his side. "How could you let me sleep in so late?" I demand, although the meaning of those newspapers isn't lost on me. He must have been installed there for quite some time. "And why aren't there roofers banging around overhead?"

He closes the paper he'd been reading and adds it to the stack. "I also took the liberty of asking them to reschedule. I thought you could use a lie-in. Before you tell me exactly what kind of a tyrant that makes me, will you please swallow these?"

He holds out his hand and drops two pills into my palm. I'm tempted to give them back to him on principle, but my head aches sickeningly. I'm also profoundly thirsty, my mouth like sour cotton. Settling for a meaningful glare, I accept the painkillers and gulp down the entire glass of water by my bedside.

"Do you think you could manage some toast with the tea?" he asks. "Or perhaps an egg?"

"Toast sounds good, thanks," I say and, before he can gloat about it, "but only because I know you'll sit there being polite and distant until I eat something. Did you get any sleep at all?"

"Enough," is his mild reply. "You were snoring too loud to notice, but Rachel came and sat with you for a few hours this morning."

"I don't snore."

"My mistake. Your airways must have been taken over by a demon. Temporarily, I'm sure."

I ignore him as a matter of principle. "Where's Rachel now?" I ask.

"Attempting to persuade my mother to let her melt down

some of the silver to make bullets for a gun that, as of yet, doesn't appear to exist. It didn't seem worth dissuading her."

Despite my determination to stay annoyed with this man, I have to fight to stifle my laugh. "How can she make bullets for a nonexistent gun? Does she think they're a one-size-fits-all deal?"

"I didn't think to ask, and, considering my mother has taken it upon herself to barricade not only her person, but every piece of silver we own, in her bedroom, I doubt she'll have an opportunity to find out." Nicholas rises to his feet in one elegant movement, holding out his hand and keeping it there until I slip my own into it. I think he's going to turn mushy and maudlin, but all he does is give my palm a quick squeeze. "I'll go down and get your breakfast ready. You'll want to freshen up, I'm sure."

The reason for his hasty departure down the stairs—and his somewhat lackluster gesture of affection—is made clear as I enter the bathroom. Someone has also made an attempt at repairing the ravages of the roofers in here, but I hardly care about the dusting of plaster or the strategically placed pots. I'm far too horrified by the vision presented in the mirror.

I know, from my long experience of head injuries, that outward swelling is a good sign. It means the wound is external, pushing out where there's plenty of room to spread. My brain, though still a little foggy, appears to be fully intact.

To be confronted with the reality of what this looks like on the *outside*, however, is another thing altogether. Especially when my sleep was being watched over by a man whom I hope will someday see me naked.

"I look like Frankenstein's monster," I moan as I finger the stitches along the side of my brow. They protrude painfully from my swollen flesh, the skin red and stretched around them. That alone wouldn't be *too* bad, since I can just swoop my hair over most of it, except that the entire side of my face around it is a huge, puffy purple bruise.

If I didn't know any better, I'd say Dr. MacDougal did a bad job on purpose, trying to make me look as much like a hag as possible out of spite.

"It would be just like her," I mutter to no one in particular.

And it would be, too. That woman is obsessed with appearances. I've known it from the start. I've never met anyone so determined to present the image of a happy, unified family to the world, so resolved on foisting her stepdaughter into the Hartfords' path. She wants everyone to believe she's the perfect wife, the perfect doctor, the perfect everything—when really, she's just as petty and fallible as the rest of us.

"Son of perdition," I mutter, catching my own eye in the mirror's reflection. For the briefest of moments, I feel sure it's not *me* looking back, but my sister. Before the accident, there was always a calm assurance to her gaze, a wisdom I doubt I'll ever manage to duplicate. I'm so certain, in fact, that I lean forward and press a kiss on those cracked, dry lips. "Winnie, you brilliant minx. I don't know why I didn't realize it before."

There's no answer, of course, but that doesn't dissuade me. If anything, it only makes me move that much faster as I rummage around in my makeup kit to repair the ravages of last night's mishap.

But not *too* fast, mind. Some things aren't worth rushing.

"I figured out Oona's cake."

I reach the bottom of the stairs a few minutes later, my makeup intact but my hair still undone, the long strands hanging heavily to my waist. Nicholas prefers me to wear my hair down like this, but it's rare for me to style it in anything but my usual ornate braids and coils.

"I thought you said you just wanted toast." Nicholas appears in front of me bearing a tray with my breakfast. As was the case with yesterday's eggs, he's taken his time over the task. Not for him a mere scrape of butter across a piece of bread. Oh, no. The tray he's holding bears a pot of marmalade that I *know* didn't come from this house, a folded napkin made of linen, and even a single daffodil nodding its head at me from a small vase.

A daffodil. Because I once said, in passing, that they were my favorite.

My knees grow weak, and I falter. Once again, Nicholas is there without my needing to ask, one hand holding his tray, the other holding me.

"To the sofa, my dear," he says. "And then I'll get you all the cake you want."

"I don't want cake," I protest. Still, I let him guide me to a seated position while he sets the tray in front of me and begins preparing my tea exactly how I like it. "I'm talking about Penny's cake."

"But you called it Oona's cake. Are you sure you're feeling well?"

"Oona's *metaphorical* cake." My hands shake as I lift my teacup and sip, but it has more to do with excitement than exhaustion. "Nicholas, what do you know about the MacDougal marriage?"

He pauses in the act of applying a generous helping of marmalade to my toast.

"Are she and Ian happy, do you think?" I ask. "As in, *really* happy?"

As is his usual custom, he gives my question serious consideration before he answers. He waits until he hands over my toast and settles back in his chair before speaking. "It can't be easy, losing a wife in childbirth the way he did," he eventually says. "And remarrying so soon after."

"But people do that all the time. Plenty of blended families and second marriages are happy ones. What I want to know is, is their relationship a successful one? In the eyes of the world, I mean?"

"In the eyes of the world, yes."

The careful diplomacy of his answer tells me much more than he realizes. "But not in your eyes."

My astuteness doesn't cause so much as a blink. "No."

I wait, allowing him a moment to gather his thoughts and explain. He takes his time with the task, crossing one leg elegantly over the other, but I'm not disappointed with the results.

"Oona MacDougal is a smart woman and a strong one," he says. "I've always admired her for that. Only the bravest and most determined souls can stick this village out long enough to carve a space in it."

There's a message in there for me, I'm sure of it, but this isn't the time for self-examination. "But?" I prompt.

He sighs and scrubs a weary hand along his jawline. "But Ian MacDougal is none of those things, I'm afraid. He never has been."

I think of the apologetic, slightly cowed air of the man and nod my understanding. Ian MacDougal seems to be a decent schoolmaster and a good father, but he's not the sort one would pick out of a crowd. Or, if I'm being honest, an intimate gathering of friends.

"The problem with smart, strong, determined women is that they have a tendency to know their own worth," Nicholas continues. He feigns an intense interest in his fingernails. "That's not an easy thing for some men to accept."

"Some men?" I echo. The next question that hangs on my lips has nothing to do with the state of the MacDougal marriage, and everything to do with the kind of man Nicholas Hartford III is, but I don't dare ask it.

He answers anyway, his gaze lifting and locking on mine. "Weak men. Small-minded men. Men who can't recognize a good thing when it shows up on their doorstep with tarot cards and promises to upend their entire worldview." He holds my stare a few seconds before shaking himself off. "Well? Are you going to tell me what this has to do with Penny's cake?"

As much as I'd like to unpack the first half of Nicholas's comment—and the fact that I don't care much for tarot cards as a general rule—I can't ignore the more pressing needs of this investigation. Especially since so much of the day has been wasted already.

"The lovers," I say. Since he has no way of knowing what I'm referring to, I trace the shape of the showdown snakes on my untouched toast. "It's the MacDougals. The perfect couple, harmonious in all things. Or so Oona wants everyone to think."

He blinks. "You might want to start this at the beginning."

At this point, I doubt I *could*. So much has happened in the past week, so many people's lives touched by this murder.

"The short version is that I believe Oona was being blackmailed by Sarah Blackthorne. All of them were—the general, Penny, Oona, half the villagers with a secret to hide." I lick the marmalade from my finger and pop the triangle of toast in my mouth. "Sarah kept track of it all in the notebook I was telling you about yesterday. Each villager was assigned a page in the book, and some of those pages had numbers and the wealth symbol—a record of the money she got from them."

"This is the notebook Oona took from Rachel and Lenora?" he asks. I could kiss him for his ready understanding. One of my favorite—and least favorite—things about this man is how little escapes his notice.

I nod. "Theirs was just a copy I had them make. Every villager's secret is in there. You said it yourself—the general isn't really a general, but his symbol was the one for war. Oona and Ian aren't really happy, but they were presented as the ideal lovers. And Penny's cake is no miracle of baking science. She admitted it to me yesterday. She buys them from a bakery a little ways north of here—and don't look at me like that, because I didn't pry the name of it out of her. I didn't have the heart to, not after all she'd gone through."

He looks only slightly conscious stricken. "It seems like a terrible waste, is all."

Spoken like a man who's never been the victim of blackmail. "The exact figure isn't clear, but it sounds as though Sarah got quite a bit out of her by threatening to tell everyone the truth if she didn't pay up," I say. "She must have been extorting everyone that way—Oona MacDougal included."

"I think you'd better show me this notebook," he says.

"Unfortunately, I don't have it anymore." Losing a valuable piece of evidence isn't a thing I like admitting, but there's no denying it any longer. "I've looked everywhere, but I can't seem to find it. I think Oona must have stolen it from me."

He casts a careful look around him. "Oona broke into your house?"

"Yes. No. I don't know." I hold a hand to my temple. For once, it's not intended to give the impression of fake mysticism. There's still so much pain throbbing there, so much fuzziness I can't seem to shake. "Between the roofers and the pair of us coming and going, I don't know when she would have had a chance. But she couldn't get the copied version away from Lenora and Rachel fast enough. And then, last night while she was stitching me up, she was almost taunting me about having tossed it out—and with the medical waste, where I have no chance of recovering it. Without either the copy or the original, everything I say is just conjecture and hearsay. And she knows it."

A thoughtful pause settles over Nicholas. I think he's going to say something in Oona's defense, chastise me for flying off into the realm of fantasy, but the question he eventually asks is both simple and surprisingly astute. "Where did the notebook come from in the first place?"

I halt. I've spent so much time lately trying to decode that notebook, to determine why it's missing and where it's gone, that I forgot how mysteriously it came into my life in the first place.

"I don't know," I confess. "It just appeared in my living room one day. Lenora and Rachel disclaim any responsibility for it, and I can't see Inspector Piper planting it as evidence—especially not since the paper it was printed on came from his aunt, who's already in trouble for growing the wolfsbane."

Nicholas just nods and watches me, following along as I work through the convoluted threads of my memory.

"My living room was a disaster area, because the girls had been over the day before to go over all the werewolf lore they'd gathered from the villagers." I glance up. "That was the same day Lewis came over to talk to me about something that was bothering him. He was agitated and shifting around. He knocked into that table right there."

We both look at the table in question. I've since put away the elephant tranquilizers and old *Horse & Hound* subscription, but I can picture them as clearly as if seeing a vision. He was sweating and nervous and had hit the table with his hip. Everything went flying, falling into the already messy heap of books from Lenora and Rachel. How easy would it have been for a notebook carried in a pocket or the waistband of his pants to have joined the fray?

"Lewis King," I say on a long breath. My eyes fly to Nicholas's, which contain nothing but a calm acceptance of my conclusions. "He must have found the notebook while he was searching for the papers in his aunt's house. He must have—Nicholas, he *knew*. He knows about the blackmail scheme. I'm sure of it."

"How sure?" Nicholas asks. "'You want to ask him a few questions' sure, or 'you're ready to call Inspector Piper' sure?"

I close my eyes and try to sift through all the facts I've assembled about Lewis King over the past few days. His relationship with his aunt, strained and cold, but still very much a part of his life. His obsession with making money, which he never seems to have enough of. His belief that he's being cursed. His increasingly werewolf-like symptoms. His hyperhidrosis.

I can't tell the exact moment it all clicks, but my eyes snap open and I jump to my feet, heedless of the way my joints protest the sudden movement.

"We have to call the police," I say, my voice surprisingly calm considering the conclusions I've just reached. "And an ambulance."

"An ambulance?" he echoes.

"Yes—and fast." I don't wait to explain. "I'm pretty sure that whoever poisoned Sarah Blackthorne is also trying to murder Lewis King."

Chapter 17

"I believe this is the part where you tell me how you knew Lewis King was passed out on his aunt's kitchen floor."

I cross my arms and stare at Inspector Piper, refusing to budge so much as a centimeter. "Not until you promise."

He consults his notebook, which from my vantage on the other side of the interrogation room where I'm being held, I can see contains the image of a whale spouting water from its head. "Let's see . . . You and Mr. Hartford say you arrived at one thirty-two, but the call was put in for an ambulance six minutes before that."

"Promise me, Inspector. It's important."

"So either you peeked in the windows and saw him on the ground—and then lied about it—or you knew ahead of time that he'd be there."

"Or I'm the one who poisoned him and I developed a guilty conscience at the last minute," I add. I approach the table and tap the paper. "Make sure you include that one."

Inspector Piper stares at me as he blows an enormous bubble out of what I'm certain is an unsafe amount of chewing gum.

"Ms. Wilde, need I remind you that Lewis King has been transported to hospital, where his chances of survival are still in question?"

"Of course not. I'm the one who told you what to tell the paramedics. Peter, *please*."

My use of Inspector Piper's first name gives him pause. He snaps his gum and stares at me, his beady eyes unblinking.

"I know you already talked to Nicholas, so there's no need to waste time with this whole double interrogation method," I add. He's still not blinking, so I indulge him with a summarized version of events. "Lewis has been showing symptoms of the wolfsbane poisoning all week. The sweating, the thirst, the confusion—it was all there. He was probably feeling nauseous and dizzy, too, but I never thought to question him on it. I was too distracted by thinking those were signs of his transformation into a werewolf."

"Ah, yes." He flips the pages of his book to one that accurately, if not helpfully, shows a picture of a dog-like creature. "That would be the one who supposedly attacked you last night?"

I yank the notebook out of his hand and promptly sit on it. "I'm not giving it back until you agree to let me do this my way," I warn. "Someone in this village has been poisoning Lewis King for the same reason they poisoned Sarah Blackthorne—to stop the blackmail. They also tried to kill me last night by luring me off a cliff. We have to stop them before they try again."

Without his notebook, Inspector Piper seems at a loss about what to do with his hands. He waves them ineffectively before deciding to clasp them on the table in front of him. "If you're worried about your safety, I could always keep you in here until the investigation is complete. I wouldn't mind."

Despite the gravity of the situation, a laugh escapes me. "I'm sure you would. And if it were just me you needed to protect, I might take you up on it. But you can hardly lock up me, Lenora MacDougal, Oona and Ian MacDougal, Rachel Hartford, Nicholas Hartford, *and* Aunt Margaret. They've all seen or heard about the Book of Shadows. Where would we fit?"

The inspector looks around the small, cement-lined room where I've been held for the past hour as if trying to imagine the seven of us living here indefinitely. He sighs. "All right, Ms. Wilde. If—and I mean *if*—I play along with this scheme of yours, what's the point? According to your conveniently misplaced Book of Shadows, nearly everyone in the village has a reason to want Lewis King dead. The fact that he's still alive is all we have going for us. I don't see what telling everyone he died will accomplish."

That's because Inspector Piper suffers from a severe lack of imagination. Fortunately, I have enough for the both of us.

"He shouldn't *be* alive," I say, ignoring the inconvenient truth that were it not for Nicholas's well-timed tackle last night, I wouldn't be alive, either. "He should have been dead days ago, but he takes atropine for his hyperhidrosis."

"And you know this because . . . ?"

I emit a fake cough. I also adjust my position so I'm not sitting quite so squarely on the corner of his notebook. It's starting to poke. "I have my ways. How I know isn't important. But atropine, in case you weren't aware, is—"

"An antidote for aconitum poisoning. Yes, Ms. Wilde, I do occasionally come up with a nugget of information on my own."

He pauses and waits for me to continue, which I take as a good sign that he's coming over to my way of thinking.

"As long as Lewis remained alive and a potential blackmailer, the killer was frantic—worried. It's probably why he made an attempt on my life last night." I delicately finger the stitches on my temple, trying not to think of how near to success he'd come. "The closer I got to figuring out that Book of Shadows, the more likely it was that I'd talk to Lewis King and piece the rest together. One of us needed to be taken out of the picture. And since Lewis had enough atropine in his system to prevent the wolfsbane from doing its job, it made sense to try me."

"But you're still alive."

"Yes."

"And you don't have the Book of Shadows."

"No."

"Nor do you have a suspect."

"Neither do you," I point out. He doesn't have to sound quite so smug about it. I might not have *a* suspect, but I do have several dozen of them. That has to count for something. "Which is why I think you should make the announcement that he's dead. With Lewis out of the picture and the evidence missing, the killer will start to feel secure again. Until, of course, I take advantage of tonight's full moon."

"Ms. Wilde, I cannot, in good conscience—"

It's time to play my full hand. "Someone is working very hard to give the impression that this village is beset by a werewolf. The slaughtered animals. The missing pets. The wolfsbane dug up from your aunt's garden when there were four other perfectly murderous poisons growing alongside it."

Not to mention the hunched creature luring me out over the landscape last night, his every footstep secure.

"The moon has always had a strong influence on our world, Inspector," I say. "Even Stonehenge is believed to have lunar correlations. If you'll just indulge me for one night, I think I can deliver your murderer. Or at least help you narrow the list."

He snaps his gum. "Just one night?"

"Of course. Tonight's full moon is all I need to pull together the powers of the—"

"Spare me the mystical homily, Ms. Wilde," the inspector interrupts. He glances at his watch and sighs. "All right. I'll hold off on making a formal announcement about Lewis King until tomorrow morning, but that's all I can promise. What you do from there is no concern of mine. Legally, I can't stop you from holding a public gathering or performing made-up rituals in the dead of night."

"How do you know it's a made-up ritual?" I demand.

He doesn't answer. All I get is a long, careful look and a pained shake of his head. "And for the love of everything, please don't make me bring you in on indecent exposure charges. I don't get paid nearly enough."

"You're *finally* getting around to dancing in the moonlight, and I have to stay home and babysit?"

Nicholas is waiting for me outside the precinct, leaning against his mother's Land Rover like a chauffeur awaiting his pickup. As I approach the vehicle, he pulls open the passenger-side door and helps me in. All that's missing is a cute black cap on his head to complete the picture.

"It's not ideal, but someone has to keep an eye on Rachel and Lenora," I say as he lifts himself into his own seat. "They're the only ones, with the exception of me, who've seen the completed Book of Shadows. I can't risk having them at the Retribution Ceremony."

His eyebrow twitches at that last part, but he merely says, "Ah, yes. Not at the Retribution Ceremony. What was I thinking?"

I laugh and wait until he pulls the car out before speaking. "I just need to get all the villagers involved in Sarah Blackthorne's blackmail scheme in one place, and this seemed as good a way as any. I don't think another fête meeting will do the trick."

He sighs but doesn't argue. He never does. It's one of the things I like best about him.

"Once I see them together, and watch how they act when I sacrifice the Book of Shadows by the light of the full moon, I'll know more," I add. "It'll work—I'm sure of it. You know how good I am at reading people, Nicholas. I can prove it to you.

Right now, you're wishing you'd crashed that plane into the Pyrenees, after all."

Now it's his turn to laugh, a low chuckle he combines with a rueful shake of his head. "Actually, what I wish is that I'd had you in the plane with me. Besides, how do you propose to sacrifice the Book of Shadows? You don't have it."

"Well, yes, but none of the villagers knows that. Sarah could have had dozens of copies. That's why I have to perform a sacrificial ritual. To lay all threats of blackmail to rest along with the spirits of the fallen. The killer won't miss a chance to witness that firsthand. Pull over in front of the vicarage, will you? I have a few errands I need to run before I head home."

He obliges, but with a silence I know presages another of his thoughtful ruminations.

"I won't be hurt," I say before he can speak. "I don't plan to eat or drink anything that doesn't come from a sealed package until the murderer is found, and the entire village will probably come out for the ceremony, so there's safety in numbers. If it helps, I also solemnly swear not to chase any werewolves who appear under cover of night this time."

There's no laugh this time. "Eleanor, you don't have to do this."

"Of course I do. Even if Aunt Margaret would be willing to step in my place as the Witch du Jour, the whole point is that *I'm* the one who—"

"Ellie. Stop."

I didn't heed his warning to stop fast enough last night, so I'm careful to do so today. Especially since he called me Ellie. Other people might use my nickname with easy familiarity, but Nicholas Hartford III isn't one to let his formality go without a fight.

The Land Rover is parked at a semiawkward angle blocking the main road, but he doesn't heed this as he turns to me and clasps my hands in his own. "You have nothing to prove to these people."

I open my mouth to reply, but he presses my fingers tightly. I feel that pinch as though he's clasping my heart in his hand—it's squeezing the air from my lungs with a grip that's painful in its intensity.

"You are *not* Sarah Blackthorne," he says, his voice rough. "No, don't argue. You might be able to convince Inspector Piper that your motives are self-serving and mercenary, but I know better. I know *you*. You couldn't care less about selling your potions."

On the contrary, selling my potions is the entire point of all this. Without a means of income, I have no choice but to pack up and return to my former life. To the wandering and searching, the never-ending pursuit of entities I can neither see nor touch. If I want to stay in this village—and I do—I have no choice but to recoup what's left of my reputation.

"They'll come around," he says, his voice softer this time. One of his hands releases mine and comes up to cup my cheek, but it doesn't lessen the vise-like grip he has on my heart. If anything, that gesture only tightens its hold. "They'll see what I see when I look at you. They just need time, that's all. It's not worth risking your life over."

I snatch my hands away, surprised to find them shaking. "That shows how little you know about the real world," I retort.

For once, I'm not talking about the riches that set him and his family apart. Money is part of it, yes, but money is also something I'm used to doing without. Taking care of myself is an art form I have perfected. By hook or by crook—and I mean that literally—I've managed to scrape my way by in this world. And, my current difficulties notwithstanding, I know I'll keep doing it.

But Nicholas has always lived here. He was born not just

into wealth, but into acceptance. Admiration, even. Nothing he says or does, short of murder, will lower him in the eyes of the village—these warm, weird, wonderful people who share so much history, so much of their lives.

"Do you know what Penny Dautry thought after five minutes of conversation with me?" I ask. It's not exactly the line of reasoning I planned to take, but it's the only way I can make him understand. "That I was blackmailing her. That I was picking up where Sarah left off. Not because I'm a practicing witch, and not because I talk to my dead sister at night, but because she looked at me and saw a woman as miserable as Sarah had been."

Nicholas doesn't respond, just firms his lips in a straight line.

"She thought that because I'm *exactly* like Sarah Blackthorne."

Greedy. Lonely. Alone.

And determined by any means necessary not to let any of it show.

"I'm not doing this for me, Nicholas," I add, softer this time. "I'm doing it for the village. Everyone has suffered so much at her hands, paid the price for just trying to get by. They deserve some closure after all they've been through."

I open the door and swing my legs out, glad to find that they're stable. Glancing back, I offer him a tentative smile. "Lenora and Rachel will put up a fight, but don't let them wear you down. Tie them up, if you have to."

"Eleanor—wait," he calls one last time.

I almost ignore him, afraid that to linger will only give him a chance to start squeezing my internal organs again, but I turn around. "Yes?"

He looks at me for a long moment, his mouth hovering over his words. I don't know what he means to say, but he settles for a gruff, "Be careful tonight. And come see me the moment it's over."

"I will," I promise and shut the door.

I wait only until the engine kicks up and Nicholas drives off before heading into the vicarage. There are plenty of ways to spread news in a place like this, but none are as effective as the time-honored practice of a phone tree. With any luck, news of Lewis's supposed death will be discussed over every dinner table. By dessert, I hope to have the entire village out by the evergreen crossroads so I can finally lay this case to rest.

As to what will happen after, well, I can't see that far into the future. And for once in my life, I'm not going to pretend otherwise.

Chapter 18

"There are more candles down in storage if you want them," Annis says as she thrusts a box of votives into my arms. "They're probably as old as this place is, though, so I can't promise they'll light. Especially if it rains during your vigil."

I glance up at the darkening sky, where the clouds are still holding themselves around the fringes of the horizon. The weather report is inconclusive regarding whether or not the moon will be visible tonight, but things are looking good for me so far.

"This should be plenty," I say. "And I'll pay you back for all of them."

"Nonsense. I'm more than happy to contribute to such a worthy cause. This sounds exactly like what the village needs. Poor Lewis. Whatever he was guilty of, he didn't deserve to die for it."

The box of candles easily weighs twenty pounds, so I brace it on my hip. It eases the weight in my arms but not in my heart. Annis had been so devastated to hear of Lewis's death, so enthusiastically supportive of my desire to bring the community together in the middle of the night, that she'd started the phone tree at once. I can't help but feel like a monster.

Looking at her now, those kind eyes brimming with unshed and authentic tears, I know very well that I *am* a monster.

"Annis, you know it's not actually a vigil I'm planning, right?" I ask.

"Memorial service, then."

"Not really that, either."

"Prayer circle?"

"Um . . ."

Annis smiles. It's one of her most serene smiles, the kind that makes it seem as though nothing can touch her. "You're going to have to give me something, Ellie. I was hoping to write those candles off as a charitable donation, but I can hardly put it down as a Wiccan orgy."

With that, any fears I might have had that Annis is unaware of my true intentions are put to rest. I have no idea how this woman is able to find so much good in every situation, but I find her nothing short of miraculous.

"A pagan ritual is the best I can do, I'm afraid," I say.

"I might be able to work with that." She nods as if in dismissal, but something about the way she holds herself gives me pause. I'm rewarded for my patience a few seconds later. "Will this be enough, do you think?"

"I'm not sure." Since I've already told so many lies to her already today, honesty is the only option I have left. "I should probably admit that only half of my goal tonight is to let those who were being blackmailed know that their secrets died with Sarah and Lewis. I'm also hoping to jolt the murderer into making a mistake or revealing a clue of some kind. I know you never imagined that one of your parishioners could do something like this, but I'm certain it's one of them."

I hold my breath, waiting for her judgment.

"That's not what I meant," she says. "What I was really asking is, will it be enough to finally make you feel like you belong?"

I'm riveted in place, the candles growing heavier by the second. "What are you talking about?"

"Maybe nothing." She leans forward and presses a quick kiss on my cheek, careful not to jostle the injured side of my face. "But I think you'll be surprised how many people show up tonight—and not just because this promises to be more entertaining than the time Randall Humboldt got his head stuck in the bike rack outside the general store. You have more friends around here than you realize. There aren't many people who would risk their lives for the sake of the truth. Even fewer who would do it with such panache."

I can't think of anything to reply to that, which is just as well because Annis releases a low laugh and waves a farewell.

"See you at midnight, Ellie," she says. "I can't wait to see a pagan ritual up close."

If I'd realized that church candles weighed as much as a small child, I'd have stopped by Mrs. Brennigan's house first. My errand with her is a much shorter—and lighter—one.

"Oh, Madame Eleanor!" She appears on the doorstep before I have a chance to knock, though I do manage to set the box of candles down without straining my back *too* much. "Is that for me? I don't recall . . ."

"Ordering twenty pounds of wax candles?" I push the hair out of my face. I never did get around to putting it up in my usual braids, which means the long strands are flying in every direction. "I should hope not. These are for the ceremony tonight. Which, incidentally, is what I came by to talk to you about. Are you on your way out?"

"Unfortunately, yes. Can it wait?"

Not really, no. The candles will do a good job of outlining a circle around the evergreen crossroads, and the elderberry cordial I intend to spill all over the ground will serve a double purpose of glinting under the moonlight like blood and helping to spark a small, highly controlled bonfire in the center. The one thing I don't have, however—and the one thing I need more than anything—is that blasted Book of Shadows.

"This is going to sound like a strange request, but do you have any of those floral notebooks that Margaret Piper makes and sells at the Saturday market?" I ask. "She said you requested some to sell at the fête, but I was hoping you might have one or two lying around."

"Oh, Lord. Yes. Dozens of them. I don't know why, but I always buy pretty stationery in the belief that I'll write my magnum opus on it someday. Did you want them?"

"Yes, actually," I say and toy with the idea of telling her the truth. If she's going to be present at the ceremony tonight, she'll surely notice that the book I'm going to cast into the flames in an attempt to lay this blackmailing nonsense to rest looks suspiciously like the one I borrowed from her house.

But she makes it easy on me.

"Oh, perfect. If you're taking donations in to Annis, you can add them to the heap. That will save poor Margaret from having to make more. They're in the library. Do you think you can find them on your own? I'm terribly late as it is."

"Absolutely," I say, feeling even worse about my falsehood now. Mrs. Brennigan has no real reason to trust me, but here she is, letting me into her house to snoop around as I see fit. It's a fake psychic's dream come true.

"Thanks, love. I don't know what I'd do without you."

I do. Most of it includes a long, carefree life free of lies, deceit, and dancing in the moonlight.

It doesn't take me long to locate the library. The Brennigan home is Edwardian in design and construction, which means it's tall and skinny, most of the ground floor designed for looks rather than use. As such, the library is located near the front.

It's a dark and stately room, but the books aren't the heavy, leather-bound tomes one would expect to find on the shelves. In true B&B form, it's all creased paperback novels and travel guides—the kind of light reading that would appeal to guests on a repairing lease in the country.

I find the notebooks stacked along a shelf behind a studded desk chair. At the sight of them, my heartbeat picks up, so similar in design are they to the Book of Shadows. Those twine spines, the delicate hand-pressed pages . . . The only difference is that they appear to be made mostly of violets and buttercups instead of those pink tea roses. If I were an attendee at the ceremony tonight—or, indeed, the murderer—I wouldn't be able to tell the difference.

Even though I highly doubt Mrs. Brennigan is hiding the real Book of Shadows in a library she just invited me to peruse at my leisure, I take a moment to flip through each one, holding my breath until I see the blank pages peeping back at me. Only one has any writing in it, and it appears to be the start to a cozy mystery set in Chicago in the roaring twenties.

"If this is her opus, she needs to seriously consider finishing it," I say as I chuckle over a few of the lines. "Poor Mrs. Brennigan. The one thing she's ever suffered from is a lack of confidence. I'm going to make her a creativity tonic."

My promise thus made, I put the half-written mystery back on the shelf, along with one of the nicest-looking buttercup notebooks so she can keep going if she's suddenly visited by her muse.

"It's not there."

I pause in the act of turning around, clutching the half-dozen notebooks to my chest.

"I've already looked, but I'm sure you know that, don't you?"

"I wasn't aware you were still in the village," I say, struggling to keep my voice level. My pulse, having leapt at the sound of that voice, takes off in a skittering pattern.

"It's not in any of Lewis's bags, either. I was just over at my aunt's house, going through his things. How one man could have been so opposed to owning an iron, I have no idea."

There's nothing for it but to turn the rest of the way to face the carefully shellacked hair and tight-fitting shirt of none other than Richard King. For once, he's not smiling, all those shining white teeth of his tucked behind a deeply etched frown.

"I was so sorry to hear about your brother," I say, even though it sounds inane in the face of what seems to be alarmingly like a murder confession. "This must be so hard for you, coming on the heels of your aunt's death as it did."

"I know he had it in his possession at one point." Richard takes a step forward. He's still far enough away that I could easily dodge around the opposite side of the desk, but I don't dare move. "He told me as much the day he stole my car. But he misplaced it, he said. *Misplaced it.* Can you imagine that kind of carelessness?"

Yes, I can, if only because it's right on par with a young woman who recently suffered a blow to the head allowing herself to be trapped in a library with a man twice her size. I wish I'd thought to ask Mrs. Brennigan what kind of errand she was running. It would really help me to know what kind of a timeline I'm looking at here.

"He reassured me by saying he thought he might have left it at your house." Richard's teeth finally make an appearance, his smile as eerily fake as his tan. "You don't happen to have it, do you?"

"Not anymore," I say and, since it seems like the most likely way to get out of this alive, "I left it with Inspector Piper."

Richard releases an eloquent string of curses that could only come from a man who makes his living indulging in public discourse. I watch with a kind of detached wonder, almost as though seeing him from behind a pane of warped glass. When he lets the mask fall like that, his emotions coming through the careful television personality façade, he looks even more like his brother.

Lewis is the rougher version, obviously, the uncut stone to Richard's flashy diamond, but there's no denying the similarities. In fact, when he runs his hand through his hair in a gesture of obvious annoyance, the resemblance is uncanny. Those same tufts of hair, that same cherubic face . . .

He looks almost like the picture Rachel drew. The picture she showed to the train station workers. The picture they affirmed was the man who arrived last Wednesday, with plenty of time for murder of all kinds.

I jolt where I stand, scattering the notebooks all over the ground. The sound of those pages flapping seems to recall Richard to a sense of his surroundings. Also to a sense of gallantry, since he comes forward to assist me in gathering them up again.

But the gallantry is only a shield. Without bothering to scoop up the fallen books, he grips my arm with a strength it's impossible to ignore. The hard press of his thumb is going to leave a deep bruise on my skin, but it's not nearly as deep as the bruise to my ego. It's a strange set of priorities, I know, but I can't believe I didn't see this coming. I'd been so *sure* that one of the villagers was the murderer. Richard is a little smarmy for my tastes, but he seemed so harmless.

There's nothing harmless about the way he yanks my arm, however, pulling me away from the desk and across the floor.

"If you gave the inspector that notebook, then you're just going to have to get it back," he says. The cultured accents of his voice are at odds with the menacing way he manhandles me.

"I can't take evidence away from a police station," I protest. "Not when it's already been logged and examined. I'm not a magician."

He halts. During that short pause, I think the wisdom of my remark is going to prevail, but he stares at me and shakes his head before uttering a low laugh. “No, but you are a witch. That’s the next best thing. Come on. We have to hurry before the Brennigans get home.”

I’ve read enough books about kidnappings to know that my best chance of survival is to raise as much of a hue and a cry as I can while I’m still around civilization and can reach help. The moment Richard gets me in his car or out of reach of the neighbors, all hope is lost. There will be nothing to stop him from rubbing me all over with wolfsbane.

That, therefore, is precisely what I do. Without waiting for him to realize my intentions, I open my mouth and release an earsplitting scream that Lenora would easily recognize as that of a banshee.

Richard takes instant exception to this. With another of those eloquent bursts of profanity, he lifts his fist and prepares to silence me through any means necessary.

“Not my stitches side,” I plead, but it’s too late. For the second time in as many days, my head is struck with a blow that leaves my brain rattling. This time, however, my brain decides not to fight back. The painful rip of my stitches bursting open is followed by a bright flash of color and, finally, darkness.

Chapter 19

Strangely enough, this isn't the first time I awake to find myself kidnapped and bound by a murderer.

There seems to be a profound lack of imagination exhibited by the killers in my life. When in a pinch, they resort to the most obvious means of restraint, which is to affix my wrists and then stand back and watch as I struggle to free myself.

Though to be fair, Richard isn't standing back. He's sitting. And from the zooming sensation that's making my head spin, I'm guessing we're in a car.

"Oh, good," he says as my head bobs to an upright position. "You're awake. I was afraid I might have killed you."

"Afraid not," I croak, my mouth dry. "Witches are like cats. Our lives tend to keep cropping up."

Moving my jaw causes some of the dried blood encrusted to the side of my face to loosen and break off.

"Here. Drink this." He holds out a water bottle and, as if just now remembering that my hands are tied and wedged awkwardly behind my back, he swerves the car over to the side of the road. It's a strangely considerate gesture, pulling over to hold a water bottle to my lips, which naturally causes me to recoil. I'm not ingesting anything this man has to offer until I figure out where he's taking me—and why.

"Go on," he urges. "You need your fluids. You bled an awful lot. Why did you bleed so much?"

I'm guessing it's because he reopened a head wound with the blunt edge of his fist, but I refrain from saying so. Mostly because he still has the water bottle pressed against my mouth, and opening it will allow him to pour the contents down my throat.

"Suit yourself," he says and withdraws the offer. He also pulls the car back onto the road, allowing me a moment to appraise my surroundings. We're in the teal car—a thing I know not just from the glint of color out the window, but also because there's an alarming rattle coming from the undercarriage.

From the nearness of the sun to the horizon, I'm guessing it will be dark within the next half hour or so, which means it's another four hours until my midnight appointment with the lunar goddess and anyone will think to come looking for me. I almost—*almost*—regret sending Nicholas off to take care of Lenora and Rachel, since he'd come in handy right about now.

But I definitely don't want those girls mixed up in this. Not now. Not considering the lengths Richard appears to have gone to kill his relatives. I can only imagine what he'll do to someone who doesn't share his genes.

"Where are you taking me?" I ask when it becomes apparent that we haven't strayed too far from the village. Given how much time has passed, we should be well out of town by now, heading toward London or the coast or wherever it is people go when they want to hide a body. But I recognize a few farmhouses off to the right, and I can see the tip of the church tower standing off in the distance in the sideview mirror. If I had to take a guess, it looks an awful lot like he's been circling around until I woke up.

To interrogate me? To torture me? I don't like my odds either way.

"You know what?" I say, my panic rising. "If you still want me to get that book from Inspector Piper, I might have thought of a way to get in—"

He cuts me off with a short laugh. "We're not going anywhere near that place. How much did you tell the inspector anyway?"

"About the blackmail scheme?" I think fast, wondering how best to play my cards.

It's difficult, since I don't know which ones I'm holding. Richard King was obviously involved in his aunt's blackmailing and the records kept in the Book of Shadows, but the extent to which he played a role is unclear. Nor am I perfectly sure why he had to resort to murdering his aunt and brother. It's possible that he wanted Sarah's insurance money and lied to me about it being given to the Tennis Foundation, but he has to know that two family members dead of poisoning and his name listed as beneficiary is what they call an open-and-shut case.

I never liked Richard for this crime, and sitting here in his car, whizzing toward an unknown destination with my hands tied behind my back, I'm forced to remember why. It's the same reason I had a hard time believing it of Lewis. Neither of them are what I'd call *good* men, the one caught up in his own fame and the other his financial schemes, but general male selfishness isn't the same as guilt. It usually takes something more—some push, some threat—to cross the line over into murder.

Then again, I *am* tied up and bleeding. It's possible that I'm wrong.

"He knows as much as I do," I say. "That your aunt kept a log of everyone in the village. That she hid their true identities behind the symbols she assigned them. That she used their secrets to extort money from them to the tune of tens of thousands of dollars."

He takes his glance from the road long enough to stare sharply at me. "That's all?"

Even with my whirling, bleeding head, I know what he's really asking.

"He also knows that she's been giving the money to you all these years," I say. "And that Lewis didn't know about it until he found the Book of Shadows in your aunt's papers. He confronted you about it, didn't he? Is that why you poisoned him, too?"

I don't realize that I'm not wearing a seat belt until I start flying. With my arms bound behind my back, there's no way to protect my head except to curl myself into a ball and hope my body takes the brunt of the impact. It does, but my forehead still thumps against the glove box, adding to the already whirling cacophony of sound and sensation inside my skull.

I have no way of knowing how long I stay there, huddled against the dashboard, nausea warring with my desire to get as far away from this car as I can. The latter wins when Richard emits a low groan. Like me, he wasn't wearing any restraints when he slammed on the brakes and brought us to a tearing halt, which means he has yet to regain full faculty over his senses. I'm not sure how his head is faring, but his chest appears to have hit the steering wheel, temporarily robbing him of his ability to talk.

That doesn't stop him from trying, however. "Not . . . me . . . ," he pants. "Only . . . wanted . . ."

I don't bother waiting around to find out what Richard King wanted. Money, obviously, and enough of it to force his aunt to sell her cute stone house on the hill. And then, when that wasn't enough, he made her turn to blackmail to keep the tap running. I can't help but feel a pang for poor Lewis, who'd obviously stumbled onto this scheme out of the blue.

He came to me because he thought he was being cursed. Because of the book he'd found, because of what his aunt had done to the village. Because, even then, his brother was poisoning him, making sure that he, like Sarah, would never be able to tell the truth of his misdeeds.

And me. I have to get out of here or Richard will try to silence me as well.

My hands are still bound behind my back, so I have to turn to face my captor as I fumble with the door handle. The position makes it possible for me to shove the door open and stumble out, but not before I get a good look at Richard's face. In this position, with my adrenaline throwing everything into highlight, he looks even older than before. His face is pale underneath the makeup, the roots of his touched-up hair showing a line of gray.

"Please . . ." he says.

I don't let my sympathy hold me back. On legs that wobble at every joint, I turn and flee.

By the time I make it to the farmhouses we'd passed by earlier, dusk has come and gone, leaving me plunged into twilight. The moon will be full and luminous by the time midnight rolls around, but for now, it's nowhere to be seen. This means I have to pick my way over the terrain much more carefully than I'd like, my steps slow enough that I don't accidentally stumble over rocks. Without my hands to catch me, a fall like that could be devastating.

Now that I'm closer to the gently rising hills, I recognize them as the ones from when I walked Lenora home—those strange, swelling lands that hold her house in the palm of a hand.

"I've never been so happy to see a MacDougal in my life," I say as I scamper down the nearest rise. I can hardly be blamed for it. After a day like mine, I'm feeling oddly nostalgic for a familiar face.

Their house isn't lit as I approach, no signs of life bustling in or around the yard. Even in the dark, however, I can tell that the back is just as pristinely kept as the front, an immaculate green lawn hedged all around with prickly rosebushes. In fact, the only signs that a family actually lives here is a pair of bicycles leaning against the brick and a freestanding greenhouse surrounded by empty pots and upturned bags of soil. Both of those things make sense: the bikes for the children, the greenhouse for the parents. Lenora had mentioned that her parents were keen on gardening, even if her brother did cut all the heads off their flowers.

"Hello?" I call, bypassing the greenhouse to kick at the back door to the house with all the strength I have left in my legs. "Is anyone home? Mr. MacDougal? Dr. MacDougal? George?"

No one answers. I kick harder, but that only results in a sore toe added to the rest of my injuries. I turn my back to the door and try the handle, but am unsurprised to find it locked. However safe this village is in the normal way of things, when there are murderers at large, you remember to lock the doors.

I cast a nervous glance back the way I came, wishing my head didn't hurt quite so much. My vision is slightly blurred, my ability to make out shapes in the night somewhat diminished. I don't *think* Richard has followed me here, but it's not something I'm willing to risk.

Partly because the idea of taking shelter to catch my breath and my bearings is one that appeals strongly to me, and partly because I'm hoping I'll find a pair of gardening shears that will get this rope off my wrists, I head in the direction of that greenhouse.

As I'd hoped, this building remains unlocked. I turn my back to the door and snick the handle, slipping inside the crack without anyone noticing.

My sigh of relief is loud even to my own ears. My whole body shakes from a combination of adrenaline and exhaustion, and I want nothing more than to sink to the ground and close my eyes for a few minutes. I know better than to give in to that urge. The second I stop moving, I'm going to have a very difficult time getting going again. The last thing I need is for Richard to catch up to me napping on the floor of a greenhouse less than a kilometer from where I escaped his clutches.

It's darker in the greenhouse than it was outside, so I have to squint to make out the greenhouse's contents. It's not a well-organized space, as far from Oona's neat clinic as you can get, with scattered piles of soil, seedlings knocked on their sides in their tiny pots, and various gardening tools littered throughout. I find the shears fairly easily, however, as they're hanging from a hook near the back window.

"Thank goodness for little boys," I say as I beeline that direction. George probably used the shears to remove all the flower heads and, hoping not to get caught, neatly hung them back up. It takes some careful maneuvering before I'm able to get the rope pressed against one of the blades, even more awkward up-and-down shifting as I saw against it, but I manage to get my hands free after a few minutes.

The joints that have been pulled and tugged into position scream in agony at their release, but I force myself to get the blood flowing again. Richard had the foresight to dispose of my cell before he shoved me in his car, but I should be able to break into a window to get to the MacDougal's phone and call for help.

I'm so elated at this new turn of events that I don't quite understand when help turns around and calls for *me*.

"Eleanor! Oh, Eleanor!"

"Madame Eleanor, please come out. This isn't fun anymore."

"We're awfully close to the house. I don't think she can have come this far."

I recognize one of the voices as belonging to Lenora and another to her stepmother, which strikes me as strange for a number of reasons, not the least of which is that Nicholas is supposed to have both Lenora and Rachel hidden away in the safety of Castle Hartford. Too relieved at being rescued to question this anomaly further, I open my mouth to call out for them to rescue me.

. . . And stop myself before I make the mistake of issuing a sound.

I'm not sure what causes me to cast a look toward the lowest ledge of the potting shelves, unless it's that brief purple-blue flash of the flowers growing there. At first glance, it looks a little like the flax flowers I've taken to planting at the evergreen crossroads, which is the only reason I give a double take. There have been far too many coincidences with those crossroads for me to leave anything up to chance.

But as my gaze fixes on the flowers, I realize that flax would be a far more welcome sight.

"What the devil—" My words are a whisper, but my body is a scream as I fall into a crouch and draw closer. I keep my hands fixed firmly at my sides, all of my concentration on not accidentally falling on top of or touching those flowers. "Oh, Oona. *No*."

There's no denying what I'm looking at. Purple buds. That hooded floral shape. It's the uprooted wolfsbane, and with nary a precaution put in place around it. There's literally nothing stopping Lenora or George from rampaging in here and handling the plant—touching it, putting their fingers in their mouths, an accidental poisoning a mere inquisitive exploration away.

"Madame Eleanor!" Lenora calls again. Her call sounds fainter this time, as if she's drawing away, but the other voice—Oona's voice—sounds perilously near.

"Stay where you are, Lenora. I'm just going to check the—"

I make a quick survey of my weapon choices, of which there are several. If I don't like the idea of holding the wolfsbane out in front of me like a talisman to ward off evil, I can opt for George's flower-lopping shears, a heavy potted plant, or what looks like a hoe in the back corner. I'm debating between the last two when Oona's voice draws away again.

"What's that?" she asks, sounding irritated. "Lenora, honestly, I don't know what you expect me to do—"

Neither do I, but I heave a sigh of relief as Oona's voice fades away. I wasn't looking forward to hitting her over the head with a hoe. Then again, being left alone with my thoughts isn't particularly pleasant, either. They're far too busy dwelling on all the signs that have been staring me in the face since this investigation started. Not Richard King and his confession of blackmail, but this evidence of more.

So much more.

One: Oona and Ian, the disgraced lovers, two more in a long line of villagers being blackmailed by Sarah Blackthorne.

Two: Oona's outrage at seeing Lenora and Rachel with the Book of Shadows, not to mention her immediate confiscation of said book.

Three: Oona's extensive medical knowledge of poisons and her regular contact with Sarah Blackthorne, both as her doctor and as she administered first aid the night of the attack.

Four: Oona's love of gardening and this village, in no particular order. The gardening gave her ample opportunity to tend to the wolfsbane, as the evidence in this greenhouse suggests. The village gave her motive—and lots of it. Nicholas said as much this afternoon. She spent so many years struggling to carve her path here, underwent so many fights to earn acceptance. I understand better than anyone how hard that must have been for her. To have it threatened by a greedy woman and her greedier nephew must have been an agony.

I knew the murderer had to be a villager. I knew I couldn't be that wrong.

But victory, such as it were, has never felt so hollow. Oona MacDougal has never been my favorite person around these parts, but I thought we were reaching an understanding. It felt almost as though we were approaching that promising land where friendship, not wolfsbane, blooms. Friendship isn't a thing I offer or accept easily, and to be so catastrophically wrong is a thing that doesn't sit well with me.

Unless . . .

"She's not here, love. Let's go."

I hesitate, wondering whether it would be better to go after them and put Lenora under my protection or to let them leave and head straight for Inspector Piper with what I know, but there's no need. The decision is made for me.

"I'm just going to peek in the greenhouse first. I want to grab something."

There's nothing for it after that but to equip myself with the hoe. Gripping it tightly, I muster all the energy I have left in me and hold it over my head. As much as it pains me to physically hurt a human being this way, it has to be done.

I know now what I have to do.

Chapter 20

"You should have seen the way she took Oona down." Lenora stands in the center of a circle of villagers, all of them hanging on her every breathless word. "One second she was standing there, getting ready to attack, and then . . . *thwap*."

Not unsurprisingly, several members of her audience give a startled jump.

"She knocked her right over the head. And saved my life, I bet. Oona was going to grab the poison for me next."

I don't bother correcting her. Lenora was nowhere near her stepmother when the fateful blow was struck, but I can forgive her exuberant exaggeration. Everyone shares in the sentiment—and I mean literally everyone. All of the faces gathered outside the police station are familiar ones, the villagers out in droves to witness the ending to this story.

I doubt this is the way they expected it to go after all the excitement of their evening. Apparently, Mrs. Brennigan took one look at that box of abandoned candles and scattered notebooks in her library and assumed the worst—especially when there was a substantial amount of my blood spattered over the top of them. As a criminal, Richard King could use some training, but I forgive him for his shortcomings. After all, he doesn't have much experience. His aunt did the dirty work for him, merely handing over the cash whenever he stopped by to make his demands.

Once it was discovered that I was missing, Annis started the phone tree up again. This time, however, it wasn't to invite the villagers to my moonlit ceremony. It was to set up a search party and track me down. In absence of the naked dancing, I imagine my dead body turning up in a ditch somewhere was the next best thing.

That we're all gathered now, with only an hour until midnight, is an irony that isn't lost on me.

I scan the crowd, looking for one face in particular, disappointed when it doesn't appear. "Lenora—promise me you'll stay with Mrs. Brennigan until I come to get you," I say. "Under no circumstances will you go home with anyone else. Is that understood?"

She's perplexed by this command, but she nods a solemn agreement. Mrs. Brennigan agrees, too, her protective arm going around the girl's shoulder. I don't like leaving Lenora alone—not like this, not when I still have one last thing to do—but I trust Mrs. Brennigan to hold her fast.

"I still have to make my statement," I apologize as I step inside the door to the police station, which is buzzing with all its late-night activity. Between potential murderers being hauled in for questioning, a kidnapping victim being released from a greenhouse, and Richard King getting carried from his car in a stretcher with restraints holding him down, they're rather busy. "I'm sure we'll all find the closure we seek soon."

I leave the villagers to their low-murmured variations of "I'd never believe it of Oona MacDougal" and "I always knew there was something off about her" and head inside. Inspector Piper is expecting me, his hip against the counter and an aura of pained acceptance about him.

"Well, Ms. Wilde?"

I shake my head. "He's not here yet. I can't imagine what's keeping him. Actually, I *can* imagine it, which is what has me worried. Do you think—?"

"It's a likely possibility." He tilts his head toward the back, where the interrogation room once again waits for me. This time, however, I'm not the one who's being questioned.

"Where's Lenora?" Oona demands the moment I walk through the door. She looks much as she always does, neat and precise, her features sharp, but there are dark circles under her eyes that seem to be growing by the minute. Getting hit over the head with a hoe will do that to a person, even though I did it as gently as I could. "And George? Are they being looked after? Who has them?"

"Mrs. Brennigan has Lenora, but we still haven't seen George," I say.

She makes as if to bolt up out of her chair, but a look from Inspector Piper has her staying put. "Around what time did your husband take him?"

She casts a bewildered look around the room. "I don't know. Seven o'clock or so—when the search party started. I picked up Lenora from Castle Hartford, and Ian took George." Her bewildered look takes a decidedly nasty turn as it points at me. "We wanted to help find Eleanor as soon as possible and thought it would be best to split up."

Inspector Piper coughs. "Yes, well. Technically, you *did* find her. Or, rather, she found you."

"What are you going to do to me?" Oona asks.

"As of right now, nothing but ask you to be patient," he says. "Ms. Wilde believes that having you here would be the best way to draw your husband out, and I'm inclined to agree. Considering the lengths to which he went to preserve his reputation in this community, he'll most likely be here demanding your release at any moment."

"No he won't," Oona says sadly. "He doesn't care about me at all. I'm beginning to think he never did."

In this, however, Oona is mistaken. As if on cue, Ian MacDougal's slightly lilting burr sounds in the distance. "What's going on here? Why is my wife being detained?"

"George," Oona asks with a pleading look my way. "See if he has George."

I nod and slip out the door before Inspector Piper has a chance to tell me to stay put. He hasn't been too pleased with my handling of the situation thus far, but there's no denying that I already hand delivered him one criminal. Richard King confessed to knowing of and benefiting from his aunt's blackmail scheme within minutes of being detained.

As for the other criminal, well, he's not in handcuffs yet, but he will be soon. Especially since it looks as though two of the larger officers on the force have just blocked off the front door.

Ian MacDougal stands in the middle of the police precinct with George, one hand resting heavily on his son's shoulder. My first priority is to make sure that little boy will get through this in one piece and live to tear the wings off of dozens of flies, so I put on a smile as I approach.

"Thank goodness you're here, Ian," I say in a deceptively breathless voice. "Oona's been asking for you since they brought her in. Hello, George. Would you like to come check out the vending machine with me? They have three different kinds of onion crisps."

George's face lights up at the prospect of this simple treat. "Can I have all three?" he asks and, without waiting for an answer, "I'm glad you're not dead, Madame Eleanor."

"I'm glad too," I say. I prepare to walk him back to the vending machine to ply him with onions and potatoes in hopes of easing the sting of having a parent who's a murderer, but Oona ruins it by appearing in the doorway.

"George, thank goodness you're all right!" she cries and drops to her knees before him.

The boy looks highly embarrassed to be embraced and smothered with affection in front of so many police officers, but he accepts the kisses on his cheeks with an air of one resigned to his fate. It's that, more than anything, that tells me my instincts were spot on.

Well, that and the fact that Lenora has been confiding all of Oona's similar crimes to me over the past week. Forcing her to drink beet and spinach smoothies. Wishing she'd choose to apprentice at the clinic with her instead of with a witch. Pushing her into friendship with a girl who shares her interests and intelligence. Casting herself in the role of bad guy by taking away the Book of Shadows because, well, Satanism.

Oona MacDougal is hardly a *soft* woman, but she is a good one.

And a smart one. Too smart to poison Lewis King with a substance she knew would be counteracted by atropine, anyway. As his doctor, she had to have known better than anyone that aconitum would never work on him.

Her husband, however . . .

"Ian MacDougal, you are under arrest for the murder of Sarah Blackthorne and attempted murder of Lewis King."

Moving as one, Oona and I usher George out of the room and toward the vending machines. There are some things a child should never have to witness firsthand. The arrest of his father is one of them.

"How's your head?" I ask as I dig around in my purse for all the spare change I have before handing it to Oona. Police station snacks don't come cheap.

"It hurts. How's yours? If I'd have known you were just going to rip all those stitches out, I wouldn't have been so careful with them."

I wince and turn to face Oona, an apology hanging from my lips. She sees it and gives George several bags of the potato crisps with instructions to take them over to the corner, where he can enjoy them as far away from her as possible. "I hate the way the onion ones smell," she explains to me, but we both know that's a lie. She just wants George out of the way while we talk.

In addition to a good woman, she's also a good mom. A *great* one, probably.

"What's going to happen to them?" I ask. "After Ian is arrested, I mean?"

She seems surprised by my question. "Nothing, I imagine. It won't be easy, getting them past this, but they're resilient. George will probably either turn to stealing candy from the local pick-and-mix or setting fire to anthills. Lenora's rebellion will most likely take the form of following a certain psychic around town and trying to sell potions to unsuspecting villagers. That'll be fun for both of us."

I can't help chuckling at the picture thus conjured—especially since I suspect she's right. The laughter doesn't linger, though. "You're sure you'll keep custody of them?" I ask. It's the one thing that's been worrying me the most. With their biological mother dead and a father in prison, they'll most likely become government wards.

"Absolutely. I'd like to see anyone try to take my children away from me."

"*Your* children?" I echo.

"Well, of course they're mine. They always have been. I legally adopted them the day Ian and I were married."

At my continued look of bemusement, Oona shakes her head. "Have I shocked you? And here I thought the Great Madame Eleanor was on to everything. The children are the only reason I stayed as long as I did. It certainly wasn't for Ian. He never would have let me take them with me, even if he didn't particularly want them for himself. He only cared how it reflected on him."

I can't help thinking of what Nicholas said about Ian—that he's a weak man, a small one, one who would never stack up to the woman he married, and who probably resented her for it every day of his life. It seems he was more astute regarding their relationship than I was.

I'm beginning to think he's more astute about *our* relationship, too.

"He was so determined to bury our problems, to save face in the community even when Sarah kept demanding more blackmail money out of him," Oona continues. "*You* overheard our argument that day at the house. *You* know."

Actually, I know nothing of the sort. I'd been so sure that the topic under discussion was me and my role as Lenora's mentor that it hadn't occurred to me to dig deeper. How's that for myopia?

"He'd spent all our savings by that point." She heaves a sigh. "I think that's why he resorted to poisoning poor Sarah and her nephew. I wouldn't give him another penny—mostly because I don't have any more. That big house, the perfect façade . . . Ian insisted. He always insisted. But he couldn't keep it up without me. That was the arrangement you overheard us discussing."

"You gave him the perfect wife," I say.

She nods sadly. "And he gave me my children."

I'm not sure what to say to that, so it's just as well that George takes advantage of the momentary lull in conversation. "I'm thirsty," he calls from his snack corner.

"Of course you are. You just ate six times your daily sodium allowance." Oona sighs. "Do you have any more change, Eleanor? I didn't think to grab my purse before you knocked me unconscious."

I wince. "Sorry about that. I couldn't think of how else to get you in here. I wasn't sure you'd believe me if I told you I suspected your husband of murder."

"You might have been surprised. I learned a long time ago that Ian MacDougal wasn't the man I thought he was. I should have known something was off when our cat died like that."

"Died?" I ask with a careful look to make sure George isn't listening in. "But I thought . . ."

"That he disappeared? That was another lie we told the world, but at least it came from a good place." She grimaces, as if remembering. "Rather, I thought it was a good place at the time. We wanted to protect the children. I found the poor thing about a month ago under one of the rosebushes. He used to go tomcatting around Margaret Piper's garden—I remember sending Ian to investigate, to see if any of her poisons looked nibbled on. That must have been what sparked the idea to kill Sarah Blackthorne."

I think about all the other missing animals, of the werewolf scampering over the countryside last night with fresh carnage in its hands before it lured me toward the cliff's edge. "Do you think he would have tested the poison . . . ?" I begin, too horrified to continue.

"On other people's pets? Yes, unfortunately. Ian has a lot of qualities I don't admire, but he's not the sort to rush into something without knowing what he's getting into. Especially once he found that it wasn't working on Lewis." She levels me with a careful stare. "Take my word for it and hold on to a good man the moment you find him. They're not so plentiful that you should take them for granted."

I can't pretend to misunderstand her. "It's not like that with me and Nicholas."

"No?" she asks. "You could have fooled me. He's the one who took over the search party from Annis—he had the whole village organized within minutes. I've never seen anything like it. In my line of work, I've witnessed a lot of men worried for their partners' well-being, but never one as grim and determined as that one. If everyone hadn't immediately come to your aid the moment they heard, I have no doubt he would have torn the countryside apart with his hands trying to find you."

"No, really—" I begin, unsure which part of that I'm objecting to. Nicholas coming to my rescue or the fact that I can't believe the village came together for anything but my untimely demise.

"He loves you, Eleanor. The whole village does. Those aren't gifts you want to take lightly. People die for that kind of thing." An inexpressibly sad look takes over her expression, and I don't have the heart to contradict her. "People kill."

Chapter 21

For a man who supposedly loves me, Nicholas proves difficult to track down.

It's officially midnight by the time I approach my house, the moon luminous and full overhead, but I don't feel the least bit like dancing. Not only does every bone in my body ache after the day's events, but I'm feeling unaccountably depressed by the way things have turned out.

I should be elated—I've solved the murder, found my place in the village, and made a new friend. Even the news about Lewis King is positive. According to the latest hospital reports, he should make a full, if painful, recovery.

But there's no denying that Oona's sad story has left a gaping hole in my heart. Not just for her children, who are going to have a lot to deal with as more of the facts surrounding the case become known, but for all those who had to die along the way—human- and animal-kind alike.

"Oh, Beast," I say as I near my back door. "Will I ever see you again? Or did you fall victim to Ian MacDougal, too?"

"I thought I told you to come see me the moment you finished tonight."

I scream and whirl as a male voice accosts me from near the garden wall. Although I know in an instant that it's Nicholas—the soothing sound of his clipped baritone is unmistakable—I can't help holding a hand to my rapidly beating heart.

"What are you doing, standing around like that in the dark?" I demand. "Do you have any idea what I've gone through tonight?"

"No, but from the look of you, it can't have been pleasant. Are there *more* stitches on your face now?"

There are. Before I left the station, Oona patched me back up again—this time with the addition of three more stitches along my brow. They hurt a lot more the second go-around, but she promises that I won't look *completely* haggard once they're gone.

"It was Ian MacDougal," I say. "He's the one who murdered Sarah."

Nicholas nods as though that makes perfect sense.

"And a little bit of Richard King, too. He's the one who kidnapped me."

He nods at that, too, his calm acceptance of the news doing much to settle my nerves. So, too, does the way he offers me the crook of his arm and tilts his head toward the field out behind my cottage. It's a ridiculous thing to do, to take me out for a casual midnight stroll after everything that's happened, but I accept his escort anyway.

"Where are we going?" I ask as he adapts his long, lean stride to match my own faltering steps. At this rate, he'll probably have to carry me back. "I don't mean to be rude, but what I really want right now is a hot bath and my bed."

"Even more than you want me?" he asks archly.

"Well, yes," I admit. "By, like, a really big margin at the moment."

Over the low sound of his chuckle, another voice sounds. This one is lighter, softer, and oh so familiar. *Silly Ellie,* it says, ringing out clearly in the night. *Always so practical.*

I start. I know better by now than to be the least bit surprised to hear my sister's voice carried on the wind, but I can't help it. "Winnie, you perfect wretch!" I cry, heedless of the fact that Nicholas is watching me. "I could have used you a hundred times this past week. Where have you been?"

She doesn't answer. I'm tempted to stop walking—and talking and eating and sleeping—until she speaks up again, but Nicholas gives a mild cough and answers for her.

"I believe you'll find her out in the stables."

"The stables?"

"It was one of the first places I looked when you went missing." His voice is gruff. "I'd appreciate it if you wouldn't do that again, by the way. I find I didn't care for it."

"I didn't care too much for it, either," I mutter, but I can't help the way my footsteps feel suddenly light, my heart even lighter. "I'm sorry you were worried. I didn't expect anyone to kidnap me in broad daylight."

"That's because you've always underestimated your effect on people. Come on. It's only a little ways from here."

There's so much I want to say to Nicholas, so much I want to ask him, but none of the words feel right. From the tales Oona told, I have Nicholas to thank for saving me today. He organized the villagers and spearheaded the search after Annis put out the call. He took to the hills to find me no matter what the cost.

To look at him, however, you'd think he did nothing more than read a few newspapers before changing his shirt for dinner. He's calm and collected, not the least bit ruffled as he leads me out under the full moon to the sound of my dead sister's voice.

In other words, he accepts me as I am. The murders and the kidnappings, the head wounds and the voices from beyond the grave—none of it ruffles him. They're part of who I am, which means he embraces them without question.

I want at least one of them to be named after me, my sister says, interrupting me before I can corral my thoughts into words. *And not the weird little one, either. You can name that one after Liam.*

Once again, she floats away into the distance. I don't mind as much this time because we've drawn within view of the stables. It's a much shorter trip now that there are no hunched Ian MacDougals in the distance, carrying off his poisonous evidence and leading me over cliffs.

"In the third stall on the right," Nicholas says as we approach the cavernous opening. There must have once been a door there, but it's since fallen off the hinges to leave nothing but a moldering pile of wood and debris. Most of the stables are like that, actually, an architectural hazard as decrepit as it is beautiful. "I'll wait out here and keep your sister company. Come find me when you're done."

As he hasn't let go of my arm yet, I'm finding it difficult to comply with this request. I discover why when he transfers his touch from that of gallant escort to a serious, stern man clutching me by both hands. "I mean it this time, Ellie. No sneaking out the back. No climbing out the roof. *Come find me.* I'm not leaving here unless you leave with me. I never will."

Flooding sensations of guilt and desire move through me. He has every right to be annoyed with me, since I've done nothing for the past few days but push him aside, but I'm not familiar with the protocol in situations like these. He's done so much for me, *is* so much to me. Forget things like the money I owe Penny and the roofers. The real question is, how are you supposed to pay back a man who wants to give you the world?

"Nicholas, I—"

I'm prevented from saying the words on my lips by a sound from inside the stables. At first, I think it might be Winnie again, but there's nothing human about that cry. There's nothing canine about it, either, which is my other guess.

"Beast?" I ask, turning on my heel. I'm almost ashamed of how quickly I forget about Nicholas, but I can hardly help myself. That was a meow I heard. *Several* of them, in fact.

I pass the first stall, heedless of my surroundings and the distant scent of long-decayed hay. "Beast, are you in here?"

I pass the second stall, too, barely noting that the door to that one looks as though it was ripped off its hinges. "Was Nicholas right this whole time? Have you been fattening yourself up on defenseless baby mice?"

I reach the third stall, this one dark and gloomy and the perfect setting for my kindred spirit to hide. "You'd better be injured. You'd better be missing a leg *and* an ear. You'd better be—"

I drop to my knees almost at once. There isn't nearly enough light in here for me to make out the exact condition of my cat's health, but there's no mistaking the luminous yellow glow of her eyes. Or that she appears to be surrounded by wriggling, squirming bundles of fur, each one mewling a little bit louder than the one next to it.

They're defenseless babies, all right, but they aren't mice. And from the proprietary way Beast licks each one, I'm guessing she has no intention on eating them anytime soon.

"One, two, three . . ." I count each tiny head as I encounter it. All three kittens are sleek and dark like Beast, save for the weird little one Winnie demanded I not name after her. Not that there's too much weird about her. A crooked hitch to her tail and a twisted white tip on each ear might not make her a pedigree, but the moment I lift the tiny creature in my hand, cupping it like the MacDougal house, I know she's perfect. And not just because a small pink tongue dashes out and kisses my hand.

At least, not *only* because of that.

"Two seconds in, and she's already shown me more love than

you ever have," I accuse Beast, but there's no malice in my voice. There's only low crooning and a creeping sense of contentedness I didn't know was possible.

Three kittens, three little miracles, triplets born in a cozy bed while murder and mayhem blazed around them. I'd been so worried that Beast had made a foolish mistake, allowed herself to be caught in a trap or by a werewolf's claws, when all she'd done was take herself off to have her babies in peace.

"And you went with her, Winnie, didn't you?" I ask. "This whole time, you've been right here keeping watch."

When she doesn't reply, I drop a gentle kiss on the white-tipped kitten's head. "I don't care what she wants," I say. "Your name is Winifred, and you're going to be as snuggly and trainable as any silly old puppy."

As if aware of her new role, the kitten gives a small yawn and snuggles herself deeper into my palm. That alone would be enough to make me feel the comfort of my sister's presence, but a breeze picks up and moves through the stable, carrying with it the light scent of Nicholas's signature bergamot scent.

That's not the only thing that comes with it. Understanding follows not too much later.

Nicholas Hartford III, rich and powerful though he may be, is out there waiting for me to finish what I need to do. He's standing watch for me until I'm safe at home again. He's giving me the time and space I need to realize that of all the wild and mysterious things I believe in, a man caring about me shouldn't be the most fantastic of them all.

It is, though. It's fantastic and wonderful and, apparently, mine for the taking. All I have to do is reach out and accept.

As much as it pains me to abandon these precious bundles now that I've found them, I set the kitten down next to her mother, leaving them to their bath. I know they'll be safe here. Like that brothel madam overseeing her domain—or like Oona

MacDougal fighting for the children she knows are her own—Beast will ensure they come to no harm.

After all, she was smart enough to flee the damp and the danger to carve herself a safe space to call home. That, more than anything else, is what everyone needs in this world.

Including me.

Chapter 22

"Two dozen hand-pressed notebooks from Margaret Piper, as promised."

General von Cleve drops a box on the table in front of me, his face red with the exertion of his errand. He pauses to extract a handkerchief from his pocket and wipe the beads of sweat gathering on his brow.

Sometime in the past three weeks, Sussex decided it had deluged us long enough. Almost overnight, we went from cold rain to a sun so painfully bright that every woman walking down the street has been transformed into a walking garden party. I've never seen so many wide-brimmed floral hats in my life.

"Are you really going to sell these at the fête?" Nicholas asks as he picks up one of the notebooks and turns it over in his hand. He's "helping" me inventory and price the donated goods, by which I mean he's mostly standing outside the vicarage questioning my decisions. For a man so determined not to participate in the village's customs, he's been spending an awful lot of time at the planning meetings lately.

Then again, it could just be that he enjoys the pleasure of my company. According to him, it's the only way he has a chance to see me anymore. I've been in quite a bit of social demand lately.

"And for fifty pounds apiece?" he adds with a tsk. "That's a bold choice."

I stick a price sticker on the box without batting an eyelash. "These are the infamous witchcraft books that uncover murderers and lay werewolves to rest, thank you very much. I already have preorders for most of them." I turn to the general with a sweet smile. "I hope you remembered to thank Margaret for her contribution."

"You can thank her yourself," the general says with a thumb hooked over his shoulder. "I saw her milling around the village square on my way here."

I'm not surprised. Something about the sunshine—or the fact that the infamous fête takes place tomorrow—has brought just about everyone out of doors and into the community spirit. I have no idea who's going to buy the massive stack of doilies and homemade tea cozies that have been piling up, but at least we won't run out of goods. My elderberry cordial is likely to make a big hit. Annis uncovered another box of ancient candles to be put up for sale. And Penny has donated not just one, but two of her chocolate cakes.

Her *real* chocolate cakes, only slightly sooty on the outside from baking pans that will probably never get clean again.

Even the MacDougals stopped by earlier to wish us luck. Oona, Lenora, and George aren't venturing out *too* much in public yet, but I like to think it's because they're busy at home snuggling with their new kitten. They named her Eleanor, but to avoid confusion, she goes by Nora. William, the only boy of the litter and already showing signs of turning into a menace, is slavishly devoted to his new owner, Mr. Worthington.

As for Winifred—Freddie for short—well, she's staying with

me and Beast. Beast is terribly possessive of the little thing. I doubt I could give her away even if I wanted to.

"Wait," Nicholas calls as the general shoves off in the direction of the pub. "One of these books already has writing in it."

"Oh, that's probably just Mrs. Brennigan's mystery novel." I put a hand out to accept the book from Nicholas, but he's busy flipping through the pages, his brow pulled tight. "It's good, right? I think she might be onto the start of a great new career."

"Uh, something tells me this isn't a novel." He allows the pages to fall open to the front, where the familiar scrawl of a lumpy pentagram reaches my eyes.

"No way." Instead of waiting for him to hand me the book, I jump to my feet and snatch it out of his hand. After the night we caught Ian MacDougal, I assumed the notebook would show up somewhere in his personal effects, but it's remained stubbornly missing. Inspector Piper says that it was a good thing Ian confessed, or my carelessness may have cost him the case. "I knew I didn't lose it! This is it, Nicholas—the original. All the markings are here. You and your mother, Penny, Old Man Petersham, the MacDougals . . . Wait a minute. There's one missing here."

I hold the book open to showcase the jagged-edged remnant of a page removed from somewhere near the front. I'm afraid I'm going to have to take a full catalog of the villagers to know for sure which one it is, but I happen to glance up at the general's rapidly retreating form and realize I don't need to go that far.

"That miserable sneak," I say, unable to suppress a short laugh. "I *knew* he wasn't there to repair my roof just out of the goodness of his heart. Green tea, indeed."

Nicholas looks a question at me.

"He helped himself and the roofers to tea when I came to get you, remember?" I ask. I make another quick flip through the notebook but, as expected, find nothing resembling the markings of war. No matter which way I look at it, the general's page isn't here. "He must have taken the notebook from my bag then. That whole thing—the thatchers and the story about me being the daughter he never had—it was a cover to get access to the notebook so no one would discover the truth about him."

"I didn't know the old man had it in him," Nicholas says. Neither did I, but I imagine that given the opportunity, he'd have made a great military tactician. "What are you going to do with the book now?"

I turn it over in my hands and sigh. "Give it to Inspector Piper and tell him I found it under a couch cushion or something. Oh, dear. He'll never let me live this one down."

Nicholas lifts one amused brow. "Couldn't you just tell him the truth?"

"How could I? The general never did let me pay him back for the roofers. Turning him in now would only make me the worst kind of snitch."

"Are there different levels? How interesting. Which snitches are the acceptable kind?"

I ignore him, as per my usual custom. If he doesn't understand the subtle nuances of my personal moral code by now, I doubt he ever will. "Well, that solves *one* of the mysteries that's been bothering me. That only leaves poor Regina. Ian never did confess to killing her, you know. The Gilfords' dog, yes, and the cat he left on my hill. A few of the other cats found by Animal Control lately, too, but he drew the line at small mammals."

"What's that, love?" Aunt Margaret makes her way up to the table. "I see you got my notebooks delivered safe and sound. Mind you don't sell those to just anyone. They're from my special batch and should be handled carefully."

Nicholas pauses in the act of stacking them together and glances at his hands. "Er . . . your special batch?"

Margaret's trill of laughter reaches the top of the church bell tower. "Not that kind of special, young man. Peter made me move all of my poisonous plants to a locked greenhouse. No more accidents, he said. He doesn't think his credibility can take it."

"Then what makes them special?"

She winks. "I danced naked under the full moon for two hours. The lunar goddess is a very powerful force, you know."

Nicholas coughs and shoots me a glance. That glance is tender and loving and, yes, mocking. It's the look I like best, the look that lets me know that although we haven't gotten all the kinks sorted out between us just yet, there are still plenty of full moons left.

"Alas, I *don't* know," he says. "There always seems to be a murder or kidnapping that gets in the way."

"Or a wind chill factor," I point out.

"Well, expect a lot more where these came from," Margaret says. "My garden hasn't been this abundant since, well . . . Let's just say my begonias have never looked so good. This year promises to be a prolific one."

"Your begonias?" I echo. Why do those sound so familiar?

"The Gilfords have been experiencing a good spring so far, too. And the Humboldts. And don't even get me started on what's happening over at the Cherrycove farm. The asparagus are already shooting to the skies."

"Wait a minute." I close my eyes and picture the evergreen crossroads, which have lately started showing the tender green flax shoots, as I predicted. I don't know *all* the farms bordering that area, but if I recall correctly, those are all within a stone's throw.

Or a wayward pig's wanderings . . .

"Margaret, no." My eyes snap open again, my stomach like lead. "You didn't. You wouldn't. Her *heart*."

She blinks benignly at me. At least, I *think* it's a benign blink. That theory undergoes a dramatic change when, as if from out of nowhere, a crack of lightning splits the sky and rolls of dark clouds circle in from the horizon. The rumble of thunder precedes an onslaught of sudden rain by only a few seconds.

Nicholas jumps to action almost immediately, grabbing boxes and running to hand them to Annis's waiting arms at the vicarage door. Half of the wares are going to be ruined after this, but I find myself too mesmerized to help him, my feet rooted as if planted into Mother Earth's very veins.

"The pig's heart," I repeat, softer this time. Even though I'm soaked almost all the way through from the deluge, I swear Margaret remains untouched, her puffs of silver curls still perfectly dry.

"Well, of course, love," Margaret says as she unfurls an umbrella and places it over her head before anyone else can notice the way the rain splits around her. "How else was I supposed to absorb her power?"

Keep an eye out for
More adventures featuring
Ellie and her friends

Coming soon from
Tamara Berry

And don't miss
The first in the series
SÉANCES ARE FOR SUCKERS

Available now from
Kensington Books